**“Really a dandy thriller.**
**The *Marathon Man* is definitely a winner.”**
***—The Cleveland Plain Dealer***

“There are two literary virtues that one wishes hadn’t become cliches: ‘It’s a good read’ and ‘It exists on several levels.’ One wishes these hadn’t become cliches because they are two obvious virtues of William Goldman’s *Marathon Man.*”

*—The Washington Post*

“A slick, professional job . . . Goldman has [his] craft well under control.” *—The Boston Globe*

“A cliff-hanger . . . International skulduggery, clandestine mayhem, and sweet revenge.” *—Fort Worth Star Telegram*

“Stiff competition to such classic enjoyments as sex and fattening foods. *Marathon Man* has the makings of a very rich dessert for mystery lovers.” *—Washington, D.C., Star-News*

“Dazzling . . . Funny and savage, baffling and logical . . . Try not to let anyone tell you how it ends.” —IRWIN SHAW

“Brilliant ‘entertainment’ in the Graham Greene sense . . . This book gradually eases you to the edge of your chair, then keeps you there with that combination of terror and pleasure that only the superb thriller can achieve.” *—Library Journal*

“An immobilizing thriller . . . [that] should run rings around any other book of this kind.” *—Kirkus Reviews*

ALSO BY WILLIAM GOLDMAN

FICTION

The Temple of Gold (1957)
Your Turn to Curtsy, My Turn to Bow (1958)
Soldier in the Rain (1960)
Boys and Girls Together (1964)
No Way to Treat a Lady (1964)
The Thing of It Is . . . (1967)
Father's Day (1971)
The Princess Bride (1973)
Marathon Man (1974)
Magic (1976)
Tinsel (1979)
Control (1982)
The Silent Gondoliers (1983)
The Color of Light (1984)
Heat (1985)
Brothers (1986)

NONFICTION

The Season: A Candid Look at Broadway (1969)
The Making of "A Bridge Too Far" (1977)
Adventures in the Screen Trade: A Personal View of Hollywood and Screenwriting (1983)
Wait Till Next Year (with Mike Lupica) (1988)
Hype and Glory (1990)
Four Screenplays (1995)
Five Screenplays (1997)
Which Lie Did I Tell? More Adventures in the Screen Trade (2000)

SCREENPLAYS

Masquerade (with Michael Relph) (1965)
Harper (1966)
Butch Cassidy and the Sundance Kid (1969)
The Hot Rock (1972)
The Great Waldo Pepper (1975)
The Stepford Wives (1975)
All the President's Men (1976)
Marathon Man (1976)
A Bridge Too Far (1977)
Magic (1978)
Mr. Horn (1979)
Heat (1987)
The Princess Bride (1987)
Misery (1990)
The Year of the Comet (1992)
Maverick (1994)
The Chamber (1996)
The Ghost and the Darkness (1996)
Absolute Power (1997)
The General's Daughter (1999)
Hearts in Atlanta (2001)

PLAYS

Blood, Sweat and Stanley Poole (with James Goldman) (1961)
A Family Affair (with James Goldman and John Kander) (1961)

FOR CHILDREN

Wigger (1974)

# MARATHON MAN

WILLIAM GOLDMAN

BALLANTINE BOOKS
NEW YORK

A Ballantine Book
Published by The Ballantine Publishing Group

 Published in the
United States by The Ballantine Publishing Group, a division
of Random House, Inc., New York, and simultaneously in Canada
by Random House of Canada Limited, Toronto.
Originally published by Delacorte Press in 1974.



www.randomhouse.com/BB/

Library of Congress Catalog Card Number: 00-193203

ISBN 0-345-43972-4

Cover design by Carl Galian
Cover photo © Jana Leon/Graphistock

Text design by Holly Johnson

Manufactured in the United States of America

First Ballantine Books Edition: July 2001

10 9 8 7 6 5 4 3 2 1

FOR

Edward Neisser

# INTRODUCTION

# MARATHON MAN
# (The Events Leading Up To)

I had been a novelist for close to twenty years before I began *Marathon Man*, a story very different from anything I had ever tried before. The reason for the timing was that Hiram Haydn, my brilliant and beloved editor, had recently died. To this day I have no idea what my career might have been had he either (a) died sooner or (b) never been my editor at all.

I wrote my first novel, *The Temple of Gold*, in 1956, when I was twenty-four, and when it was accepted for publication by Knopf, that became the seminal event of my creative life. Shortly after its publication, I began to hear of an editor at Random House named Hiram Haydn. He was by all accounts decent, real smart, a teacher, a scholar, a novelist himself, and pushing fifty. This last was crucial for me—

—I have always been in search and in need of father figures.

So I fantasized that someday I would have Hiram Haydn as my editor. I had no idea that "someday" was just around the corner. I believed during these years—and yes, I am aware how totally nuts this is—but I truly believed that to justify the fact that I didn't have a real job, it was essential for me to publish a novel every twelve months.

I wrote my second novel in 1957—*Your Turn to Curtsy,*

*My Turn to Bow*—still my favorite title of all of my stuff—and submitted it to Knopf. What can I say about their reaction? Did they love it? No. Did they have problems with some of it? More than a few. Hate it? Don't be an optimist. They loathed, despised, and detested it so much they *denied it had ever been submitted to them.*

I was free to go to Hiram. I called his office, found he was on a long vacation. And so crazed was I to get published each and every year, I trudged through snow and sleet, like your favorite postman, to try and immediately find another publisher to accept me. I got a couple of quick rejections, natch, so in desperation, I gave it to a girl I knew from Oberlin who worked for an editor to give to her boss.

*She* thought it was so terrible she wouldn't dream of doing that. "You should learn to know your characters," this secretary told me, and sent me on my way.

Doubleday took it. And I will always be grateful. I became a little less grateful maybe when they told me they didn't think much of my novel, but that perhaps someday I might write something commercial and they were willing to gamble a couple of thousand dollars—my advance—on my future.

My next book, *Soldier in the Rain,* they also had zero faith in, but they would piss away the few thousand again in the event that the book after that was something they could sell. I told them I wanted to try elsewhere. They said fine, but don't expect a whole lot.

I gave *Soldier in the Rain* to Hiram Haydn who loved it, and the publishing relationship of my career began.

Hiram had left Random House at this time to start, with two other publishers, a house of their own, to be called

Atheneum. They brought out three books simultaneously to start things off, *Soldier in the Rain* being one of them. And no story I can tell you better explains what has happened to publishing over the last forty years than this one now.

Because one of the tenets of Atheneum's basic contract was that they did not and *would not* include an option clause. If they published you, and you weren't happy, well, they didn't want unhappy writers and you were free to go elsewhere.

One weeps.

I was with Hiram from 1958 through *The Princess Bride* in 1973 when he, alas, died. He was a great believer in my talent, and boy, do we all need that. He also liked the kind of stuff I was turning out during that period. Hard as it may be to accept now, if you think of me as a Hollywood writer, my novels at that time were seemingly charming but ultimately serious and depressing stories, in which the most sympathetic character always died horribly.

Not wildly commercial stuff. (Though through some miracle, I always found an audience in paperback after the books all stiffed in hardcover.)

Then I had maybe the dumbest idea of my life—to write a long novel, *Boys and Girls Together.* Took me three-plus years and in the middle of that, I stopped to work on Broadway for awhile.

When I came back, I was blocked.

No fun, that. I had six hundred pages done, no idea how to get back to it. I was living in a small apartment on Eighty-sixth and York in Manhattan and had taken the bedroom of a guy's apartment on Eighty-eighth and York to write in. (Sounds nuts, I know, but it worked out.)

The OJ crime of that period—we are back in '63—was the Boston Strangler. And one morning, I read an article in the *Daily News* that stated that the newest theory in Boston was this: There were *two* stranglers, not one.

That morning, on that short walk up York Avenue, a novel literally dropped into my head. Based on this notion: what if there were indeed two different stranglers, and what if one of them got jealous of the other.

I sat down at my desk and in a few minutes, outlined the plot.

The plot of what, though?

Until coffee that morning, I had been trying to figure out how to return to *Boys and Girls Together*. Was this just another neurotic ploy to set me back further? I was totally capable of such nuttiness, I knew that. So I spoke to a couple of friends about this *heffalump* that had suddenly landed on my desk. We agreed that the important thing for my sanity was to get back to my half-finished novel.

But *if* I could write the strangler book quickly—I think ten days was the time agreed upon—it couldn't hurt me. If I could finish in that time, fine; if not, pitch it and try and finish the long book.

I wrote the strangler book—eventually it would be called *No Way to Treat a Lady*—in the prescribed number of days. To make it seem longer, I wrote it with as many chapters as I could, each chapter beginning on a fresh new page, thereby cheating but adding bulk at the same time. (Some chapters were all of one *word* long.)

The book finished, I gave it to Hiram. As a kind of a "look what I found," surprise.

He read it, said that he had no idea how to edit such a book. I should be at work on *Boys and Girls Together*, not this. He suggested that I publish it as a paperback original under a pseudonym.

I did.

Harry Longbaugh became the author (the real name of the Sundance Kid, proof that even though this was several years before I wrote that movie, I had been thinking about it for a very long time).

*No Way to Treat a Lady* went into galley proofs, Cliff Robertson got hold of it, got hold of me, said these words I will never forget: "I read your screen treatment." I remember thinking "Shit, that was no screen treatment, that was a *novel.*" (I had no idea what a screen treatment *was.* I had never, at that point, seen a screenplay, much less a treatment.) I always thought the reason Robertson might have been confused was the insane look of the book, all those weird and truncated chapters. The point being? Well, Robertson's subsequent hiring of me to write a screenplay is what got me into the movie business.

And totally changed my life.

Through all my fifteen years with Hiram, I kept getting these ideas for stories that were different from what I was writing for him. (I remember I had *Magic*—about a ventriloquist and his dummy—for a very long time.) But I never considered writing any of them.

And never would have had he lived.

But now in 1973 he was gone, and when I next sat down to tell a story, it turned out to be a thriller, *Marathon Man.* If you love a genre (as I love thrillers and spy novels and hard-boiled detective novels), you're stuck with your passion, and what you hope for is someday to be classed with those writers who moved you. My guy was Graham Greene. Of course you know you can't reach that level, but hope is a thing with feathers and away you go.

In a thriller you start with a villain. (Obviously, that's not a rule, there are no rules, but it's what I did and I bet if I ever write another one, I'll do it again.) I started with Mengele, the most intellectually startling of the Nazis. (An M.D. *plus* a Ph.D.) And I knew this: I needed to get him to America. But why in the world would he come? (Mengele, when I began fiddling with this story, was either alive in South America or had been alive in South America, choose one. Living secretly or palatially; I chose palatially.)

But this was one of the brilliant minds of his generation. Why would he be so dumb as to risk his world to visit America? I was reading the papers one day when the answer came. An American doctor, in I think Cleveland, had begun doing a then-revolutionary operation, heart sleeve surgery, and people were streaming in from all over the world. Mengele would be among the needy.

From the start I have had an unerring brilliance when it comes to narrative and here was just another brilliant example. Mengele would come to Cleveland for surgery. Mengele *had* to come to America, the reasoning was rock-solid perfect. I had scored another coup.

One day I was just walking around—I get a lot of ideas just walking around, also at the ballet, just sitting there drifting—when thank God reality thudded home. *Schmuck*, what kind of a villain is he if he's so fucking frail he needs *heart surgery*? *Asshole*, what kind of thriller do you have if the villain is already *dying*? *Ahhhhhhh*.

I don't know if it's true for other writers, but for me, when a piece of material becomes urgent, there is only a certain window of time in which it can be put down. If that passes, the window shuts, the material is dead, often forever. I had never tried a spy thriller, owned the standard lack of confidence, felt a certain sense of panic setting in.

Then I read an article about how some Nazi leaders had accumulated great fortunes by knocking the teeth out of their prisoners and melting the gold down, or taking jewels from their colons, where desperate men and women had been hiding their valuables for centuries. It all fell in. The name, Szell, I chose from the great conductor—just saying it made me feel sadistic. The reason for visiting—to get his diamonds. (The only man he trusted—his father—the man who had been in charge of the fortune in America, is killed in a car crash in the opening.)

So Szell has to come. A doctor, a monster, a Nazi, but I wanted worse, I wanted more—so bless you Melvin P. Klein (not his real name), my childhood dentist who did not believe in novocaine, because one afternoon Szell became, suddenly and forever, a dentist. I had my villain. And I knew he had to torture someone because I remembered the pressure from my childhood, of being helpless in Klein's chair with his knee forcing me down to keep me from squirming, unmindful of my pain.

Babe, the hero (Dustin Hoffman in the flick, Olivier played the dentist), appeared because I had become fascinated with this notion: what if someone close to you was something totally different from what you thought? In the story, Hoffman thinks his brother (Roy Scheider) is a businessman where the reality is that the man is a spy. Who has been involved with the Nazi, Szell.

Once I had that, the rest was essentially mixing and matching, figuring out the surprises, hoping they would work. (You never know. I don't, anyway. Same is true of screenplay writing. Each time out is just as scary. I wish it weren't so, but there it is.) So now I had my torturer, my method, and my victim, and early on in the novel I gave Babe a toothache. At the time I was building this into a book, I went to see my gum guy, a wonderful periodontist, a joy. He never hurts people, plays Bach on the radio, is fascinated with restaurants, as am I.

We are talking of a genuinely kind and decent human being.

He asks what I am writing and when I am about to leave I tell him and mention that Babe has a cavity and what I am about to do to him—

—and—

—and—

—and I will never forget the look that dropped onto his face. "Oh no," he said, quietly, his eyes all dreamy. "No, Bill. Forget the cavity. You want pain. You want genuine unforgettable pain. You want pain that would make you want to die. Bill, listen to me—*have him drill into a healthy tooth.*"

On and on this sweet man went, talking to me of the glory of anguish, of how it would be impossible to keep any secrets if someone were drilling into a fine, strapping tooth. I have rarely been more frightened. Here this sweet fellow I'd known for twenty years was Jeckyll-Hyde-ing as I watched. He wouldn't stop. The level of agony would be unsurpassable. Death would be preferable. The memory of being destroyed in the chair would never leave you . . . bliss. . . .

He's still my gum guy. But now I get nervous when we're alone.

I wrote the novel over the summer of '73. In my pit in the fashionable Upper East Side of New York City. Few ever saw my office. Somehow George Hill got in one day, looked around, and termed the place "scrofulous" and though I wasn't quite sure of all the meanings, the sound matched the chaos.

I worked in a place that was *scrofulous*.

Late one afternoon (I always worked regular hours; it was important to me to pretend to have a real job) as I was waiting for the elevator, a neighbor left her place, moved alongside. She had the contiguous apartment, was reputed to be a shrink, and we had disliked each other for a very long time, owing to a swimming accident (there was a pool in the basement of the building) when she felt I had been unruly and cut off her lane.

So we are standing there.

And she turns to me.

Glares.

Speaks thusly: I CHUST VANT YOU TO KNOW (she was from Europe) ZAT I KNOW EFFERY-SING ZAT IS GOING ON IN ZERE.

I don't know that I was ever more surprised.

Because NUSSING was going on IN ZERE. NUSSING *ever* went on IN ZERE. Just me and my pit trying to make it through another day. The elevator came and we rode down in silence. And I still remember her total contempt for me.

I get home, tell my then wife and we instantly agree the woman is mad.

Later that summer we rented a house in Massachusetts, a nightmare of a place with a murky pond owned by an architect/builder who must have hated children. He built his dream palazzo with staircases but without banisters. Coming down from breakfast was an adventure. But we survived and one day I am tippy-toeing to lunch with my kiddoes, Jenny and Susanna, then ages ten and seven.

And they cannot stop giggling.

I ask why and finally they manage to ask me this question: did I know that I talked when I wrote? I was reworking a screenplay, *The Great Waldo Pepper,* and I said that I absolutely did not talk when I wrote. They said I did. I, being mature, replied "did not." Did. Not. Did. And then, in triumph, they started quoting back some of the morning's dialog. (Until that moment I had no idea that I did that.)

But all I thought of at that moment was the woman who knew EFFERY-SING ZAT WAS GOING ON IN ZERE. Because, you see, she was just on the other side of a very thin wall.

And I had been writing the dental scene that day.

Is it safe?

Huh?

Is it safe?

What?

Is it safe?

Is *what* safe?

Is it safe?

Is it safe?

Is it safe?

And later, Szell going, "You seem a bright young man, able to distinguish light from darkness, heat from freezing cold. Surely, you must prefer anything to my brand of torment, so I ask you, and *please* take your time before answering: Is it safe?"

And then Babe screaming and the top of his head coming off and . . .

. . . and at last I realized why she looked at me in that terrible way . . .

We were anxious that Olivier play Szell but when director John Schlesinger went to see him, he was dying again, and could barely move one side of his face. The part was his if he could play it, but who knew? I was working in London with Schlesinger one day when the phone rang. It was Richard Widmark asking if he could read for the part. Yes, he knew about Olivier, didn't care. (Widmark had made one of the memorable film debuts in *Kiss of Death* playing the madman Tommy Udo, who pushed a crippled woman down a flight of stairs. In today's bloodbath era of violence, that would probably be a comedy scene. But back then, no one who saw it forgot it.)

Widmark came to Schlesinger's home. Tall, educated, a

perfect gent, he had pretty much memorized the role and when he read the dental scene with a slight German accent, he was sensational. We took a cab back to his hotel together afterwards and talked of Sandy Koufax, who his daughter had married.

I never saw him before that afternoon and have never seen him since. But no one who was almost in a movie I've been involved with has been as fine.

The only two moments from the novel that wrote easily for the movie were the ones near the end with Szell in the diamond district, finally being spotted by the Jews, and the dental scene. I've written about the rehearsals with Hoffman and Olivier in *Adventures in the Screen Trade*. But this happened, too. We had hired a dentist to be there to assist Olivier and we all sat around this large table for the first script reading. A big moment for me. An Oscar-winning director, Schlesinger. Wonderful actors like Hoffman and Scheider and Bill Devane and of course Olivier (one of my heroes, along with Willie Mays and Bronko Nagurski and Irwin Shaw).

And I am, as I always am at such moments, tired and scared.

I'd written several drafts of the novel and a lot of versions of the movie and I was whipped and I hoped, at last, I'd gotten it down okay. Because I didn't have much more to give the project. That happens to a screenwriter, at least to this one. You've thought about it so long, done it so often, in your head or on paper, that you start to get punchy, silly, dry. I wanted the reading to work so I could leave it behind, begin to rebuild my head.

The reading more than worked, it went *wonderfully*. There was a pause after the ending. A treasured pause. A sense of contentment in the air—

—and then, from some dimwitted blue, the *dentist* starts talking. "I don't know about the rest of you, but frankly, *I* have a *lot* of problems with the screenplay . . ."

*Nightmare.*

If you write movies, you never know who the enemy is. Someone is going to fuck you, that's a given. I knew Hoffman was the enemy—he felt he was too old for the role and he was right, of course. I knew Schlesinger could be an enemy; he only took such a commercial piece of work for the same reason that all the good ones do—the fear that their careers are in trouble. But those two were momentarily happy. I was free, I was home and dry. Until this *dentist* turns into Brooks Atkinson.

I *screamed* at him. "You're here for teeth! Leave the goddam script alone!" He did not know how crazy writers can be. The fact is truly this: if I'd had a gun and thought I could get away with it, the guy was dead.

I was out of the loop during shooting and postproduction, I was out of the country when the film opened, working in Holland on *A Bridge Too Far*. But the first Saturday night after I landed, I went to a big Times Square theatre and sat in the back on the right, my preferred spot when I am involved with a flick, easy for fleeing.

Lights down, picture starts. Certain things are immediately clear: you don't get people of that talent to work on a genre film very often. The actors were superb. I wanted to marry Sir Laurence. I kind of relaxed, sitting there in the dark with my popcorn. It was an absolutely decent film. I kind of liked it.

But a little over halfway, I realized something awful: the audience *hated* it. The aisles were *crammed* with people leaving. I was stunned. "Wait," I wanted to shout out to them. "It's not so terrible. There's good stuff coming up. *Please. Don't go.*" (This is a screenwriter's worst fear—that you have misconceived so badly, they hate you so much that they cannot even survive waiting another hour to resume their normal lives.)

"*Wait,*" I almost cried to them, "I've got surprises for you!"

Nothing would stop them.

I slumped in my seat. I had never missed my target by so much before. The aisles were emptying now with the dental scene hard on the horizon.

Hmmm.

I was caught up in it. Delighted by the way Schlesinger had done it, all of it indirection, no bloodbath moments. Just shots of eyes and faces filled with fear. Very classy. The audience would have liked it if they had stayed around.

The fact is, they *had* stayed around. They didn't hate the movie, it was just they had heard about the dental scene and decided not to risk it, had gone for popcorn. Back they trooped when it was done, sitting happily, as did I, till the movie ended.

Final dental scene memory.

I was Out There (the only way I can think of L.A.) in '92

when I got a twinge of pain that I knew meant this: root canal. I chose to ignore it, hoped it would stay bearable until the end of the week when I could get back to New York.

It didn't. I asked around, got a specialist, went to see him. The fellow worked in an office of specialists, a long railroad car of root canal guys. I sit in the chair, he starts to work.

And to chat. "What brings you to Los Angeles?" he starts and I already know, you should pardon the expression, the drill. I either lie and say I sell corn futures or tell the truth. Which is no fun because I am *waaay* too old to be giving my credits, and that is how this scenario frequently ends. I decide to buy time.

"Business."

"And what kind of business might that be?"

The crossroads question. I go for it. "I'm a writer."

"What kind of writing is it that you do?"

Pause. "Books and movies."

"Hmmm. Interesting." And now the most hated question of all. "What movies have you written that I might have seen?" (Often they haven't seen any.)

I am totally in his power, understand. Tilted way back. He is a big man and seems bigger, looming over me. To hell with it, I decide. Go for the gold.

"*Marathon Man.* Both the book and the movie."

Pause.

The information registers. Every dentist on both sides of the Iron Curtain knows *Marathon Man.* Excuse me, he says. He is gone, but after awhile he comes back, gently works at my mouth till he is done. I thank him. Get up to go.

And as I walk into the hallway I see this whole corridor

of dentists, all of them staring at me from their cubicles. He had told them all who he was punishing. I was not used to the attention. All these men, staring at me. I was, within the confines of that suite, famous.

Everyone in the movie business is a star fucker. Never happened like that to me before, never since. But right then, at last, I was twinkling. . . .

# BEFORE THE BEGINNING

Every time he drove through Yorkville, Rosenbaum got angry, just on general principles. The East 86th Street area was the last holdout of the krauts in Manhattan, and the sooner they got the beer halls replaced by new apartment buildings, the better off he'd be. Not that he had suffered personally during the war—his entire family had been in America since the twenties—but just driving along streets peopled with Teutonic mentalities was enough to set anyone's teeth on edge.

Especially Rosenbaum's.

*Everything* set his teeth on edge. If an injustice ever dared to creep into his vicinity, he grabbed it and squeezed it with all the bile left in his seventy-eight-year-old body. The Giants moving to Jersey set his teeth on edge; the jigaboos set his teeth on edge, now more than ever, with their notion they were as good as the next guy; the Kennedys set his teeth on edge, the commies, dirty movies, dirty magazines, the spiraling price of pastrami—you name it, Rosenbaum started gnashing.

This September day, he was particularly choleric. It was hot, and he was late as he headed toward Newark, where his only living cronies held their weekly card game in the nursing home. Three stiffs was what they were, rotten card players and rotten people, but they could all still inhale and exhale whenever they wanted to, and when you got to be seventy-eight, that counted for plenty.

They didn't like Rosenbaum a whole lot either—the games invariably ended with shouted threats of repercussions—but he always drove over, because it was the best way he had found of getting through Thursday, which, taken as a twenty-four-hour period, set his teeth on edge without half trying. One song said "Saturday night is the loneliest night of the week," another said "Monday, Monday, how can you do this thing to me?" but Rosenbaum knew that Thursday was the one you had to watch out for. Everything wrong in his life had happened on Thursday. He had gotten married on Thursday; his children had both died on Thursday—years apart, but still both Thursday—and whoever dreamed of outliving your very own? What a terrible thing. Rosenbaum had smoked three packs a day for going on fifty-five years, and his son never once even took a puff, so who do you think got the big C? He shifted uncomfortably in his seat; his truss had been fitted on Thursday.

Eighty-sixth Street was all screwed up.

Gimbels East. Ever since goddamn Gimbels East came to 86th Street, you couldn't trust it no more. It used to be his favorite cross-town easy, ten times better than 79th Street, and only tourists took 72nd anyway. No, 86th was the place you went if you wanted to really *move*, and Gimbels East had to come and screw it up. Nobody shopped at Gimbels East except the jigaboos—what Jew would be caught dead shopping at this Gimbels? This wasn't Gimbels, Gimbels was

34th Street, across from Macy's, and this pile of nothing could try calling itself Gimbels East all it wanted—to Rosenbaum, it was Gimbels dreck, period.

He did not turn on 86th, but instead went up First to 87th before he took his left. As a number, 87th set his teeth on edge. His wife's initial breast exploratory had cost him 87 smackers. Just to see a fancy butcher, have a picture taken, get the news. "There is definitely a lump on your wife's left breast," the doctor had begun, and Rosenbaum, apoplectic at the man's stupidity, had turned to his pale spouse, saying, "See how lucky we were to have come to a genius specialist? We tell him there's a lump on your left breast and, *armed with only that speck of information,* he can absolutely assure us that the lump is a lump." He turned on the doctor now, a young cocker, probably married to a blonde shiksa. "Of course there's a lump on her breast, my God, you're a tit man, I didn't come here to ask about the lump on her face—that's called a *nose*, by the way, I don't know if they teach that kind of thing any more in medical school." "Very funny, your husband," the doctor said then to his wife, and she answered, wearily, "Not to me."

Eighty-seventh Street didn't seem so bad. Rosenbaum tooled straight up to Second without a hitch, caught the green perfectly, got to Third in little time flat. He waited impatiently for the light to change, honked his horn twice at the damn thing before it obeyed him, then jammed on the gas and roared toward Lex. Everyone said he was a terrible driver, his whole family had always been at him about that, but they knew from nothing. Not one traffic ticket in thirty-five years. A few close calls, sure, a couple scrapes here and there, three or four times some near fistfights, but *no tickets*, let 'em all go to hell, criticizing him, that was all they had ever been good for anyway, giving him grief.

Rosenbaum began to come to grief himself at the corner of 87th and Lexington. The light was red, which was no big deal—anyone could survive a red light. But the car in front of him, the car at the light, was a stupid goddamn Nazi Volkswagen, and, worse, it was waiting smack in the center of 87th Street, so he couldn't edge by to the light and then leave it behind when things turned green. Rosenbaum honked a couple of times, muttering to himself, but what could you expect from any jerk in a VW? He himself was a Chevy man, and had been since before the war. If you really knew cars, if you wanted your pennies to count for something, you drove a Chevy. Anyone who didn't was a schlemiel.

The light switched to green, but the VW didn't move.

Rosenbaum honked again, a lot louder, but the car ahead still blocked him. He could hear the motor coughing, try to catch. *"Move to one side!"* Rosenbaum shouted. *"Quit hawwggging!"*

Finally the VW started, crept across Lex, began slowly passing the back of Gimbels East. Rosenbaum rode the other car's tail now, trying to get by, but the VW would not budge from the center of 87th Street. Then, without warning, the motor died again, and the car oozed to a stop, blocking Rosenbaum completely. He leaned out the window, honking and honking, really getting his throat limbered up now: "Move-move-*move*—what the hell's with you, get off the road, you're a goddamn menace, you stupid jerk, now move-your-car-or-I'll-move-it-for-you!"

From the Volkswagen came one word: *"Langsamer."*

*Langsamer.* Slow down. Take it easy. Translate it from the German how you will. Rosenbaum was starting to perspire heavily, from both the heat and aggravation. "Don't you *Langsamer* me, you kraut meathead, *mach snell!*"

The relic in the VW leaned out the window, looked back, managed to shake an ancient fist at Rosenbaum. *"Langsamer!"* he said again.

The sight of the guy set Rosenbaum's teeth on edge. So old, practically ready for stuffing, with blue eyes, just like all the Nazis, a Hun on the loose in midtown Manhattan, faded and senile; it was a disgrace anybody let him behind the wheel of a car.

For a moment after the second *"Langsamer!"* Rosenbaum just sat there and sweated. Then he drove his Chevy forward and nudged the Volkswagen. It felt so terrific, he backed up a few feet and then drove forward, nudging it again, harder. It had been years since he had felt so instinctively like getting in the ring with a stranger. Why? Well, he was (a) in Yorkville; (b) on 87th Street; (c) behind Gimbels East; (d) blocked; (e) by a Volkswagen; (f) driven by an antique limburger-lover; (g) who was making him even later for his Thursday card game; (h) which was particularly galling since his Chevy wasn't air-conditioned, and even though it was mid-afternoon in mid-September, the temperature read 92 degrees; (i) Fahrenheit; (j) and rising.

Rosenbaum banged into the other car a third time, knocking it several feet forward before it stopped, but then it suddenly went forward again as the motor caught, heading toward Park, and Rosenbaum was surprised at first, but he gunned his Chevy, quickly caught up, and prepared to pass on the right, because he knew what his mission in life was now, and it all came down to this: pass the goddamn VW, get in front of it, block it, and then slow down to . . . a . . . c . r . . a . . w . . . l.

But the other car was having none of it—as Rosenbaum went right, so did the Volkswagen, and when Rosenbaum went left, so did the Volkswagen, and suddenly, on 87th Street, war had been declared, and that was fine with Rosenbaum, because the day a Chevy couldn't mop up a pint-sized import, we might all just as well hang it up.

They talk a lot in France about the Mistral and the insanity that possesses people when it starts blowing, and in California everybody treads softly when the Santa Ana begins to brain-bake. Well, there's a wind like that in Manhattan too, nobody's named it yet, but it's there. When a hot day turns into a real steamer and the wind swirls up from the west, blowing all the mosquitoes from the Jersey swamp straight across the Hudson—and maybe that's all this was, an aberration caused by climate, but God knows it was something, because up ahead now the lights on Park Avenue were just going into their red-to-green act, and the Chevy was pouring it on, but the VW man was keeping the lead, foot to the floor, as if nothing mattered but that the bumping madman in the car behind should never pass, never, never, no matter what, and they flew across the intersection of 87th and Park, and nurses grabbed their children and a dozen people looked helplessly around for a cop, and then they were going for Madison, with the VW starting to shake almost out of control at the effort, while the Chevy gunned and scraped, and there they were, these two guys, way over 150 years old total, fighting to the death because a stalled motor had happened in a rented Volks back by Lexington Avenue, and these things do happen all the time in cities, really, but they pass, flare-up follows quiet follows outburst, on and on, and probably this one would have passed too, except for Hunsicker.

Hunsicker was making his regular delivery, and he hated the 87th Street job because the street was narrow, but he liked the 87th Street job because around the corner toward 88th was the Lenox Hill Deli and behind the counter of that establishment Ilene worked, and every week for going on over a year Hunsicker had eaten coffee and a Danish there, because Ilene was stacked and the head was nice too, one hunk of a divorcee, only she'd never come across. She'd joke with him, sure, she'd even sometimes reach out and rumple Hunsicker's hair, but she never wanted to meet him after work. Her first husband had been a teamster, she said, and once was more than enough, if you don't mind. "But I'm different" was Hunsicker's pitch, "I'm not some jerk who gets his jollies at the bowling league, I read best sellers, all the number ones, *Love Story* I read, *The Godfather*, you name a biggie, I got the paperback," but Ilene would not relent. He was telling her that Jackie Susann's latest, *Once Is Not Enough*, marked a definite improvement for her, an advance in both content and style, when the crash came.

Hunsicker guessed it was his vehicle immediately, so he took off out the door, running like a bastard, back to 87th, and even before he turned the corner, he felt the heat, the incredible heat, because when an oil truck goes, it can incinerate a brick, and there were screams now from all over, women and kids, and as he got to 87th the flames were scorching the side of the building he was delivering to, and Hunsicker ran as far into the inferno as he could, tried to make sense of it all, but there wasn't much. It looked like two cars had creamed into each other and then spun into his truck, and from there, who knew, but my God, how many dead?

Scorched, Hunsicker staggered back to the Deli, put in one call to the firemen, a second to the cops. He sat dully at the counter while Ilene, unasked, poured coffee. He sipped at it. Something in him touched her somehow, and she came around the corner, sat alongside him, wiping his darkened face with a clean cloth. That night she went to the movies with him for the first time, and three dates after that, he scored. So it all worked out fine for Hunsicker.

It worked out fine for Bibby, too. He was a black kid, barely into his twenties, who wanted to be a photographer, and who happened to be on his way to the park when the crash took place. He was the only one clicking at the time, and he got some beauties. The *Daily News* bought a bunch and spread them across their front and center pages, and eventually offered Bibby a full-time job, so he had nothing close to a complaint, either.

And actually, call it luck, timing, proof of Divine Intervention, only the two drivers took it, and that wasn't the greatest loss imaginable either. Rosenbaum was truly a scratchy man, seventy-eight and full of unpleasant quirks, increasingly cranky, and the VW driver was even older, eighty-two, a widower who had but one living relative, a son, whom he had not seen in close to half an ordinary lifetime, and even though their blood relationship was thick as standard, any emotional interchange had long since gone by the boards; theirs was an exercise in commerce, nothing more.

This widower was a refugee who had outlived all his friends and had never bothered accumulating many enemies. Everyone called him Kurt Hesse, though that was not his name. His driver's license read Kurt Hesse, his passport read the same; doctors and mailmen called him Mr. Hesse, his barber "Mr. H"; children called him "thank you" when he scattered candy in the park playgrounds, something he enjoyed doing; and his sister, when she was alive and once she got used to it, always called him Kurt. Indeed, he had been Kurt Hesse for so long now that if you asked him his name without preparation, if you just ran up behind him and cried "Name!" he more than likely would have stammered "Hesse, Kurt Hesse" and not meant to be a liar.

His real name was Kaspar Szell, but twenty-eight years had passed since anyone had called him that, and sometimes, when he was in a dreamy state before sleep, he actually sometimes wondered if there ever really had been a Kaspar Szell and, if there had, what he would have been like had he been given a chance to live.

He died instantly in the crash. The crash killed him, not the fire. The fire only delayed identification.

The entire incident, from Gimbels on, covered less than three minutes, and at the most, in the case of Rosenbaum, less than five seconds of primary pain. All in all, it would have been hard to have wished for a happier tragedy.

# PART I

# BABE

# 1

"Here comes da creep," one of the stoop kids said.

Levy did his best to ignore them, standing at the top of the brownstone steps, making sure his sneaker laces were properly tight. These were his best shoes, the cream of the Adidas line, and they fit his feet as if divinely sculpted, never, not even on the first day, giving a hint of blister. Levy felt passionate about few items of wearing apparel, but these running shoes he cared about.

"Hey creepy creepy creepy," another of the stoop kids shouted, this one their leader, small, quick, with usually the brightest clothes. Now he made his voice very hoity-toity: "I just absolutely *adore* your chateau," and he indicated Levy's hat.

Without really meaning to, Levy adjusted his golf cap, and as he did the stoop kids, three brownstones down, hit him with the sound of their triumphant laughter. Levy was particularly sensitive about the whole cap business. He had been wearing his peakbill for years, and no one cared, but then, in the '72 Olympics, Wottle won the 800 meters for the U.S.A. and *he* wore a golf cap, Wottle did, so everyone assumed that Levy was merely an imitator.

Levy felt genuinely confident about few things in this world, but one of them was—did it sound conceited? then it was conceited—his mind. He had, for someone not yet out of his middle twenties, a relatively original mind, and he would never have copied anyone, let alone a fellow runner. Now he took a breath, trying to ready himself for the taunts of the stoop kids as he began jogging storklike down the brownstone steps. The stoop kids loved his awkwardness. They flapped their arms and made goose sounds.

Levy just hated it when they imitated him. Not because they were wrong, but because they were so aggravatingly *accurate* in their mimicking. He, T. B. Levy, did look like a goose, at least on occasion. He didn't much like it, but there it was.

The stoop kids—usually six in number, Spanish in origin—seemed to live on the brownstone steps of the house three doors closer to Central Park than Levy's own. At least, they had been perched there when he arrived in June, and here it was, September now, and they showed no signs of flying south. They were maybe fifteen or sixteen, small, thin, undoubtedly dangerous when provoked, and they ate on their stoop, played handball against the stoop steps or on the sidewalk in front, and often, late in the darkness, Levy would pass them necking and more with what he assumed were neighborhood girls. Morning till night, the stoop kids were there, sitting there, standing, playing, smoking, not caring to watch the world go by, because they were a world, tight-knit and constant, and sometimes, for that reason, Levy wondered if he didn't envy them. Not that he ever wanted them to offer him a seat. Certainly, he would have rejected such an offer. But then again, who knew how he'd behave, it was all academic, they'd never asked him.

Levy turned on the sidewalk toward Central Park, jogging his way, and as he passed them the one who *adored* his chateau said, "Why aren't you in school?" so suddenly that Levy had to laugh, because once, in June, when they had been particularly insulting to him, he had said that to them, "Why aren't you in school?" and not only had he not shut them up, for a month they'd never let him come close to forgetting it. But this was the first time in many days they'd used the line back on him, and therefore his laughter. Humor was the unexpected juxtaposition of incongruities, who had said that? Levy rooted around in his mind a moment before he decided on Hazlitt. No. Meredith maybe? G. B. Shaw? *Think,* he commanded, but the right name would not come. Levy stormed at himself, because you *had* to know that kind of thing if you were going to be really first-rate, his father would have known just-like-that, known the author's name *and* the work the quote resided in *and* the mental state of the creator at the moment of composition—were these good times for him, bad, what? Shamed, Levy jogged faster.

Levy lived on West 95th Street, between Amsterdam and Columbus, not an appetizing neighborhood, certainly, but when you were a scholarship student you took what was available, and in June what was available was a single room with bath on the top floor of the brownstone at 148 West 95th Street. It wasn't all that bad, actually: a lovely jogging distance from Columbia, just across to Riverside Park and then up to 116th, a straight shoot along the river—you couldn't ask for more than that if you were a runner.

Levy crossed Columbus, picked up his pace a bit more as he closed in on Central Park, turned left at 95th, ran one block up and into the green area itself, straight to the tennis courts, and after that it was just a little half turn and then he was there.

At the reservoir.

Whoever invented the reservoir, Levy had decided months ago, must have done it with him alone in mind. It was without flaw, a perfect lake set in this most unexpected of locations, bounded by the millionaires on Fifth and their distant relations on Central Park South and *their* distant relations along Central Park West.

Levy easily passed other joggers as he began his initial circling of the water. It was half-past five—he always ran then, it was ideal for him. Some people liked a morning jaunt, but Levy wasn't one of them; his mind was at its best in the morning, so he always did his most complex reading before the noon hour; afternoons he took notes or read simple stuff. By five his brain was exhausted, but his body was desperate to move.

So at half-past five Levy ran. Clearly he was faster than anyone around, so if you were a casual observer it would have been logical to assume that this rather tallish, sort of slender fellow with the running style not unreminiscent of a goose covered ground really quite well.

But you had to consider his daydreams.

He was going to run the marathon. Like Nurmi. Like the already mythical Nurmi. Years from now, all across the world, track buffs would agonize over who was greatest, the mighty Finn or the fabled T. B. Levy. "Levy," some of them would argue, "no one would ever run the final five miles the way Levy ran them," and others would counter that by the time the last five miles came, Nurmi would be so far ahead, it wouldn't matter how fast Levy ran them, and so the debate would rage, expert against expert, down the decades.

For Levy was not going to be a marathon man; anyone could be that if you just devoted your life to it. No, he was going to be *the* marathon man. That, plus an intellect of staggering accomplishment coupled with an unequaled breadth of knowledge, the entire mixture bounded by a sense of modesty as deep as it was sincere.

Right now he only had the B.Litt. he'd won at Oxford, and could race but fifteen miles without fatigue. But give him a few more years and he would be both Ph.D. and Champion. And the crowds would sing out "*Lee*-vee, *Lee*-vee," sending him on to undreamed-of triumphs as now sports fans shouted "*Dee*-fense" as they urged on their heroes.

"*Lee*-vee, *Lee*-vee—"

And they wouldn't care about how awkwardly he might run. It wouldn't matter to them that he was over six feet tall and under a hundred and fifty pounds, no matter how many milkshakes he downed per day in an effort to move up from skinny to slender.

"*Lee*-vee! *Lee*-vee!—"

It wouldn't bother them that he had a stupid cowlick and the face of an Indiana farmer, that even after spending three years in England he still had the expression of someone you just knew would buy the Brooklyn Bridge if you offered him the chance. He was beloved by few, known by none save, thank God for Doc, Doc. But that would change. Oh yes, oh yes.

"*LEE*-VEE . . . *LEEEEEEE*-VEE."

There he was now, up ahead and running with the firm

knowledge that no one could ever conquer him, except possibly Mercury. Tireless, fabled, arrogant, unbeatable, the Flying Finn himself, Nurmi.

Levy picked up his pace.

The end of the race was still miles off, but now was the greatest test, the test of the heart.

Levy picked up his pace again.

Levy was gaining.

The half-million people lining the course could not believe it. They screamed, they surged almost out of control. It could not be happening but there it was—*Levy was gaining on Nurmi!*

Levy, the handsome American, was closing in. It was true. Levy, so confident that he even dared a smile while running at the fastest pace in marathon history, was definitely destroying Nurmi's lead. Nurmi was aware now—something terrible was going on behind him. He glanced over his shoulder, and the disbelief was plain for all to see. Nurmi tried to go faster, but he was already at maximum pace, and suddenly his stride began to betray him, the crucial rhythm getting erratic. Levy was coming. Levy was making his move. Levy was getting set to pass now. Levy was—

Thomas Babington Levy paused for a moment, leaning against the reservoir fence. It was hard to really concentrate on Nurmi today.

For he had a toothache, and as he ran, as his right foot hit the ground, it jarred the cavity on the right side of his upper jaw. For a moment Levy rubbed the offending tooth, wondering if he should see a dentist now or not. The thing had come on only lately, and maybe it would depart as it had come, because it hadn't gotten worse, and proved a nuisance only when he ran. Dentists raped you anyway, they charged a ton for maybe two minutes' work, and there were better things to spend your money on, like books, all the books ever printed; records, too. To hell with it, Levy decided.

In the end, it didn't really matter. Once they found his weakness, they almost killed him . . .

# 2

As Scylla entered the airport bar, he spotted the toupeed man immediately, and for a moment he was undecided as to what to do, since at their previous meeting they had both tried very hard, if somewhat briefly, to kill each other.

True, that had been Brussels and business, while this was Los Angeles International and, if flying could ever be considered pleasurable, pleasure, but that didn't make Scylla's problem any less tangible: Namely, how did you tell a fellow you'd recently made a pass at destroying that now you were off duty and interested in nothing more lethal than a little conversation? You couldn't just walk up and say "Hi, how are things?" because more than likely there would be a new and unasked-for-hole in your temple before the "things" was fully sounded, Ape was that quick with a pistol.

Ape was working for the Arabs now, Libya or Iraq or one of them—Scylla could never really keep them straight—or at least he had been at the time of their Brussels encounter. As soon as he'd returned to Division, Scylla had asked to see Ape's file, knowing there would be one and also that it would be thick—Division prided itself on its ability to collect and itemize all information on any adversary.

Not that Ape had always been an enemy. He shifted

countries and allegiances frequently, but for six years he had worked for the British, and the two following that for the French. After that he tried free-lancing, but evidently that hadn't turned out well—it never really worked out well for anybody; only the inscrutable and virulent Mr. S. L. Chen free-lanced on a more or less permanent basis. After his attempt at becoming self-employed, Ape moved a good deal more quickly than before: Brazil for a while, then a quick stop in Albania before settling into his present slot with the Arabs.

Scylla stared at the little toupeed man sitting alone at the farthest stool. The genuinely remarkable thing was that he should be faced with the problem of how to introduce himself safely, because it was rare that two such as he and Ape should have gone against each other and both survived. Even though Ape was both shorter and less menacing-looking than Mickey Rooney, he had been absolutely top international level with any kind of small firearm for over a decade, whereas Scylla rated along with Chen as the two fastest at killing with either hand—palm up, palm down, right hand, left, it mattered not at all.

The logical thing, Scylla decided, was to find another bar. Risks didn't bother him, but the unexpected he always tried avoiding. He had backed several steps out of the place when he paused, because, dammit, he *wanted* to talk to Ape. You didn't get that kind of opportunity often, since when Scylla had first entered the business, Ape was one of the fewer than half dozen from any country who could lay legitimate claim to being remotely legendary. Scylla flicked back a bit, coming up with some of the others—Brighton, Trench, Fidelio—all, alas, retired. Violently.

And suddenly Scylla was in motion. He was extraordinarily quick for a man his size, especially at the start; he wasn't particularly fast, but straightaway speed meant nothing, quickness was all. He had once heard a basketball coach ask another about a young player: "How is his quick?" The phrase stuck—he had not known till then you could be both quick and slow. Scylla moved along the bar behind the stools, and when he was close enough for his move, he threw some recognition on his face and whirled in behind the little man, his powerful arms locking Ape firmly in place, and it looked like two long-lost Elks or Babbitty Rotarians suddenly finding each other and going into their semi-secret greeting as Scylla whispered, "Peace, Ape," followed by the lightning rejoinder "I've none."

Scylla took the next bar stool, impressed by the speed of Ape's reflexes; it was what made him unsurpassed with a pistol—not his aim, which was good, but that his bullet was already in the air while the enemy was still aiming. "Does that bother you?" Scylla wondered.

"What? Being unarmed? No, why should it, does it bother you?"

Scylla said nothing, his big hands clasped loosely together, fingers interlocked on the bar.

Ape flicked a glance at them. "But then, you're never unarmed, are you?"

Scylla shrugged.

"Hands are better," Ape said. "Close in, there's no comparison. If I'd had your size, I'd have specialized in hands."

Scylla thought immediately of Chen, who was far smaller even than Ape, frail, barely a hundred pounds. He would never have brought up the name, but he didn't have to, Ape did. Scylla had to smile. He hadn't the least idea where Ape had received his original training, which country, but more than likely it wasn't dissimilar to his own. Actually, all they really knew about each other was whatever was locked in the files of their different main offices. In a way, this was nothing; in another, all. They could almost, on occasion, mind-read each other, and this was clearly one of those occasions.

"The reason Mr. S. L. Chen can kill so adroitly with either hand is because he is a goddamn heathen Chinee, and that kind of thing comes as second nature to Chinks, like all coons can dance." Ape stared at the trace of whisky left in his glass. "That was supposed to be funny," he said. "It didn't come out that way though, did it?" Before Scylla could reply, the little man rode right on: "Now you'll probably go to your grave thinking I'm a treasure house of prejudice. 'Ape? I met him once. Bigoted little fart, wig didn't fit.' Another." This last was to the bartender, who nodded, went for a Scotch bottle, poured. "Make it a triple," Ape said. The bartender nodded and poured.

Scylla ordered what he always did. "Scotch, please, lots of soda, lots of ice," he said, thinking that Ape was too smart to be ordering triples. Triples were dangerous; your tongue got slow, your brain, your pistol reactions. All this was true, so of course he couldn't say it; he sought a different avenue. "It's not a bad wig," he said.

"Not bad? Jesus, in the wind here today it rose up on my head, the front part did—the back part stayed in place but the front started flapping—it must have looked like it was trying to wave to somebody." He stared at his drink. "That didn't come out funny either. I used to be so funny. Truly, Scylla. A comedian."

"I believe you."

"You don't a bit."

"Does it matter?"

"No," Ape said, before he said, "Yes, yes it does, a lot."

Scylla thought it best to say nothing.

"I picked my name," the little man went on. "*I selected my own anonym.* They said, 'What do you want to be known as?' and I've been dead bald since I was twenty-two, and out it popped, not even a pause—'Ape,' I said. After the play *Hairy Ape* by O'Neill, the American. Don't you see how funny that is? I was like that all the time, barrels of laughs."

Scylla smiled, because it was the decent thing to do, and also because it was one of Ape's passions to keep his origin secret. He spoke no language quite well enough to seem native in it, and by referring to O'Neill as "the American" he seemed to remove that country as a possible home.

"I meant that about the wig," Scylla said. "It's absolutely serviceable—not as good as Sinatra the American's toupees, but then, probably you don't sing as well."

Ape laughed. "There was a fellow once—before your time, I expect—Fidelio his name was, and he was crazed to find out where I was from. It was an obsession with him—the slightest clue, he'd track it down in his spare time. I used to pepper my speech with hints for him."

Of all the legends, Scylla was most fascinated by Fidelio, who'd been a music lover—he'd been something of a fiddle prodigy as a child, but the talent didn't carry over into adolescence, only his passion for music came along—and he'd been, from what the files at Division said, anyway, the most brilliant of any of them, from any country. "Did you know him well? Fidelio?"

"Know him? Did I know him, for God's sakes, I *retired* him—"

"You did? I never knew that—our files don't say a word about that, how did you do it? It must have been hard, God, it must have been damn near impossible," and Scylla could have gone on, but he stopped before he made a fool of himself. He felt, right then, very much like a young Joe DiMaggio saying to the Babe, "Did you really point your bat and call that home run or was it luck? Did you *know* you could hit a homer? What did it feel like circling the bases, hearing them cheer? Go on, please, it's important that I know."

Ape picked up his glass, looked at the liquor.

Scylla waited patiently. When you were talking to Babe Ruth about home-run hitting, you let him set the pace.

"I'm glad you sat down, Scylla," Ape said, still watching the whisky. "I was hoping you might. I saw you standing in the doorway." He gestured toward a painting behind the bar; the glass angled faintly toward the main entrance. "Not much of an image; sufficient, though. I almost beckoned when you started backing out."

"Why didn't you?"

Ape sipped his triple—touched it to his lips, really; nothing went down. "This is only my second, and I won't do more than taste it. I'm far from being intoxicated."

Scylla missed the thought connection till Ape said, "I didn't wave because I don't like to force myself on people. Felt in the way since childhood, I expect."

You shouldn't be doing this talking, Scylla almost said, but since it was true, he didn't. Something was cutting at Ape. Something horrid was knifing away inside.

"You were going to tell me about Fidelio," Scylla said.

"I will, I remember—don't sweat it, Scylla, I'm not drunk and about to start burbling on."

Whatever it was that Ape was anguished over would soon surface; Scylla could sense that. There wasn't much he could do but wait till it happened. Still, it wasn't pleasant waiting, so he shifted to a subject of mutual interest, the time in Brussels when they both survived. Actually, it was a chance encounter, both of them apparently after the same dead passport engraver for whatever reason, and they came on each other suddenly in the same room with the corpse, and Ape fired and Scylla swiped at him with his right hand, but his aim was bad, he missed the neck, connected only with Ape's shoulder, which was surprisingly muscled, and then Ape tried once more with a shot, but he was stumbling, it was really more a warning than an attempt to kill, and then it was over, one of them going one way, one another. "Why did you miss with that first shot?" Scylla wondered. "Not that I'm sorry, understand."

"I hadn't been drinking—I was a teetotaler then, it was over a year ago."

"Fifteen months, I think."

Ape nodded. "Shadows," he said. "Shadows are ruinous to your accuracy. I was high, I expect. I went for your brain but got the wall. If I'd gone for your heart, you'd have been uncomfortable awhile."

Scylla raised his glass. "To shadows."

Ape toyed with his whisky.

The loudspeaker announced a further delay of the polar flight to London.

Ape cursed, took a long swallow of Scotch.

"I'm going to London too," Scylla said, and he touched the First Class ticket envelope in his inside jacket pocket.

"Good. I've never had company on the damn flight before, eleven hours of nothing's what it's always been. I can't read anything deeper than a magazine on planes. Hedy Lamarr's autobiography. That was perfect polar reading."

"I'm flying Coach," Ape said, and Scylla knew what had been destroying the little man.

"For cover?"

Ape shook his head.

"Mistake, probably."

Ape shook his head again.

Scylla knew it was best to say nothing. There was nothing *to* say, really. When you did this work, you went First Class. All the way. There weren't old-age benefits and pension plans; nobody was guaranteeing job security. If you flew Coach, you did it because it fit the past they'd made for you for the particular task they'd sent you on. The only other reason was to let you know your work ratings were dropping, and once that happened, retirement was a matter of time. Only, of course, you weren't allowed to retire. Catch-23.

Except it seemed, to Scylla, an altogether shitty act, sending a legend Coach. Christ, give him a job he couldn't survive, let him go out with a little glory clinging, at least; he'd earned that.

But then, the Yankees traded Babe Ruth, didn't they.

"I've had a good run," Ape said. "Better than most."

"And you retired Fidelio."

"*And* Trench. Didn't know that either, did you? Got them both. Very same year. Shadows didn't exist for me then." He took another taste of Scotch. "You know what I was thinking before you arrived?"

Scylla shook his head.

"Do you want to?"

I really don't, Scylla thought; you don't want to hear from Johnny Unitas that he can't throw the bomb any more or have Elgin Baylor tell you that his jump shot is gone. "If you feel like talking, talk," Scylla said.

"I was thinking that there has never been a woman I didn't pay for, or a child who knew my name, or a wig that enhanced me."

"Sentimental crap," Scylla said, hoping it would work . . . Pick it up, pick it up, Mr. Loman . . .

The little man was silent for a while. Then he broke into a huge laugh. "Goddamn, Scylla, what a good thing to say." Then he actually smiled.

Scylla nodded and said, "Now get on with the damn Fidelio story or I'll go look for the *Confessions of Lana Turner* in the bookstore."

"First some ablutions," the little man said, and he hopped off the stool. "You know about that, I'm sure it's in my file at Division," and he scurried out of the bar in what was unmistakably a good mood.

The file on Ape mentioned a weakness with his kidneys and a troublesome lower intestine—there had been an operation some years back. So Scylla would have known he was headed for the men's room, "ablutions" remark or not.

He had only raised his glass with Ape barely out of sight when he decided, just-like-that, to change his ticket and go Coach—it was not a traumatic decision if *you* were the one doing the deciding. Scylla left the bar immediately, made his way to the Pan Am windows, waited surprisingly little time, explained what he wanted, got it, just-like-that, and made his way back to the bar. Probably his gesture was the same as Ape's outburst, sentimental crap, but if the Fidelio story had any texture, any coloring at all, there would never be a better time to hear it, and the Trench tale too, and Scylla made a note to say exactly that when Ape realized they were flying together, so that way Scylla could seem an interested executive on the rise rather than a premature mourner for the dead.

Scylla took his place at the bar again, and waited for Ape to return. He finished his Scotch and soda slowly.

The other stool stayed empty.

Scylla ordered a refill.

And took a sip.

Obviously, something was very much wrong.

Another sip.

It's none of your affair, Scylla reminded. He sat alone and quiet at the bar for a moment, then took a large swallow of Scotch. Probably it was the size of that swallow that determined his next actions, because he never drank a lot without the door being locked, and you certainly didn't get that kind of privacy in airport bars, which meant he was giving in to anxiety, which meant he must really *want* to hear the Fidelio story, which meant he had to do something other than sit, so Scylla got up and walked toward the men's room.

The sign on the men's-room door put it all in perspective. "Sorry, Pipe Trouble. Please Use the Facilities at the Bottom of the Escalator. Thanks." It was taped to the door, written in ink in a neat hand. Scylla nodded to himself, remembering that the escalator was a good distance away, which explained why the little toupeed man was so long gone.

He was halfway to the bar when he decided the sign was a phony. Scylla turned and went back to the men's-room door, wondering why he was so sure. Probably it was the word "Facilities"—no one said "Facilities"—you developed a sense for things after a while. He knew the sign was false, just as he knew the door was locked, but he gave it a slight push anyway.

It was locked, but locks meant nothing to Scylla, he had a way with them, and he reached into his pants pocket. Everybody was always talking about skeleton keys, writers were always writing about skeleton keys, but Scylla knew they were nothing, not unless you had a hundred different sizes and styles. Picks were the thing, and he always had one, and one was all you needed if you had the gift of touch when it came to tumblers. He took out his pocket knife, small, two-bladed, and ordinary except that he had altered the tinier blade, thinned it slightly, given it an almost imperceptible hook, so that it wasn't much of a pick really, no decent locksmith would want to take it on an important job; still, it sufficed, and Scylla inserted it noiselessly into the lock once, got the feel of the tumblers, ripped up and down, and that was that.

Scylla lurched drunkenly into the men's room, made his

unsteady way toward the sinks. There were two others in the place, a young Caucasian engineer in overalls, who was working on the overhead pipes, and a Negro janitor, who was cleaning up, pushing an enormous canvas garbage sack along. "Martinis 're killers," Scylla slurred to the black man, and he ran the cold water, tested it. "Martinis 're killers," he slurred to the engineer.

"Hey, off," the engineer said, coming toward Scylla. "Pipes are screwed up."

Scylla blinked stupidly, turned off the spigot.

"Didn't you read the sign?" the Negro said.

"Sign?" Scylla said, very perplexed. "Said men's room, 'course I read th' sign, natur'ly I read th' sign, wouldn't want a buncha ladies screamin' at me." He shook his head. "Martinis 're killers," he said to the mirror, and turned the cold-water spigot on again and put some water on his face.

The engineer turned the spigot off, while the black went for the door, opened it, glanced to see if the sign was gone. "You can't use the water, mister, really. I'm sorry, but you can't." He was very polite and sincere, and Scylla wondered who had retired Ape, he or the black, and were they Arabs or enemies of Arabs. It didn't matter much to Ape any more. He was resting, Scylla knew, at the bottom of the canvas sack.

"Sorry," Scylla said, and he meant it. Now the Fidelio story was gone, and it would have been interesting hearing about Trench too. But it had to happen. Ape knew it as well as anybody. Scylla felt regret. Sincere, but hardly more than a dollop's worth.

The black was returning quickly now. "Sign's still there."

The engineer looked up at the janitor.

"Oh, that *paper* thing," Scylla said. "Thass not a sign, what did it say?"

"That these facilities are busted," the engineer answered. "And to use the ones downstairs."

Scylla almost laughed then at his own genius—"no one said facilities, you developed a sense for things after a while." Oh, he was smart, all right, all right. They were looking at each other still, and Scylla knew they were wondering whether to let him go or not. "Here lies Scylla, undone the first time he ran into a decent vocabulary." He stood very still, drunkenly bracing himself on the sink, not remotely tempted to move until they told him to go. He was sure they would, because he was not on their agenda; they had their job and they had done it and he was none of their affair. And he certainly would never mix with them, since he had his own work to take care of. There was no possibility of more violence; it did not exist, Scylla knew that, so when the violence came, he was surprised, even more so by the fact that he was the one to start it.

Because it was then that he saw Ape's pathetic toupee in a toilet-stall corner.

The bastards had taken the little man with the troublesome lower intestine at the least dignified of times—they had wasted a legend with his pants down. "*You should have waited, Jesus Christ!*" and as they looked away from each other and toward him, Scylla went first for the engineer, not because he was nearest but because he carried a heavy wrench, and that had probably been the weapon.

He rammed up with his fingertips forced together and

lifted the engineer off his feet with a blow beneath the chin, and the black was easy, because he didn't know then whom he was dealing with, so he went into a quick guard position for another right-hand assault, so Scylla took him easily with his left, clubbing the hard edge of his hand down at the janitor's shoulder near the neck, and there was the sound of bone cracking as the black sprawled near the engineer.

"*Why didn't you wait?*"

The engineer was trying to gasp, and probably he would never speak quite the same again, while the black blinked up, dazed, trying to hold his shoulder in place, looking for some way to make his brain order the correct words.

Scylla started softly. "I think I'll take your pants down, would you like that? And then I'll put you on the squat, would you like that? And kill you. And kill you! *Would you like that?*"

"Orders," the black managed. "There was nothing about you. Don't kill us."

"You know who I am?"

"I do now," the black said. "Scylla."

Scylla looked at them, genuinely undecided as to whether to finish them. Rage still had him, so the doing would be no problem. And he would risk the getaway.

"Don't," the black said again.

The engineer continued to gasp.

Then the black saved their lives: "They never said he was your friend."

"Well, he was," Scylla said. "Yes." But now the rage was lowering. "For many years," Scylla went on, trying to keep it high. But there was no way of doing that. For Ape had been no friend. Not friend nor acquaintance nor cohort nor any other thing. They shared an occupation. What was that?

He knelt suddenly over them then, his hands in killing position. He wanted their fear, and got it. It was in their eyes and in their minds that they were going to die. "You remember this now," Scylla said, and even though his rage was going, his voice still trembled. "Always leave a person something. Do you understand me? Some little thing, leave them that. A shred will do, but there must be that shred. *Do you understand me?*"

"Yes," the black said.

Scylla brought his hands lower.

*"I understand!"* the black cried out, but he knew it was over for him then. The engineer knew he was done, too.

When he had them convinced of their extinction, Scylla rose in silence and left them there, returning to the bar, finishing his Scotch, ordering another.

What a stupid performance! Word would get back. These two would report to their headquarters, and their headquarters would contact Division very loudly that Scylla had misbehaved. Worse—Scylla had *interfered.* And of course, Division would do their best to deny the allegations.

But they would never be quite so confident of Scylla again. Oh, they would use him, certainly; he was much too valuable still to discard. But they would watch him too. Much more carefully than in the past, wondering why he had misbehaved, what was wrong with him to do a thing like that, could you trust Scylla any more or was he past it. And at the next sign . . .

There must not be a next sign, Scylla decided.

And the Arabs who hired the black and the engineer—if indeed it had been the Arabs—they would be watching him too. You had to protect your people, and it would not be unfitting for them to try to take him when he was vulnerable, perhaps break his shoulder, destroy his voice. Or, if they were really angry, perhaps break his back at the spine base, let him try living crippled a decade or so.

I must not become vulnerable, Scylla decided.

Easy enough to decide, but why had he gone wild in the men's room? Why had the sight of an illfitting wig in the corner of a toilet stall sent him into fury?

Because . . . Scylla realized—

—because . . . It was hard for him even to shape the thought—

—because I want to die with someone who loves me.

There. Out, admitted, done. And was it so terrible a wish? Was it so much to ask of life, a decent dying?

Probably.

"Check," Scylla said, and he paid for his drinks, Ape's too. On the way to the plane, he detoured briefly back to the men's room. The piece of paper was down. Scylla opened the door, stepped inside briefly, glanced around. The toupee was gone.

Scylla nodded, pleased. They hadn't bolted after he'd left them. They'd stayed around, cleaned up whatever was necessary, made the proper final checks. They were probably good men.

*Good men?*

Scylla left the men's room hurriedly, angry with himself

for the thought. What's happening to you? Five minutes ago you were near to a double closeout, and now you call them good men. He reached the Pan Am area, took his place in the check-in line. I want to die with someone who loves me.

"Pardon?" the aged lady in front of him said.

*Omigod, I'm thinking out loud!*

Scylla smiled at her. He had a wonderful smile, unforced and reassuring. The woman bought it, smiled back, turned away. You keep this up, they'll be sending you Coach soon, Scylla told himself.

The possibility set him trembling.

# 3

There were four of them in the seminar room, waiting for Biesenthal. The other three knew one another, and talked quietly together in the front. From the rear of the room, Levy watched them. He had heard of them; even while he was doing his work at Oxford, news of these three had made the trans-Atlantic intellectual grapevine. The biggest of them was Chambers, black, with a shot, so they said, at being the first top-notch Negro historian. The other two were the Riordan twins, a boy and a girl, and at Yale the word was they had the best Catholic minds since Billy Buckley.

From his position, Levy knew that from time to time he was the subject under discussion. If you had a really first-rate case of inferiority, you could tell when people were going on about you, and Levy inferred from various head movements and half-shrugs that although they certainly knew who *they* were—only the best got Biesenthal—the presence of the sweaty guy in the back was a puzzlement. I should never have run to school today, Levy told himself, pulling at his damp white shirt. It was stupid, on opening day; opening day you wanted to make an impression, not break records. Run *home*, jerk, he reminded himself. *Sprint* home if you want to, but don't come to class all schwitzing. No one respects perspiration in the groves of academe.

Biesenthal blazed in then. "Blazed" was the right word. His eyes—he couldn't help it, they just were—seemed backlit, like a pretty Western. All you had to do was just peek at Biesenthal and you could tell he was brilliant. Levy had seen Oppenheimer once, and he was the same way. Oppenheimer's shirts were too big in the collar, and his pants bagged, but stick him on the Bowery, you'd still know there was genius in the vicinity.

Biesenthal was like that. Not that his shirts didn't fit—he was totally fastidious. He could afford to be; he'd been rich going in, and his career had been, for an historian, incredibly successful. Two Pulitzers, three best sellers, numberless television appearances and interviews in *The New York Times*. Biesenthal was tireless, unflaggingly colorful, an intellectual Sammy Glick. The reason he got away with being rich, successful, and famous while at the same time maintaining his stronghold in the intellectual community was that he seemed to know every fact ever unearthed in the history of the world, which gave him an advantage over most people.

"I hope you all flunk," Biesenthal began.

That caused a certain breath intake in the room.

Biesenthal relished that. He sat on the desk at the front and crossed one well-creased leg over the other. "There is a shortage of natural resources worldwide," he went on. "There is a shortage of breathable air. There is even, alas, a shortage of adequate claret. *But there is no shortage of historians.* We grind you out like link sausages, and you are every bit as bright. Well, I say, enough! I say, let you find harmless employment elsewhere. Use your backs. Shovel your way through life. The universities have processed you for financial purposes, and so long as you could afford to pay tuition, they could afford to pay me. Progress, they called it; manufacturing doctorates was progress. Well, I say, 'Halt the ringing cry of progress'—that is a quote—who said it? Come, come, *who said it?*"

Tennyson, Levy thought. *Locksley Hall Sixty Years After.* That's right. I'm sure it's right. But what if it's not right? You don't come in sweaty opening day, and you don't make mistakes opening day. Probably it's Yeats, anyway. What if I said Tennyson and Biesenthal said, "Wrong, wrong, it was William Butler Yeats, 1865 to 1939, DON'T YOU KNOW Irish poetry? How can you expect to be decent historians if you don't know Irish poetry, and who are you, sir, and why are you perspiring in my presence? Sweat is no substitute for claret in my lexicon."

"Tennyson," Biesenthal roared. "My God, Alfred Tennyson, how can you expect to compete on a doctoral level and not know *Locksley Hall* and *Locksley Hall Sixty Years After?*"

The girl Riordan began making a neat note. Levy watched her, angry at the precise way she was undoubtedly writing down the titles along with a reminder to quickly become acquainted with the verses. "I knew," he wanted to cry out. "Professor Biesenthal, I really did, I could have quoted you lines from it." Levy shook his head. You *are* a jerk; you could have *impressed* the man.

Biesenthal jumped lightly off the desk and began pacing. He was quiet for a time, as if letting them have a good look at him, letting it sink in that they really were in Biesenthal's presence. His modern-history seminar was the most prestigious class at Columbia, with the possible exception of the Barzun-Trilling seminar in Lit, but Levy wasn't even sure they gave it any more. "We shall meet on a bi-weekly basis. I shall be here promptly, and so shall you. I promise to be dazzling at least fifty per cent of the time. On occasion I am more than that, more often only brilliant. I apologize in advance for those occasions. I do not generally see much of my students, but I will undoubtedly be on your orals board, where I will do my best, which is really quite good, to delay your acquiring your degrees. Think of me as your own particular roadblock. I am also something of a snoop, and I can cause you more grief if I know your strong points so as not to bother inquiring after them. So please, *briefly,* describe the subjects of your dissertations. Chambers!"

"The reality of the black experience in the South as it parallels the unreality of Faulkner's fiction."

Biesenthal stopped pacing. "And if there's no valid parallel?"

"That's what I'm hoping," Chambers said. "I'd love a short dissertation."

Biesenthal smiled at that.

Oh is that Chambers clever, Levy thought. Smooth, anyway. God, what I'd give to be smooth.

"Miss Riordan? Miz Riordan, a thousand pardons."

"Nineteenth-century European power alliances—a critique of same."

"And you, sir?" This to the boy Riordan.

"Carlyle's humanism." He stuttered. "Kuh-kuh-Car," he said.

"That's really a dreadful notion, Riordan. No one your

age should have any interest in something that dull. Intellectuals aren't supposed to become insufferable until they're twenty-five, that's in our charter." He turned to Levy now. "Mister . . . ?"

"Tyranny, sir," Levy managed, heart—Stop it!—pounding. "The uses of tyranny in American political life, such as maybe Coolidge breaking the Boston police strike and Roosevelt putting Japanese Americans into West Coast concentration camps on the West Coast in the forties."

Biesenthal looked straight at him. "You might consider the McCarthy business."

"Sir?" was all Levy could come out with. So, after all, Biesenthal knew.

"Joseph. He was a senator from Wisconsin. He ran a series of tyrannical purges in the early fifties."

"I'd planned a chapter on him, sir."

Biesenthal sat behind the desk now. "All rise," he said, "and depart swiftly. With one final admonition." The group stopped. "Many students are afraid that when they contact their teachers they might be, somehow, *bothering* them. Let me assure you that in my case that is totally and one hundred per cent true, you *will* be bothering me, so please do it as infrequently as possible." He almost smiled as he said it, and the others laughed. But uncertainly.

"Levy," Biesenthal said when Levy was almost out the door.

"Sir?"

Biesenthal pointed to the door. "Close," he said. He beckoned with his finger. "Come," he said. He pointed to a chair in the front row. "Sit," he said.

Levy did as he was told. They were alone in the room.

Quiet.

Levy tried not to fidget.

Biesenthal's eyes blazed down on him.

"I knew your father," he said finally.

Levy nodded.

"Rather well, in point of fact. He was my mentor."

"Yes sir."

"I was just a brat when he found me, dancing along, using just enough brains to avoid the precipice."

"I wouldn't know about that, sir."

Biesenthal would not stop examining him; the eyes would not stop blazing. "T. B. Levy," Biesenthal said finally. "I assume, since your father was a Macaulay man, that you are Thomas Babington."

"Yes sir, only I try to keep the Babington part of it as quiet as possible."

"As I recall, there was another of you; who was he named after?"

"Thoreau. His name's Henry David." That was true, only Levy never called him that when they were alone. "Doc" he called him then. It was their great and very only secret. In all the world, nobody else called him that, "Doc." Just like in all the world nobody but Doc ever referred to him as "Babe."

"Is he also a blossoming intellectual?"

"No sir, he's a hotshot businessman, he makes pots of money, and it used to be all right but lately he's showed signs of becoming a world-class dilettante in his Brooks Brothers clothes. He raves about French restaurants, and all he ever drinks is Burgundy wine. You could fall asleep listening to him tell about this one's 'finish' and that one's 'nose.' I think my father would have disowned him."

Biesenthal smiled. "Your father had great faith in precision—your names reflect that."

"How so, sir?"

"They died the same year, Thoreau and Macaulay."

"No," Levy was about to correct. Macaulay went in 1859, Thoreau lasted till three years later. Levy's hands went across his stomach. What to do, what to do? Three years was almost the same as the same year, although probably Tom Macaulay would have given you an argument on that if you'd asked him on his deathbed. "Hey Babington, you wanna live three more years or not, it's up to you, speak your pleasure, what'll it be?"

"I wasn't . . ." Levy began.

Biesenthal and those damn eyes were watching him still.

"I mean, I didn't quite realize . . . I suppose I always thought one of them died in 1859 and the other in 1862, it just shows you how wrong you can be, thanks for setting me straight."

Biesenthal hesitated a moment. "No—no, of course, you're quite correct, I was in error, they did die three years apart. I misspoke, forgive me. What I meant was, of course, that they were *born* in the same year; the same month, to be perfectly precise."

Levy could not stop kneading his stomach. They were born seventeen years apart, but you couldn't correct a man like Biesenthal twice. Not twice in one day, anyway. Twice in one lifetime, sure, but that was it, unless you wanted to major in wrath-risking. "Yes sir," Levy said.

"Do not," Biesenthal began, his voice low but constantly building, "do not, ever again, humor me!"

"I would never do a thing like that, sir."

"When was Macaulay born?"

"1800."

"And H. D. Thoreau?"

"Practically 1800."

"*When?*"

"Seventeen years later."

"*Correct me, sir!* How else am I to fathom your mind? I do not like nodders. Everyone agrees with me all the time, and it bores me, sir, it bores me. I am on the lookout for minds. Your father's I venerated. I worshipped at it. Is yours so fine?"

"Oh, no, no sir."

"That is my judgment to make, but I can make it only if you show it to me. If you continue to hide it, I can only assume you are a drone, and I shall put you down in quality with the boy Riordan. 'Young Levy? Very sad. His father had a mind one would have killed for, but the child, alas, never grasped anything more convoluted than a game of pick-up-sticks.' Would that please you?"

"You know it wouldn't."

"Why are you at Columbia, Levy?"

"It's a good school."

"Better answer, please."

"Because you're here."

"Well, that's certainly better, and it's also obviously more flattering, but it's also only, I suspect, partly true. Naturally, I checked your records today. I check anyone who deems himself worthy of my ministrations. Do you find me arrogant, Levy?"

"Oh, no sir."

"Your father did. He used to chastise me constantly. You went to Denison; if I'm not mistaken, that's one of those coed pits in Ohio."

"They phrase it differently in their brochure, sir."

"And you won a Rhodes."

Levy nodded.

"A Rhodes Scholar. From Denison. You must be extraordinarily bright to do that—all the Rhodeses I know went to Ivy League universities. How did you manage such a feat, Levy?"

"I don't know, sir, I just applied. It was most likely a weak year."

"Most likely. That would account for it. I imagine they must have gone mad at Denison. There's no doubt in my mind you must have been the first winner in the history of the school."

Levy sat there.

"Probably the first even to apply."

Levy said nothing.

Biesenthal let him sit there a long time before asking again, quietly, "Why are you at Columbia, Levy?"

"Just the way things worked out," Levy mumbled.

"That is *not* just the way things work out, Levy. Because your father was also a Rhodes and your father attended that same coed pit in Ohio and he also came here for his doctorate. There's a line in a James Bond novel, Levy—'the first time it's coincidence, the second time it's happenstance, the third time it's enemy action.' "

Levy was perspiring badly. If I ever run to class again I should really be put away, he tried telling himself, but it didn't work, because that wasn't why he was perspiring, not now.

"The McCarthy section is central to your dissertation, yes?"

"Hard to say, sir, seeing as it's not exactly what you might call written yet."

"The McCarthy section is central to your dissertation, *yes*?"

"Yes."

"Very worrying, Levy."

"It's just a dissertation, Professor Biesenthal."

"You can't fill his footsteps, I'm sorry to tell you. You may end up leaving larger tracks, anything's possible, but they will be your own, not your father's."

"Look—I'm here—you want the truth, I'll tell you the truth—I'm here because I got the best scholarship offer here and that's *all* there is to it. I'm not on any crusade, nothing like that."

"Good. Because it's been too long, there's nothing you can do to clear him."

"I know that, because there's nothing to clear, he was innocent." Levy glanced quickly up at Biesenthal.

The damn eyes would not stop blazing . . .

# 4

Scylla never did his best work in London. Not because he disliked the place. The reverse. Even when he first visited it, years before, he had somehow sensed that it ought to have been his home. His affection for the city had only increased throughout the decade of his twenties.

Then, when he was thirty, he met Janey in London and fell very much in love. That was the clincher. Now, no matter how important the work he was supposed to be doing, he could never quite force the necessary concentration. He and Janey had been an item for five years now, and even though he had yet to meet the passion that could survive five years of intimacy, things were still plenty good as far as Scylla was concerned. This very evening he had wandered after dinner along Mount Street, window-shopping and thinking of Janey back home, and then he was singing "A Foggy Day in London Town" out loud. He caught himself before he got too far into it, and no one else was near enough to hear his serenading, but it still indicated that he wasn't paying quite the attention to work that was necessary if you intended staying alive.

He glanced at his watch. It was damn cold, and it was September and almost half-past three in the morning. He blew on his hands a moment, then pulled his trench coat collar up tighter around his neck. He had bought the thing from Burberry's years ago, and he knew it was cornball, but what the hell.

He sat quietly, waiting. Waiting was something you got used to. He hated it, but sometimes you made other people wait; it set them on edge, so you did it. Any advantage was worth whatever it cost you. It was strange, but he disliked making other people wait just as much as he disliked being kept waiting himself. But he did not any more allow it to disturb him. They were trying for an advantage, and when they did appear it would be natural for him to seem nervous, anxious, even irritable, so they would think the advantage was theirs. Of course, once you had them thinking that, the advantage was yours again. That was what made him as good as anybody; he gave away nothing.

At least, when he was on his game. But in London that was never quite the case. He was vulnerable in London, though no one had yet been able to turn that vulnerability to their benefit.

Three thirty-five.

Scylla shifted his position again; the bench was simply not meant for long-distance sitting. He glanced off through the black green of Kensington Gardens to the Albert Memorial. What a gloriously supreme monument to bad taste. Ordinarily he loved it, but not when he was freezing his ass off in the middle of the goddamn night on a bullshit job like this one.

Earlier that day he had offered the Russians a blueprint for a crucial section of the "smart bomb" that the military was creaming over these days, a bomb that didn't just drop: It glided until it found its prearranged target; then it fell. What made it such a bullshit job was that the Russians already *had* the blueprint of the crucial section. Only they couldn't let us know they had it, so they would have to come to the park and agree to buy it, and after a certain amount of haggling the deal would be made. It was really all so *1984* you could throw up.

Footsteps.

Scylla took his glance from the Albert Memorial, stared across the walk to the empty bench opposite. The silly part was coming up now. No matter how long he had played the game, he could never get over a kindergartenlike desire to giggle when they went through the business with the code words. Dear God, who else might be meeting on park benches at 3:39 in the morning?

Don't answer that.

A delicate-looking girl sat down across from him in the darkness. Odd on several counts: (a) sex; (b) that they would entrust something of such supposed importance to a lady as edgy as this one. Oh, she seemed calm enough; if you weren't expert, you might assume she was placid. But Scylla could sense the pounding of her heart.

She held out a package of cigarettes, toward him.

He shook his head. "Cancerous." Jesus, there it was again, building inside him, a giggle. What if he hadn't said "cancerous"? What if he'd just said "Sorry, luv, I don't smoke." Would she have gone away? Of course not. He was sitting where he was supposed to be sitting at the time he was supposed to be sitting there. Lunacy, really. If he was ever put in charge, the first thing he was going to do away with was passwords.

She lit her cigarette. "It's a hard habit to break."

"Otherwise it wouldn't be a habit," Scylla said. And with that he breathed a sigh. At least the silly part was done with.

She stayed smoking on her bench a while, inhaling too deeply. "You are Scylla?" she said finally.

Well dear God, who did she think he was after all this? Her lack of skill was beginning to gall him. He had done far too much to have to deal with lackeys and fools. He said nothing, only nodded.

"I thought you might be female."

I thought you might be male, he almost replied, which, of course, was true; so, of course, he couldn't. He said nothing.

"Was not Scylla a female monster?"

"Scylla was a rock. A rock near a whirlpool. Charybdis was the whirlpool."

"And are you that? A rock?"

He was. On his good days, anyway. He said nothing. He knew now that she was stalling. But he did not know if it was because she was inept and new, or for some other reason.

"I am instructed to say that your price is too high."

"Are you also instructed to negotiate?" She was really very pretty, in a delicate way. He was conscious of his body, thick and muscular.

She nodded her head. "Of course."

"Well then, for Chrissakes, negotiate, make a counter offer, that's what negotiating is."

"Of course." She nodded her head again.

She was so panicked sitting there, she could not keep that from him no matter how she tried; it was as if someone were trying to kill her, and then his brain belatedly sent the message through—*not her—not her—it's you someone's trying to kill—*

And if luck is the residue of design, then he was lucky, because by instinct he raised his right hand to his throat, getting it there a brief second before the garroting wire, and as the wire pulled tight, cutting his palm terribly, Scylla thought that it would never happen now, not here, in London, but that was the logical place when you came down to it, except that logic would not explain away one fact, namely that even when he was slightly off his game, it was not possible to come up in total silence behind him, no one possessed that kind of quiet skill. And as the wire tore deeper into his palm and his brain began fogging, Scylla managed to realize that he was wrong, there was one person, and it had to be Chen, fragile and deadly, S. L. Chen the wonder, who was behind him, killing him now . . .

When he found out it was Scylla, Chen was pleased. Not out of any sense of overconfidence, but rather one of the inevitable. Eventually, it had to come down to Chen versus Scylla, better now than later, better with the attack being his to initiate rather than the other way around. In all honesty, Chen's ideal would have been to put them both in a bare room, naked save for loincloths, and let one survive. But that was not to be. Still, when he found out it was Scylla, Chen was pleased.

He was not pleased with the setup. Nothing wrong with

the darkness, nothing wrong with the park or the time of night. It was the time of year that was going to prove troublesome. Chen knew that instantly. If it had been summer, then possibly Scylla might have appeared in just slacks and a shirt, and his neck would have been vulnerable to hands. But in September there was no doubt that Scylla would be in a coat, that it would undoubtedly be chilly, which meant the odds were high that the coat collar would be turned up, and if you could not see the death spots in the neck, you could miss them, causing only pain, which might give Scylla a chance to retaliate. Perhaps even win.

Chen was very much against that, so he decided to use his nunchaku.

It was an honorable weapon, ancient as air: two hard wooden sticks connected by a wire, or leather if you liked leather.

Chen liked wire.

He was a master with the nunchaku, and to the Caucasian world the strangeness of the weapon lent it an aura of fear. Noonchuck, the whites called it. Never let Chen get his noonchuck on you.

Then came the Kung Fu movie craze, and Bruce Lee used the nunchaku, and, before Chen's horrified eyes, the sacred thing became a toy for delinquents all across the globe. In Los Angeles children used noonchunks. In Liverpool they were becoming common. *Common.* It was humiliating. Chen went to all the Bruce Lee movies and writhed.

Chen had arrived at 2:30 for the Scylla encounter. He knew the girl was to arrive at 3:30 but would be nine minutes late, to nettle the big man. Chen assumed that Scylla would arrive by 3—Chen always arrived at least that early for any confrontation, and he would have been surprised had Scylla not done the same. At 2:30, Chen made a brief but thorough examination of the shadow patches behind the bench Scylla was to occupy, and found the one he considered best—it combined a certain closeness with bushes that would not reveal anything even if there was sudden strong wind.

And then he went into his crouch.

Chen could crouch for . . . how long? A day? Certainly a day, that had been the most time he had ever spent immobile. Probably he could last longer. Perhaps there would come a time when it would be necessary. Now he froze into position, so when Scylla arrived and examined the area at 3, Chen was already a part of the background. There was nothing to reveal him. He was there before Scylla came; he would be gone once Scylla died.

He held his nunchaku loosely, a stick in each hand, letting the rough wire curve as it wanted. When it was 3:41, he stood, and his hands felt strong. They were his glories, those hands; he had worked all his life on them, for the rest of his body was frail. He had never weighed much over a hundred pounds.

Chen began moving forward.

"Was not Scylla a female monster?"

"Scylla was a rock. A rock near a whirlpool. Charybdis was the whirlpool."

"And are you that? A rock?"

Silence from Scylla.

Chen began closing.

"I am instructed to say that your price is too high."

Damn her! Chen thought, she jumped to that, she was supposed to have gotten there more slowly—of all the times for him to have to get stuck with a novice! Scylla would be on to it now. Chen wanted to quicken his pace, but when you were silent, speed was your enemy. You had to be steady, you had to be slow. Otherwise there was the risk of fabric brushing fabric, twigs snapping, thunderous sounds.

"Are you also instructed to negotiate?"

Chen was six feet behind the big man. He would have preferred to have been four, but the damn girl had ruined that.

"Of course."

Three feet behind Scylla now.

"Well then, for Chrissakes, negotiate, make a counter offer, that's what negotiating is."

"Of course," she said, and as Chen moved the wire around Scylla's throat he was already aware that Scylla had gotten his hand up. His right hand was keeping the wire from the throat. Bitch, Chen thought, but then he banished everything from his mind but business. He had pulled his wire through flesh before, and hand bones broke easily.

He put his body into perfect balance and began the kill . . .

As the blood almost leaped free of his wounded right palm, Scylla was aware that the girl in the bench across had a pistol in her hand, which was stupid, guns were stupid in the darkness, just noisemakers, any hit was a lucky hit, but even though she was wrong to have brought the thing into play, she could have taken him with it if she had moved quickly enough, because right then he was dominated by pain, and pain changed the world. Pain put a cloud around you, you couldn't see through it, couldn't act in accordance with logic and experience and training.

So, for an instant, as the wire cut deeper into his hand, Scylla was feeble and clouded and ripe for dying.

But she was slow, too slow, the moment went by.

His brain began to clear. He was Scylla the rock. *Remember that!* You are Scylla the rock and you must *do* something, *now*. He hit the words hard in his mind, because the girl was standing up with the pistol, and so what if his mind was clearing, a bullet could crush clear tissue as well as clouded, and it was Chen behind him, an equal, one of the few if not the only *because you are Scylla the rock and you must do something*!

Something extraordinary, remarkable, unique, that's all, and you have five seconds. Go.

Chen was great but Chen was small—the girl was approaching—Chen was quick but Chen was now stationary—the girl raised the pistol into firing position—so if you could budge Chen, if you could unsettle his balance, if you could manage that . . .

Scylla knew what he had to try then.

He had seen it done. Once. On a basketball court. The nonpareil Monroe matched against the genius Frazier. The ultimate in offense against the greatest defender. No one near them. Mano a mano. Monroe moved to the basket and faked right, and if you fake right, there are only two further moves remaining to you: You can fake right and go left, or you can fake right, then fake left, and go right.

Monroe did neither.

He faked right and *went* right, around Frazier, who could only stand there, watching the score.

Scylla faked right and went right.

He forced his body in that direction along the bench, and then, when he seemed as if about to slow, about to fake back left, he powered everything he had into the completion of the right move, and behind him he could sense the wire momentarily loosen as Chen's balance deserted him.

Now, with all the power in his great body, Scylla hunched forward, pulling the tiny man unwillingly with him, and when he was in balance off the bench, Scylla put all his strength into a shoulder throw, sailing Chen helplessly over him, aiming him toward the too-slow girl.

They went down hard, and the girl was stunned, the pistol skittering along the sidewalk, and Scylla saw it but so did Chen, and Chen went for it, scrabbling along the cement like a desperate roach.

Scylla let him.

His right hand was pouring blood and next to useless, and he watched as Chen got close, and then he kicked Chen's head off. Or tried to. But Chen was ready and took Scylla's foot and snapped it around, tripping Scylla down, and Scylla came back with a blow from his left hand, but it only grazed Chen's head because even on his knees, even still dazed from the shoulder throw, Chen could move, and Scylla went for another left-hand blow, and again Chen spun free, and another left-hand hit missed as Chen spun and twisted, and he really was like a roach, a waterbug that you could see and chase but somehow never quite reach, and they both went for the gun then, but it was clumsy going, and when Scylla saw he might not get it first he kicked at it and sent it spinning into silent grassy darkness as Chen chopped him at the neck, and Scylla moved enough so Chen missed a death spot, but that didn't mean it didn't hurt, didn't make his nerves shriek, didn't start his brain again to clouding, but that must not happen Scylla thought, if I cloud I'm gone, and again he missed with the left, and his right was useless, to use the right would be simply too painful, he knew that and Chen knew that, so when Scylla went for a death spot with his right, when he connected, there was a double cry of pain, and who was to say which was the greater agony, his or Chen's. All you could be sure of was that Chen's was over sooner. Gasping, Scylla stood, moved past the dead Oriental, finished the girl in silence, then started running down the path toward the Albert Memorial, wrapping a handkerchief around his right hand as he moved.

The nearest pay phone was just across Kensington Gore, so Scylla forced himself into a casual walk as he approached it, because even though it was 3:45 in the morning, you could never tell who wasn't asleep, and a running man at night meant trouble, so when there was trouble, you walked.

He inserted the appropriate coins, dialed the appropriate number, and the first ring was all that was needed. "Removals."

"Scylla."

"Yes, Scylla."

"Two. Between the Albert Memorial and Lancaster Walk."

"Injuries?"

"Hand."

"I'll alert the clinic, Scylla."

Click.

Scylla left the phone booth and waited. He didn't have to, he could have just gone, but he always liked to be around for possible eventualities.

Besides, he needed to think. Why had Chen tried to retire him? Someone had hired him—who? Why? For what happened back in the Los Angeles men's room? Possible, but he really hadn't done enough for the Arabs to kill him. They could have contacted the Russians easily enough, but the Russians would have tried sending one of their own men, not an Oriental from a country they despised. Scylla's hand was starting to throb really very badly. He shook his head—whatever was going on, he didn't know enough yet; insufficient data had been given the machine.

In seven minutes, a proper-seeming ambulance entered Kensington Gardens. Five minutes after that, the ambulance exited. All very efficient, and, naturally, nothing of any kind would ever reach the papers.

Scylla found a cab, took it to near the clinic, paid, and got out. He waited for the cab to leave; then he walked to where they would be waiting for him. His hand was worse, and he wanted to run, but running meant trouble, so when there was trouble, you walked.

Dripping badly, Scylla made his slow way.

At the clinic, everything was ready for him. They cleansed the wound, prepared a partial anesthetic.

He told them curtly he was having none of it.

The doctors assured him there would be pain.

He assured them he had been there before.

The doctor began, reluctantly, to repair the non-anesthetized hand. Scylla watched it all, every stitch. And he never made a sound.

He was Scylla the rock. On his good days, anyway.

# 5

Levy sat alone in a corner of the library, working on America in 1875. Not that specific date, actually; specific dates were garbage. His father had written, "For the pedant, dates are deities, worthy of worship, but for the true social historian, they are minutiae only, a shorthand, convenient reminders and no more. You do not ask a *Titanic* survivor, 'Let me see now, just exactly when was that?' You ask him this: 'What was it like? How did you *feel*?' And that is the job of the social historian: to make the past vibrant for the present; to emotionally involve those of us who were not there. And to make us understand."

America around 1875, Levy thought, lemmesee, lemmesee. (He had spent the previous hour on England, the one before that coupling Italy and France. Germany he was weak on, relatively, but that was because the Germans bored him so, no humor; it was almost as if back in the beginning He had ordained, "Okay, let's get this earth going, all blonds to Scandinavia, all dummies to Poland, and get the gigglers out of Germany.") Hmmm, Levy thought, 1875, 1875. Boss Tweed went to jail in New York City around then, which meant lots of big-city rulers around, Big Power men, to each town its own Dick Daley, and Christian Science began then too, old Mary Eddy and her nut notions, and when was the first Kentucky Derby? Same period, and the first telephone exchange began right almost exactly when Custer got his lumps at the Little Big Horn.

Good, Levy thought, terrific double image, the first phone exchange *and* Custer getting blasted at the same time, what a country this was then, what a mother of a place it must have been, Melville over fifty and unknown, Twain around forty and going good, Joe Pulitzer a kid, twenty-five maybe, and Mrs. O'Leary's cow had only just destroyed Chicago, and think of the inventions flying out of people's minds: Remington hustling typewriters in the East and Glidden figuring out a barbed-wire maker to open up the West and Thomas Alva with his gramophone and Bissell with his carpet sweeper, what a fantastic time, a country on the make, that's what we were, the toughest kid on the block, only we didn't really know it, and besides, we didn't want to know it, because being the toughest meant responsibility, leadership, and we were too busy hustling and humping to bother with taking over.

Levy tilted back his chair and gave it a rest for a while. Not bad on America. Superficial, sure, but he wasn't any nineteenth-century expert, hell, he was just kind of keeping his hand in, he was a modern-times guy if he was anything; still, you had to noodle these other periods around. The main thing was to know the world, every twenty-five years or so, back for a couple hundred years, and if you had that info handy, always there under your belt, then you could figure out the gaps. That was the way his father's mind had worked. It wasn't necessary to know it all or anything. Just most and the rest logic took care of. His father had loved logic, Levy too.

There was a commotion now over at a table to his left; an attractive guy and an attractive girl, punching each other kind of, but you knew they were both more interested in softer contact. Levy watched them. It was really why he did his studying here, rather than in some cubicle in the stacks. He liked watching people.

Liar.

He liked watching *girls*.

There were a couple of Barnard students that really took the old breath right away. I'm gonna have me one of them some day, Levy told himself. A looker. Please.

He jerked around then, conscious that Biesenthal was watching him. Biesenthal indicated the pile of books in front of Levy. "Your charade fools no one," he said. "You were ogling."

"Oh, no sir, it may seem that way, but I'm really doing a terrific lot of work."

"If you wanted to work, you'd get yourself a cubicle."

"I'm desperate to get one but there's a shortage now, so I'm stuck here," Levy said.

"I always studied here," Biesenthal said. "It was much better for girl-watching."

*You* watched girls? Levy almost said.

"I know what you're thinking," Biesenthal said. "I know that look—once I saw a student of mine, and I was in my car, driving along Broadway, and when I stopped at the light he stared at me dumbstruck. I asked him what was wrong, and all he could say was, 'My God, you can drive.' We *are* human, some of us, Levy. Try to let that penetrate. What were you, as you claim, doing a terrific lot of work on?"

"1875," Levy said.

"Neglect not Glidden," Biesenthal said.

"Absolutely not, sir."

"You haven't the least notion who Glidden was, admit it."

"Barbed wire, are you kidding, very important." Hey, son of a bitch, you impressed him. Mark it on the calendar when you run home. "What'd'ya think about phones and Custer?"

Biesenthal looked at him. "Custard, Levy? Your words are all running together."

"No—no, George Armstrong Custer, the last-stand idiot—the first phone exchange was going on when he got creamed, isn't that a good image, isn't that a terrific image for America, I think it's terrific."

"As your father used to tell me, 'Leave images for the poets.' " He glanced at his watch. "It's almost seven, I'm due home for dinner, walk me, Levy." He crooked his finger. "Don't bother bringing your debris. It's just down to Riverside Drive."

Levy followed Biesenthal out of the large study room. He must not think I'm a complete fool, Levy decided. I bet he hasn't asked the Riordan twins to walk him home. "I would invite you for supper, Levy," Biesenthal began as they left the library. "Except that my wife—a genuine beauty in her time, Levy, and a wonderful mother for our children—is, alas, a totally dreadful cook; not only is the food mediocre, there's never enough of it. Need I add that we don't entertain a great deal at home." They moved on out of the campus toward

Broadway and 116th. There was a book and poster shop near the corner, in the window Che and Bette Midler and JFK side by side. "Where were you when he died?" from Biesenthal.

Levy followed him across the street. "Kennedy? I was in the high-school lunch room, and somebody—he was a football player; dumb? not to be believed—and he said, 'Kennedy's been shot,' and together me and this other kid said, 'What's the punch line?' and we laughed at both of us coming out with it at once until we saw this stupid guy's face and we knew there wasn't any."

"I meant your father," Biesenthal said.

"I was kind of around, I guess," Levy said.

They slowed the pace as they began the sharp decline toward Riverside. "I've wanted you to know something," Biesenthal began. "No reason, I just did, I'm telling you for *my* good, understand that."

"Yes sir."

"I'm going to tell you a great secret, Levy—this could destroy my career, shatter it overnight if it became common knowledge—if I were a closet queen and the *Times* made it a banner headline, it would be nothing compared to what I am about to let drop now, so pay attention: I'm a baseball fanatic, Levy. Not the Mets or the Dodgers or Aaron or Mays—I love it all. I covet box scores. I still, approaching senility, sneak into the bathroom Sunday morning with the sports section and lock the door, pretending to bathe while I'm actually memorizing batting averages. All right—use your wondrous brain, Levy. For a man with my fetish, what is the most important single annual event in the universe, greater even than the Miss America Pageant?"

"The Series?"

"Correct. The World Series. And for a man in my position, nothing could be worse, because there are occasions, many of them, when I am forced to teach during a Series game. Do you know what I do when this happens?"

"No sir."

"I have had a secretary for over thirty years, and she is brilliant. I have given her the finest portable radio, and after each inning, when I am in class, I have trained her to put a most distraught expression on her face, as if the ultimate cataclysm has just occurred, and she comes into class and says, 'May I speak to you a moment, Professor Biesenthal?' and I say, testily, 'What is it, what is it, can't you see I'm busy?' and she takes me aside and while I nod with a most serious mien, she whispers, 'Oakland's gone ahead two to one in the sixth, Seaver's still in for the Mets but he may be tiring, they've got McGraw warming up.' I hesitate, as if undecided as to the proper action, then return to my students, all of whom feel honored that I have kept my time with them sacrosanct, no matter how terribly important the outside world's intrusions might be."

They started up Riverside Drive, heading toward 118th. "Your father died in March—"

"The thirtieth—"

"—and I was in class, and in she came, my wondrous secretary, even fifteen years ago she was that, and I'll never forget that same cataclysmic look on her face, and I remember thinking, 'It can't be the Series already, they haven't even started the season yet,' and then I thought, but what else can it be, what can be so terrible she interrupts with that face, and

I went to her not knowing if I was indeed senile and I'd lost half a year, and fifteen years ago it was Milwaukee with Burdette and Aaron against the Yankees with Mantle and Ford, and I was getting all the names straight, trying to figure what was happening, but she didn't use a name, she said, 'He's dead,' and then she left the room.

"I was so relieved—I hadn't gone senile—I remember actually smiling, and I went back and sat down with the students, and then it must have hit me, because I said, 'You must all leave. *You must all go now.*' They left, and an hour or so later my secretary came in with my coat and hat, and I asked how, and she said cerebral hemorrhage. 'Good,' I said, 'good, I hope he went quickly, I hope he didn't suffer,' even though I knew how dreadfully he did suffer, and I also suspected it wasn't any cerebral hemorrhage."

"That was just a first attempt to keep it quiet. Pretty feeble. It was in the papers the next morning that he blew his head off."

"Where were you?"

"In the house, down the hall. I was ten, and I'd gotten a terrific grade on a paper he'd helped me with—sometimes he was sober enough to kind of teach me. Some paper, it was this drippy page I'd written on wool, and he knew everything, I don't have to tell you that, and I thought I should let him know how well we'd done, but then I thought if I did that, it might be tough sledding, getting through supper with nothing to talk about, so I decided to save it, and then the shots came, and I remember standing in the doorway to his room, and he was out of sight from me on the floor behind a bed, but the blood wasn't, there was like a little river of it, a stream, kind of, and I remember thinking, 'Thank God it wasn't me spilled the paint,' and then I saw how pretty it was, how it helped the room, made it more colorful and everything. I don't know how long I stood there, but finally I quit the crapping around and walked to the phone and called the cops, and when they came I asked for the gun, and they said, no, it was evidence, and I said, okay, but I want the gun when you're done with it, and they said, we can't give a gun to minors, but I'm a very persistent fella sometimes, and you better believe I've got that gun now. My brother got it for me when the cops were done with it—he was twenty—and when I was legal I practiced with it and practiced with it. I'm dead with it, really I am."

They stopped in front of a fancy building with a doorman. Biesenthal waved him away. They stood alone on the sidewalk. "Why?"

"I don't know—I kept hoping McCarthy would be found alive somewhere. Then I just thought, see, I'm not all that strong physically, I'm no heavyweight contender, and I thought wouldn't it be terrific to nail some bad guys before I was done. Now I just keep it because it's mine, because it was Dad's, I don't know why I keep it. Good night, Professor Biesenthal." Levy started away.

"Tom?"

My God, he called me Tom. Levy turned. "Sir?"

"Why didn't you answer the *Locksley Hall Sixty Years After* quote? It was so obvious from your face you wanted to."

"Scared."

Biesenthal nodded. "I do frighten people, I've worked very hard for the effect. My youngest daughter calls me Ebenezer . . ." His voice trailed off.

Levy looked at Biesenthal. He's embarrassed over something, Levy thought; he's stuck.

Then the words came in a burst: "I wept when he died, I wanted you to know that."

"It wasn't a good day for any of us," Levy said.

# 6

Scylla stood at the entrance to the Castle and stared down at Princes Street. It was growing dark quickly, but Princes Street remained the most beautiful thoroughfare imaginable; nothing else in Edinburgh compared with it, nothing else in Scotland, nor Britain nor Europe nor this or any other world. It was a gift from the Almighty, as if someone had taken all the finest shops on Fifth Avenue and set them across from Central Park but then, instead of having it just be any old greenery, had made a great hill hundreds of feet high, topped off by a mighty gingerbread castle. If you had to pick a street to die on, you couldn't beat Princes.

Stop thinking about dying.

But he couldn't help it. He stood in the chill air watching the lights in the lovely stores, Forsyth's and Lilywhite's, mainly pondering mortality, or, rather, the lack of it. His right hand throbbed, the stitches on fire. It was his own fault; he was closing his fists too frequently, rubbing his hands too often.

Just because Robertson was late.

If it had been anyone else, no cause for worry. But Robertson was legendary for his promptness. If you were in Beverly Hills and he called from Beirut saying, "Meet me

Tuesday on Mount Everest, the north wall, halfway up, two thirty," well, you had better have one hell of an excuse if you got there at twenty of three.

Look on the bright side—it might just mean that his car got held up in traffic or a tire went flat. Logical, except Scylla could see the traffic on Princes, and it was moving smoothly, and more than that, if Robertson had gotten a flat, he wasn't the type to fix it—he'd just pull to the curb, hail a taxi, and arrive, as always, precisely when he said he would.

There was no bright side.

Robertson was late because he was dead. The question was, did he fall or was he pushed? God knows, with his history of heart disease, he could have toppled over anytime. Not only was he overweight, he smoked heavily and drank too much and ate only rich foods, so, logically, a stroke made sense.

But strange things had been happening, most recently the business with Chen, so it was possible Robertson had died violently. Scylla hoped not. Even though theirs was strictly a business relationship and at least in part illicit, having nothing to do with Division and Scylla's regular work, he still hoped that Robertson had gone in his sleep, shortly after finishing his favorite meal of a double order of smoked salmon and an underdone *entrecôte* steak on a plate with almost any vegetable, just so it was smothered in hollandaise, and an extra large portion of profiterole for dessert.

Scylla hesitated. Robertson owed him money from their prior transaction, perhaps twenty thousand dollars, but Scylla knew he had been in Edinburgh too long already, he ought to get the hell out and on to Paris; these extra side trips up from

London had to be quick, so Division wouldn't get particularly interested.

To hell with it, Scylla thought as he started down the hill to the street, I'm going to see what happened, I just want to make sure he didn't suffer. Robertson ran the finest antique shop in Scotland, specializing in old jewelry, so perhaps that was why somebody got him. Greed. A plain and simple heist, and Robertson protested too vehemently and the thieves got panicky and started killing.

Scylla liked Robertson. They had relatively little in common, and yet he felt a fondness for the fat old queer. Once, when he was making a delivery, Robertson's parents had arrived unexpectedly, and they all four went out to dinner, and Robertson immediately became much more subdued of speech, far less flamboyant with his gestures, and they dined at the Aperitif on Frederick Street, where a proper fuss was made, since Robertson was a steady and a heavy-tipping customer. And what was the main subject of conversation?

Girls.

It was all very sweet. His parents honestly did not know that their Jack was one of the major queens of western Europe. And Robertson carried it off so well, seeming to be genuinely depressed about his bachelor state, saying that no girl would have him, he was too fat and unattractive.

Scylla had the taxi drive past Robertson's shop on Grassmarket. It was totally dark. No sign of life. The building next to it was empty, and to Scylla it all felt of death and decay. After one more block, he got out, paid the driver, walked back to Robertson's store, and stood across the street, watching. Nothing inside. No movement.

Scylla crossed over and picked the front lock easily, the hooked blade of his knife having no trouble with the tumblers. Robertson lived in the rest of the house above the shop, and Scylla made his silent way to the stairs and up. Robertson's bedroom was on the third floor, and as Scylla reached it, the door was open enough for him to see the outline of the mammoth shape of the dead man sprawled across the bed.

Scylla entered the room, then stopped, stunned.

Robertson was *snoring*. The fat bastard wasn't dead, he was asleep. Scylla flicked the bed lamp on and said "Jack—Jack?" and Robertson blinked his eyes in wild astonishment, staring, *he could not stop staring*, and Scylla realized, Jesus, all the time I thought *he* was dead, he thought *I* was dead, that's why he never came.

Scylla sat rigidly in the chair by the bed lamp. "Why didn't you come, Jack?" he asked.

"Our appointment was for tomorrow," Robertson answered grumpily.

"You thought I was dead, didn't you?"

"I can't answer something as silly as that now, can I?"

"Why did you think I was dead?"

Robertson pushed the sheet off his body. "Scylla, dear God, what is this gibberish?"

"I can make you tell me things, Jack. Don't make me do that."

Robertson sighed, threw back the covers. "If we're going to argue, at least let's do it in the kitchen, I'm hungry. I'll just get my robe," and he crossed to the closet.

Scylla sat in silence by the bed lamp, his hands in his lap, his foot on the cord.

Robertson put his robe on, and from the other side of the room said, very distinctly, "You will never, *never* threaten me again, is that clear enough?" There was a tiny pistol in his hand.

Scylla made a sigh.

"Answer me, goddamn you."

"Jack, it's your life on the line now, you don't understand these games, don't say another word, *please.*"

"Just put up your hands."

"Jesus, that's original."

*"I'll kill you."*

Scylla put up his hands.

"Now you listen to me," Robertson said, standing across the room, a gigantic shadow. "You will never threaten me again, because what we've been doing, the stealing off the top, it's all written down—every transaction has been carefully annotated, and it's in a sealed envelope at my solicitors', and if I die it will be opened, and there are instructions as to who to give the information to, and I would think you would have considerable difficulty surviving once the news gets around."

"You were stealing off the top long before I got involved."

"Meaning?"

"I just wondered if that was all written down at your solicitors' too."

"Yes. Everything."

Scylla shook his head. "None of it is. You're a secret fellow, Jack. Your fine parents don't know about your proclivities, and I think you enjoy living in shadows, and I don't think you'd ever tell anybody anything, much less write it down."

"You want me to kill you?"

Scylla shook his head. "You've got it wrong, Jack; it's you that has to die."

"Keep your hands up—"

"Certainly, but hear me now, Jack, a moment ago, when I said 'Please don't say any more,' I meant that—if you'd stopped then, if only you had, it might have been all right, but now, you see, I have no choice, because if I don't kill you you'll know that Scylla can be threatened, and threatened successfully, and once you know that, well, you'll have the better of me, won't you, you'll be able to do what you want with me, and no one must ever be allowed that power."

"How can you threaten me? I've got the gun—"

"Because I'm invisible," Scylla said, kicking at the light cord. The room went black.

Robertson fired at the chair. A little popping sound. Then silence.

"Scylla?"

Nothing.

"I know you're alive—your body didn't fall."

"No fooling you, Jack, is there?" From another part of the room.

Robertson fired again. Another popping sound. "You haven't got a chance," Robertson said.

Another silence.

"Poor me." From another part of the room.

"I'll say I caught you robbing the shop."

"Listen to the panic in your voice, Jack."

"Don't move!"

"I already have."

*"Stop."*

"I already have." Scylla crouched easily along a side wall.

"Don't you see—you can't win—I've got the gun—"

"And I've my hands, Jack." Whispered.

"Scylla—listen—"

More whispering. "Don't fire again . . . drop it when I say so . . . if you fire again, you better hit me . . . because if you miss, I promise you you'll die for hours . . ."

"It's not written down—you were right—let me give you your money—"

"We can't go back—if I let you live, you *will* write it down—there's no trust, not any more, so all it comes to is, how do you want to die?"

"I don't want to die, Scylla."

"Well, you must. But it can be painless."

"I was sorry when I found out you were dead—truly, Scylla, I like you, so do my parents, they never fail to ask after you."

"Lovely people. Tell me what you know, Jack."

"Nothing. I just got a call from Paraguay saying I would be given a new courier. I had to assume you were dead."

"Of course. I'm coming for you, Jack. Drop it, *now*!"

The gun hit the floor.

"Good boy, Jack; now go to bed."

"No pain. You said."

"Lie down."

The sound of the mattress compressing.

"Do you want it to look like a suicide? You could write a

note explaining, worry about your heart, about becoming a burden. You could tell your parents how much you cared for them."

"I'd like that, Scylla."

Scylla plugged the lamp back in, took out his handkerchief, picked up the gun. "Where's your note paper, in the desk?"

Robertson nodded.

Scylla brought him pad and pen. "Be as personal as you want, Jack. I think it would mean a great deal to them."

Robertson wrote the note while Scylla waited patiently. When Robertson was done, Scylla glanced at it. "You're a good man, Jack; they'll remember you warmly. Close your eyes."

Robertson closed his eyes.

Scylla was amazed that he had trouble pulling the trigger. It had nothing to do with the fact that the wildly fired bullets imbedded in the walls would make suicide, at the very best, suspect. It was simply that his physical work lately had either been in self-defense or brought on by strong emotion, but this, this now, was the core of the job, the meat-and-potatoes part, and if that started getting difficult . . .

Scylla aimed the pistol at the temple, could not squeeze.

"Tell me about your lunch today, Jack." *He could not squeeze the trigger.*

"Why?"

"Because . . . I want you thinking of food, of profiterole and vintage port, because . . . these last years would have been miserable for you . . . another stroke lurking round the corner and then nothing to eat beyond celery, so I want you to know . . . I'm doing you a favor, aren't I, Jack . . ."

"For God's sake, Scylla, *you promised no pain!*"

Scylla fired, hitting the temple in the proper spot. He placed the pistol carefully in Robertson's hand, let the hand fall naturally.

"Be there soon, Jack," Scylla said.

It was true, it was true. Scylla sat staring at the body. I'm just like you, Jack, except you're prone.

I'm dead, but I won't lie down.

# 7

Babe sat in his corner of the library—he really thought of it as "his" corner, "his" table, and always resented it when anyone else was planted on the farthest-from-the-door-in-the-left-hand-corner chair. He sat hunched over, punchy, all because of the Italians—the goddamn Italians were *ruining* him. Their names were driving him maaaaaaad.

Most people fretted over Russian names, and sure, they had a point, it wouldn't be fun going through life having to spell Feodor Mikhailovich Dostoievsky every hour on the hour. But at least there was only one of him. You said "Dostoievsky," everybody knew you meant the guy who wrote those biggies.

But when you mentioned a Medici, did you mean Lorenzo or Cosimo (1) or Cosimo (2)? And which Bellini, Gentile or Giovanni or Jacopo? Not to mention the Pollaiuolo boys, Antonio and Piero. And who but a fiend could have come up with not just Fra Filippo Lippi but also Filippino Lippi? And all but the Medicis were painters or sculptors or architects.

Babe leaned back in despair. I'll never get it, he thought. I'll just be a second-rater, that's what they'll put on my tombstone, "Here lies T. B. Levy, he couldn't even get the Italians."

Maybe he wasn't cut out to be a good social historian. It was a bitch, knowing everything, but then his father had, and Biesenthal managed it, so it wasn't impossible, just no breeze.

You'll never beat Nurmi if you think this way, either—that was a task, running the marathon, and so was this, a task, that's all it was, and just as you had to sometimes force your body, the same held with your brain. Levy grabbed one of the art books he had sprawled all around the table and opened it to some stuff by the Pollaiuolos. Okay, he told himself, look at the work, what does it tell you? Antonio did things one way, Piero another. They were human, they had their quirks, just like thee and me. So find the man behind the canvas. The old bean's all you've got, so use it. Think. Logic.

Then she walked into the library, and logic went right down the tubes, out the window, vanished, kaput, gone.

From his spot in the corner, Levy went into his gaping act. Short blonde hair around startling blue eyes, all of it packaged in a shiny black raincoat. It was to die over. My God, Levy wondered, still staring across the room, what must those eyes be like close up? Better: What must they be like if they were close and *cared* for you?

Quit the self-torture—back to the Pollaiuolos. Levy closed his eyes and tried to concentrate first on Antonio, then Piero, separating them ever so slightly, ferreting out little key differences that might aid him in his . . . in his . . .

Forget it, Levy decided, opening his eyes again so he could peek some more at the girl.

She was kind of glancing around the room now, arms full of books, obviously looking for a table. *Right here,* Levy wanted to shout; near *me*. It was the logical place for her. He was alone, there were seats for six, so lots of space available, room to stretch out in, only even as he outlined the virtues of his spot in the corner of the enormous study room, he knew in his heart it wasn't about to happen.

Beauty had a way of avoiding him.

It was true. His class at Denison was universally admitted to be the homeliest in the college's history. And try finding a lovely Rhodes Scholar sometime. It was his fate, he knew, to fall in love with Venuses and marry a plugger with a face like a foot.

The truth was, girls were a problem. Not that he didn't adore them on general principles. It was just this: No girl he had ever cared for had given him a tumble, and none of those who wanted him could he ever convince himself to crave equally in return. Every girl who came after him was all the time so smart; there wasn't a Phi Bete at college who didn't eye him at least once during his undergraduate days. And he dated a lot, was intimate with a few, but they bored him. Just because *they* were smart and *he* was smart, they always assumed he wanted intellectual conversation. And he hated it. Give him a waitress with a C cup and a sweet soul and probably he would have settled, and gladly. But it never worked out. It never had and it never would—omigod, Levy thought, she's walking in this direction.

He quick picked up a book and flipped it open, and if she did sit at his table, what would he do? Just play it cool, that was the only way. When they're gorgeous, they're used to all the approaches, so let her approach you. Just bide your time and wait, and when she asks to borrow your eraser, just maybe casually slide it over to her, but don't let her think you're impressed, because the glamor girls were used to impressing everybody, and once they've got you they give you the heave, orange peel, that's all you are to them, and *Jesus, Levy, you don't have an eraser!*

Well, he just had to get one or it was all over, so he stood and looked around the room. The girl Riordan was studying on the far side, and she was the type that always had erasers, so he started toward her, knowing that she was going to think he was trying to start something serious with her. That was the way the homely ones always felt about him. If he said, "Pardon me, could you lend me a sheet of scratch paper," they always thought he was practically proposing. Still, it was worth it, because now he would be away from the table, so he wouldn't feel unhappy when the Vision sat elsewhere.

"Hi, excuse me," he said to the girl Riordan. "I'm the guy sat behind you in the Biesenthal seminar, and I wondered, could I borrow an eraser, please?"

She smiled at him. Wedding rings danced behind her eyes; Levy could see them sparkling. "What kind?" she inquired. "Ink? Pencil? Art gum?"

"Just your ordinary everyday eraser would be fine, thanks."

"Faber Eraser Stik's *my* favorite," she said, handing it to him. "You can keep it. I've got others galore."

What kind of a human person has a favorite eraser? Levy pondered. The size of the disclosure shook him, because someday this creature would be head of the department, probably at Bryn Mawr, and she'd mark down some student from an A to a B because the student liked a Dixon Ticonderoga over a

Faber Eraser Stik when it came to neatening up smears. "Thanks, I really appreciate it," Levy said, and he turned.

And there she was. Seated. Reading. Alone. At *his* very own corner table. The blue-eyed wonder.

Clutching his Faber, Levy moved in a very businesslike manner back to his seat, sat down efficiently, picked up a book, opened it, and without even giving her a glance began to study. He was at one of a line of three chairs; she was across from him, on the far end of a similar line. Levy stared at his book intently until a movement of hers caught his eye, and he quickly looked over. Nuts, he thought as he saw her taking notes with a yellow pencil; she's got her own eraser. He went back to his book and waited, because he wanted a look at her face without her being aware, so when she was deeply involved in her book, when she'd turned six or eight pages, he moved his eyes toward hers.

She was, there was simply no room for argument, something. Probably she wasn't beautiful. Garbo was beautiful, maybe Candice Bergen might be someday. This one here was only pretty. Pretty like Jeanne Crain or Katherine Ross, no more than that. Perfectly pretty was all. This one—

Bergman in *For Whom the Bell Tolls*! That's who she reminded him of, with the short blonde hair and the eyes and . . .

. . . the eyes were really not to be believed.

So blue, dark, and deep, and—quit staring at her, don't do it too long, give it a rest—Babe admonished himself a few more times before he thought, dammit, it was too late, he had gaped too long, she had felt it.

And now she was looking back at him. "Yes?" she said.

Only she didn't mean "yes." She meant bug out, take off, kid, get away, boy, ya bother me.

"Huh?" Levy said, brazening it through as best he could. "You say something? I didn't catch it."

She gave him a look, went back to her reading.

Well, Levy thought, I may have managed to get her ticked off, but at least I didn't cave.

Twenty minutes later, she grabbed her raincoat, left the room.

Levy started gathering his books so he could follow her, until the Holmes in him deduced she wasn't going anywhere permanent, since her books were still spread out on the table top. Levy left his own books in a similar condition and, after a suitable wait, picked up her trail, keeping her distantly in sight. She walked on through the library and out to the cool foyer, threw her shiny raincoat over her shoulders, opened her purse, lit a cigarette, started smoking. Then she turned, and spotted him following her.

It was a tough moment; he couldn't just stop dead, that would give it away, and he couldn't hide, she'd seen him. The only out was to head for the foyer too and have a cigarette, and the fact that he didn't smoke wasn't terribly bothersome to him until they were in the foyer, alone, and he had nothing to do except stand there like a fool, but he was in too deep for that now, so without a beat he said, "Match?" right into those punishing eyes.

She hesitated, handed some over.

Levy took them, thinking, *dummy,* first you ask for the *cigarette*, *then* you ask for the match. Now he was forced to mime searching through various pockets before he gave her what he hoped was his Cary Grant smile along with "I'll need a cigarette too, I'm afraid."

She hesitated a little longer, then gave him one.

Levy lit up. "Next you'll probably think I'm going to ask you to smoke it for me," he said, giving her as unforced a chuckle as he had around right then.

She half turned away from him.

Levy was more than contented with her profile. She was just so pretty. Not the greatest shape that ever came off the assembly line. Better than Grace Kelly but no Sophia Loren. Kind of more buxom than willowy but still short of zoftig.

They smoked in silence for a while.

"You don't even inhale," she said, surprising him.

"Not while I'm in training," he managed, delighted he could come out with anything at all. Since she wasn't interested enough to ask what he was training for, he told her anyway; he hated incomplete thoughts, a heritage from his father. "I'm a marathon man," he said.

She seemed less interested than ever.

You're losing her, Levy shouted where it echoed throughout his body. Not that you ever had her, but come on, hit her with a little something interesting, show her what a fool you're not. "Cigarettes," he shrugged desperately. "I can take 'em or leave 'em alone, but it's a funny thing, though, women are really hooked on 'em, the *Times* had a big article on that just the other day, how women can't stop smoking the way men can, wonder why that is." You just insulted her sex, dummy, suppose she's a Libber, how do you so effortlessly find just the wrong thing to say?

In the foyer, the Vision at last turned back to Levy, looked him dead on. "Why are you following me?"

Levy flung down his cigarette and stomped on it, just in time to avoid a coughing fit. "Following you? *Fol*lowing you! You must be some kind of crazy is all I've got to say. Who you think you are, Jackie Onassis? Why the hell should anybody follow you? I mean, I don't want to crumble your ego or anything, lady, but *you* sat at *my* table, I was doing just fine until you butted in, I was all spread out and doing terrific research and then you came, so if anybody's following anybody it's you following me, and if you want to follow me, it's no skin off my nose, people sometimes follow me, girls and like that, but you'd *never* hear me corner them with an accusation, I mean, when people act nutty you've got to leave them room to retreat in, room for diplomacy, that's the way I am when people follow me, anyway, gentle, understanding, and . . ." He would have gone on, except there was no reason to: She just snuffed out her cigarette and hurried out of the library into the night.

"Lies," Levy wanted to cry out after her, "I was following you because you're just so pretty, I'm nothing, a schlepper, I can't even run a whole marathon yet, but try me again, please, I promise I'll make you smile."

She was gone.

Another dazzling introduction executed by everybody's favorite Casanova, the legendary T. Babington Levy. Levy stood there awhile, contemplating the entirety of his latest campaign. Rarely, if ever, had such ineptness been shown. Why, he got this target so ticked she'd fled without even her books, and when you got someone *that* mad—

—her books.

Levy dashed back into the libe, scooped up his own research, hers, bee-lined to the out-of-sight magazine area behind the librarian's desk.

Five minutes later, the Vision was in the entrance to the room and heading fast toward the corner table, where her books had been. She hesitated, looked around, took a few steps, glanced back, left.

Fifty minutes later, Levy was buzzing her name in the foyer of her rooming house near campus.

She answered via intercom. "Who, please?"

It wasn't the best connection in the world. "Miss Opel?" Her name was Elsa Opel; well, no one was perfect.

"Who is this?" Her accent—Swiss maybe? Maybe Slav, he was rotten at accents, for a great historian, anyway—was considerably more pronounced when she had to force her voice than it had been in the foyer.

"Tom Levy—the marathon man."

"And you've come for another cigarette, is that it?"

Levy laughed. "No, no, it's just you forgot your books and I figured they might be important, so after I was done studying I brought them on over—it's right on the way to my place, no big deal or anything."

"That's very kind," she said, and pushed the button, allowing the door to unlock.

Levy saw her standing in the doorway toward the rear of the place, on the main floor. "Here," he said, and he handed them over.

She nodded. "Thank you. Good night."

"Good night," Levy said. Then he said, "Your name and

address were on the inside of your notebook, in case you're wondering how I knew where to come, Miss Opel."

"I wasn't, but again, thank you. And good night."

"Good night," Levy repeated.

"You say 'good night' but you don't go anywhere."

"I twisted my ankle on my way over here," Levy explained. "I was just giving it a rest."

"You weren't limping when you walked down the hall."

When it came to lying, he really was the worst. "If you're a marathon man, you don't like to give in to pain."

"Where were you hiding?" she said then.

"Hiding?" Levy replied, wondering whether he should start to ready his supply of outrage again, as he had in the foyer when she'd first accused him of following her.

"I came right back when I realized my forgetfulness. The books were gone. Yours too."

"Gee, I don't see how that's possible," Levy said, "I was studying right there the whole time."

"I must have gotten confused. Thank you, Mr. Levy. Good night." She closed the door.

"Behind the librarian's desk. I was hiding there," Levy replied from the corridor.

She opened the door, looked closely at him. "Why?"

"It seemed like the best place to hide."

"No, not why were you hiding *there*, why were you hiding at all?"

"Well, I couldn't have you catch me making this million-dollar heist of your school books, it would have been too embarrassing."

"Are you embarrassed now?"

"Oh yes. Humiliated."

"Is that why you're perspiring?"

"Partially. I ran over here. I run every place."

"Why did you go to all this bother?"

"It wasn't so much bother, really. You do live kind of on my way home. I mean, it's not totally out of the way."

"Do you always pursue people who sit at your library table, is it some kind of fixation?"

Levy shook his head, nodded, shrugged, nodded again. "Because you're so pretty." It was the wrong thing to say; he knew it the minute the words were gone.

"It just happened, I didn't work for it."

Levy made one last try for a retrieve. "Well, I can't very well rave on about how smart you are, I don't even know you, you may be a real dummy, and I'm done lying to you."

"But you'd like to know me."

"Yes, ma'am."

"Because I'm so pretty?"

"That's got a lot to do with it."

"How old are you?"

"Twenty-five."

"And are you always so incompetent with women?"

"Oh yes; this is actually way above average for me."

"Well, I'm twenty-five too, and you're probably very nice, and in ten years you may be twenty-six, but right now I'm a nurse and I haven't got time."

But I'd make you so happy, Levy wanted to say. Then he thought, Listen, schmuck, don't keep news like that secret, tell *her*, you got nothing to lose, she's flushing you anyway. "I'd make you so happy."

She was really stunned.

"I would, it's true," Levy hurried on. "I'd learn all about nursing—I'm smart as a whip—we could have these great long terrific talks about tourniquets—"

She burst out laughing.

"You will see me again, sure you will, say it."

"You shouldn't beg people—"

"I'm not begging, for Chrissakes, nobody's begging, why the hell should I beg, I'm junior Phi Bete, I was tops in my Rhodes group, a first breezing, and lemme tell you something, people with that kind of record don't go around begging things from dopey nurses who smoke—what kind of a nurse smokes, don't you know anything? If you can't tell begging from beseeching, you've got no chance with me."

"If I do see you again, will you promise to shut up?"

I'm winning, Levy thought. Imagine that. He nodded his head.

"All right," she said after a moment. "All right. I'll see you again." And then, surprisingly, she reached out and sadly touched his cheek. "But it won't come to anything."

"You can't tell," Babe said, watching her eyes. She looked so damn sad, she really did, so why did that make her even prettier?

Elsa rubbed her fingers against his skin. "Yes I can," she answered softly. "Regret is the best we can hope for . . ."

Alone, she lit a cigarette, smoked it all the way down, put it out, lit another. Then she picked up the phone and called Erhard. "He is terribly sweet," she said. "Very naïve, very kind."

She listened a moment.

"I'm sorry if I sound depressed. I'm not, I'm tired."

Another pause.

"Yes, I think it's fair to say that he finds me attractive."

Pause.

"How much time do I have?"

Long pause.

"I'll do my best." She closed her eyes. "With luck, in a week he'll love me . . ."

# 8

Babe got out his aging Remington and began to pound.

Doc? This is me and you better sit down. I mean it, it's that important, that incredible, that gravity suspending. (Omigod, you're thinking, he's in love again—once more the kid brother's head over heels.)

Right.

Doc, Doc, I don't know where to begin—

(Begin with her buck teeth, you're thinking; start with how her thin-haired skull glistens in the moonlight.)

Wrong.

(Nothing wrong with the teeth or the hair? Odd. The last one had fewer strands than bicuspids. Hmmm. No boobs but a great mind. Or maybe *three* boobs and a great mind, which?)

Neither, and go to hell.

(Must have been a field hockey champ back in school. Calves like Bronco Nagurski, shoulders like Larry Csonka, but a nice complexion from all the outdoor effort.)

Close your hole and *listen to me*—I've known her a little over a week, and each day when I go to pick her up I think I'm crazy, no one's *that* terrific, but each day she's more terrific, more tender, more divine, perfect, impeccable, immaculate, utopian, consummate, indefectible, sublime. And I'm understating.

(Probably I can get you a quick admission to Menninger's.)

Let me start with the faults: her name, I've got to admit, is Elsa Opel.

(Nothing wrong with that, I once had a car named Opel.)

And she's my age, Swiss, and a nurse—

(Look on the bright side, could have been a stewardess.)

—other than that, faultless. Other than that, a head-spinner. All my life, I've been drooling after other guys' girls. You don't know what it's like to watch the other bastards drooling after mine.

(A drooler, is she? That what you're trying to hint? Nothing wrong with drooling. One of the better things you can do with saliva, actually. Limited substance, saliva. Any other impediments? You better tell me now. Pin-headed maybe? Didn't you get interested in a love at Denison who verged on being pin-headed?)

Everyone makes mistakes. But not this time. Oh Doc, Jesus, it's so fantastic please get your ass down here to meet her. New York isn't that far, come on. I want to see your head spin, I really do. See, there's one thing I haven't told you.

(Okay, hit me with it, I'm braced.)

She loves me back. She really does. A beautiful girl, a beautiful, non-competitive, sweet, sensible girl, and she *cares* for me. After all these crummy years, my cup is running over.

Sumbitch,

Babe

# 9

Scylla lay in bed blinking.

In his dream, he had been too slow, and that was not a good thing, even in dreams that had never happened before. And of all people, it had been Mengele who had beaten him.

Mengele, the chief of the Auschwitz experimental block, the doctor they called the Angel of Death, the one who had gone almost mad trying to breed blue-eyed humans as a kennel master tries to breed drop-eared dogs.

They were in Mengele's lab, it was Auschwitz, but Scylla was calm. He towered half a head over the death doctor's five six, and more than that, the door was open, and the door led straight to freedom. Scylla had never been to Auschwitz, had never met Mengele, but in dreams such things happened, and this was happening.

"I'm in despair," Mengele said.

"Why?"

"I cannot make the baby's eyes come out with the proper shade of blue. Yesterday in frustration I threw a baby high into a fire. It was a terrible thing for me to do, letting my emotions get control like that."

"Control is important for us," Scylla agreed.

"I just thank God you're here at this moment to help me."

"How can I help you?"

"I need skin. I want to transplant skin, and you have just the shade I'm looking for."

Scylla shrugged. "A patch of skin is nothing. Take it."

"No, no," Mengele explained. "A patch does me no good, I need all your skin, every bit of it, you must let me skin you."

"I don't think I'd like that," Scylla told him, taking a quiet step toward the open door and freedom.

Mengele made no move to follow. "You must listen, it's a great blessing I offer."

Scylla shook his head. "Without skin people could see right through me."

"That's the blessing—don't you understand, the world would see right through and you wouldn't have to lie any more. Think of the weight that would lift—no more lies. No more point to lying, because there would be no skin to cover you and the world would know the truth when you spoke it. You have lied so much, admit it."

"Yes."

"And you long to end it, admit that too. You have so many fabrications going, don't you want to sometimes scream the truth?"

"*Yes.*"

"Well, that is the chance I offer you. Everlasting truth. Peace. The rest only the honest ever know."

"*No.*"

"Don't let your emotions gain control." He held out his tiny surgeon's hands toward Scylla.

Scylla fled for the open door.

But he was too slow.

Mengele beat him to it, shut it, and it locked. They were alone in the lab now. Mengele began coming for him.

He, Scylla the rock, who could kill with either hand, began backing from the tiny lunatic. He, the great Scylla, retreating before nothing, a frail physician who couldn't even make eyes come out the proper shade of blue.

"Why do you fear me?" Mengele wondered.

"I don't. There is no fear in my body."

Mengele held out his hands.

"I'll use force," Scylla promised.

"Oh please, please, none of that," Mengele said, and with his tiny hands he led Scylla to a table, laid him down. "There will be no pain, I promise. I'll just make a small cut from your forehead to the base of your neck and pull your skin right off. It won't hurt any more than disrobing from a pair of pajamas." He began to cut. "You see," he said as the knife split Scylla's skin, "there isn't even any blood," and he put the knife down, pulled the skin off. "Let me get you a mirror, your veins are quite beautiful," Mengele said.

"No!"

"Here," Mengele said, and he handed the mirror over.

Scylla managed one look at himself before he woke up blinking.

Wow.

He lay still, concentrating on the ceiling, winded, empty.

He had no idea of what the dream indicated about the state of his mind, but he did know this: Whatever it was, it was getting very dark down there.

He rolled his muscled body out of bed and sat, rubbing his cold hands together. Scylla the sponge, he felt like. Scylla the soft.

Cut it!

He stood, grabbed his Scotch bottle (had it really been full when he started to bed last night?), and moved to the window of his room in the Raphael. He drank while he looked out at the Arc de Triomphe. What was the time? He glanced at his watch. Coming up to half-past five. After midnight in America, Janey would be dead asleep. If they ever made an Olympic event of sack time, Janey was a cinch to qualify. Beauty sleep.

Scylla dressed, walked downstairs, woke the concierge, got a ton of tokens. It was all an unnecessary precaution, because if he was tapped back home, what difference did it make if they'd bugged the Raphael on him? Habit. He felt better on the move.

Anyway, he needed the air. It was dark when he stepped outside and began hunting up a pay phone. He never worried about the night; he was big and big-shouldered, and he could kill with either hand, and sure, a mugger wouldn't have any way of knowing that last, but still, he moved like an athlete and he had size, and muggers had never bothered him.

He found a spot near the Arc and after a good deal of pidgin French and dials and beeps and king-sized waits, finally he could hear Janey's sleep-filled voice coming through. "Huh? Wha?—who? What time is . . . oh, never mind," and then, finally, "Hi."

"This is the answering service," Scylla said. "Didn't you leave a wake-up call?"

"A *joke*?" Janey wailed. "Three thousand miles in the middle of the night to make a funny? People have been jellied in aspic for less."

Scylla began the segue into code now; at first it had irritated him, the inconvenience of it all. Now it was sort of a game you had to play at a party to humor the host. "Are you awake enough to take down some stuff ?"

"Only partially, I'm afraid."

"Partially" was the crucial word. "Wide awake" meant there was nothing much going on. "Partially" meant there were items that Scylla ought to know about. "I'll sign off then. The reason I called was to tell you I'd be back three days early, but since you're only partially awake, I won't bother you with information like that. You're not mad at me for waking you."

"Never," Janey said. "I had to get up anyway, the telephone was ringing."

They ended on that joke, both hanging up, and then Scylla had ten minutes to wait. His return "partially" meant he would call again, to the pay phone in the basement garage of their apartment building. Ten minutes was how long it would take Janey to get roused, dressed, out the door, and gone.

It was still before six, and cold. Scylla shivered with it, and wondered why he had left his Scotch bottle back by his bed table, where it could do no one any good. He could not, as he paced the dead street, think of one good reason why he didn't just quit and take off with Janey for London and rent or buy a little mews house maybe, and sit around watching the telly and visiting the greengrocer and living the way you were supposed to, happily ever et cetera.

To hell with Division not letting you quit until it wanted to retire you. If he were rich enough, if only somehow he could get like Croesus, he'd bribe his way out, or at least try, and if that didn't work he could buy an island in the goddamn Pacific and fortify it and let The Division do its worst.

An island in the Pacific, Jesus—Scylla shook his head. Maybe it was a good thing he'd left the Scotch bottle back at the hotel, if that's the way a few swigs were going to affect his thinking. Keep the Croesus notion, though; at least it gave him a culture hero to think about.

Scylla placed the second call, went through all the beeps and sounds again, and then he had Janey back.

"Where are you," Janey began, obviously upset.

"On the loose in gay Paree, it's a very swinging place. Or is that London? Let's go to London, I'd like that, would you like that?"

"I mean, exactly where? On the street, in a hotel? Why aren't you asleep, it isn't even six yet."

"Dream woke me. I just took a walk."

"You're alone, then?"

"All."

"You better be, you bastard. I hate it when you go on trips without me. How bad was it?"

"The dream?" Scylla shrugged his big shoulders. No point to lying. Janey always sensed that kind of thing, anyway, he had no way of knowing how. From his tone, probably. "Very. Extremely, even."

"My doctor always recommends Scotch."

"Didn't work."

"Get back here; that's what *I* always recommend. The best cure I know is me."

"Taken once every four hours."

"Dream on—you're not that young any more."

"You'll pay for that kind of talk, you tawdry bitch."

"Call me Janey; all my friends do."

Scylla listened, making sure that the upset was gone from Janey's voice. Then he proceeded with the business at hand. "Why the 'partially'?"

"Kaspar Szell was killed."

"Wow."

"I knew you'd say that."

"When?" Scylla said.

"Almost two weeks ago in Manhattan. The Yorkville section. He was in a car and another guy tried cutting around and they smashed into an oil truck. Total incineration. I think that's why the news took so long getting around. Identification wasn't all that easy. He was using the Hesse name, and besides, nobody ever heard of him anyway. But it's done. You still there? You're not saying a word."

Scylla grunted.

"Upset?"

"I guess—I don't really know. I can't take it all in yet."

"Is it going to cause that many changes?"

It already had. He couldn't be sure, but probably there was some connection with the death in New York and the Chen business—even though Chen was simply a free-lance assassin, still, somebody had to do the hiring. And then, of course, poor Robertson had mentioned a South American call informing him that there would be a new courier. Scylla thought a moment; he had to make an answer, but there was no point in troubling Janey with specifics; just a general truth would do. "Many changes? Only everything."

"Wow," from Janey.

"Conservatively speaking," Scylla said.

# 10

"Cold?" Levy asked.

Elsa shook her head, no.

They were sitting on a rock by the lake in Central Park. Below them, their rowboat moved lightly as bursts of evening winds skittered along the water. Levy knew she was lying, because, in the first place, he had a sweater on and she didn't and *he* was cold, so there was no way she could avoid being just the least bit uncomfortable. And it was getting colder because his stupid tooth was hurting worse. It always did when the weather chilled. It was that front tooth on the top, and he did his best to cover the cavity with his tongue. They really ought to be getting back, he knew. But they'd been sitting there for an hour now, since the sun had started leaving, and it had just been so damn terrific that he didn't want to be the one to tear it.

Elsa put her arm around him. "Not so cold now," she said.

Levy kissed her gently. At first he had been rough with her, because he thought she wanted that, manliness, machismo; a girl this gorgeous must have seen her share of winners, and he wanted to measure up. But she'd shied from that, and after a night or two of necking he realized that what she wanted was what he was: tender. Oh, he didn't look it—he looked angles and bone, sharp-elbowed, much too clumsy to be soft. But it wasn't so. He liked necking, he even liked holding hands. Although that was probably against the law nowadays for anyone under thirty. Not that screwing was so terrible; Levy had done some of that too, though not with Elsa, not yet, anyway. Screwing was fine and orgasms glorious, but, at least in his limited experience, it was also rough and quick, too rough and too quick, and where sex was concerned, he was never in a hurry. Sometimes, in the back of his mind he realized that he was probably very good at sex and that if he had been handsome, he would have been as much in demand as a caterer at holiday time, but he wasn't handsome, and it wasn't so terrible.

Elsa touched his cheek. "Such a lovely face," she whispered.

"Everybody says that," Levy told her. "Even on the streets, strangers come up to me."

In the darkness, she smiled at him, ran her tongue along his lips.

"That's very inventive," Levy said. "Do it again, why don't you, just to be sure you've got it."

She ran her tongue along his lips again.

"I take pity on waifs and weirdos, you're a very lucky girl."

She put both her arms around him now. He could feel her body trembling.

"Hey, you're just freezing. We really ought to be turning the boat in anyway."

"Let me freeze, I've just loved this so, just talking, go on."

Levy kissed her neck softly, grazed it with his lips.

"Homer Virgil," she said. "Before you asked was I cold, you were telling about him. Was he famous, your father?"

"Old H.V.? Well, not like Ann-Margret or Donny Osmond, but for an historian he did okay."

"Such a terrible name for a child."

"That was my grandfather's doing—he gave all his kids terrible names—see, he was the principal and head teacher and chief cook and bottle washer in this little Midwestern school, and he claimed that it didn't matter, all anybody heard was the Levy part anyway. There weren't a whole lot of Jews in central Ohio in those days, believe me. He loved the Greeks and the other oldies. One of my uncles had Herodotus for a middle name. He's dead now, my uncle—I don't mean to imply that's what killed him, but it couldn't have helped him a whole lot either."

"Your father is also dead?"

"He is also dead. Cerebral hemorrhage. Out of the blue, totally unexpected."

She watched him in the darkness.

"What?" he asked.

"Nothing."

He hesitated, wondering if he could go on, clear it up, but it was doubtful that she knew; she hadn't been in the country then, and even if she had, she would still have been a kid, and besides, H.V. hadn't been *that* famous.

She kissed him very hard, then quickly stood, stretched her arms high. Babe watched. It was a clumsy gesture, but on Elsa even clumsy was pretty.

Then things stopped being so pretty, because as Elsa

smiled and whispered "Come," and started for the boat, there was a sudden sound from the bushes behind them, and the limping man appeared for the first time, back-handing Elsa in the face, knocking her off balance and down.

Levy watched it, and it was as if he had been a spectator to a street play—it came so quickly there was no chance for involvement, just spectating, and there she was, his one true woman, being beaten by a savage limping man. *"Hey!"* Levy shouted, and started after them, but too late, because there was another sound from the bushes behind him, and then the big-shouldered man was spinning him around and crashing a fist into Levy's face.

Levy staggered, blood spurting, but he didn't go down, and his nose felt broken, and Elsa was being pulled toward the bushes now, the limper trying to yank her purse free and Levy started to say "Let him have it!" but the big-shouldered man never let him get it out, because he kicked Levy hard in the stomach and Levy gasped, crashed to his knees on the rock, and then went to all fours as the other man hit him again, hard across the cheek, and Levy rolled down. The big-shouldered man pulled him toward the bushes, started grabbing for Levy's wallet, and Levy instinctively made a protective move, which was stupid, because all it got him was a knee slammed into his back, and the blood from the first punch was smearing now, his tongue stinging of salt, and it was his fault, he shouldn't have stayed late in the park, only tourists were that dumb, and he lay very still while the attacker tried getting his wallet, but he was having trouble, Levy's back pocket was buttoned and the guy couldn't rip it clear fast enough, so he kneed Levy in the back again, hit him again across his broken nose, and Levy started coughing from the blood, and he could hear Elsa almost crying, and if that limping son of a bitch was touching her he'd—he'd—

—he'd what?—

—nothing—not a goddamned thing—if they wanted to rape her he was helpless, or even if they just wanted to pound the shit out of her on general principles he was helpless, his nose was broken, he felt as if his ribs were smashed, and they could do what they pleased, he was helpless—

*Helpless!* The word forced its way past the blood and into his brain, and the reality of it was so humiliating that Levy somehow found it in himself to kick at the big-shouldered guy, and he landed a good one, and the enemy cried out, and that was a triumph, you couldn't deny that, but unfortunately it didn't last long enough because as Levy tried to make it to his feet and over to Elsa the big-shouldered guy was back, all business now, banging away with big hands at Levy's face, swelling it out of shape until Levy fell, half-conscious.

Then they were both standing over him, the limper with Elsa's purse and the big-shouldered guy with Levy's wallet. "We have your wallets and we have your names, and addresses." The limper patted Elsa's purse. "And if you report this to the police, we will know and we will come for you."

Elsa was crying now.

"And next time will be bad," the big-shouldered man said. "You understand 'bad'?"

Levy lay there.

Then the muggers were gone.

Levy slowly crawled toward Elsa. ". . . Were you . . ." was what he said. Touched, he meant, molested.

She shook her head, no. She understood him; that was the truly splendid thing about them—they understood each other. Everything. "The purse only." She began to come apart then, the reaction setting in. "Just the purse," she said again. "I'm fine."

Levy held her very close. "Both fine," he managed. He didn't want to ever let go, but when he started smearing her with his own blood, there wasn't much else he could do . . .

# 11

Doc

I don't think I'm going to send this, which somehow frees me to write it, but if I do, remember I'm not myself, I mean, I'm a little off my feed, I'm not going bonkers or anything.

Doc I just got mugged, I got the shit kicked out of me, I'm not upset about that—no, bullshit, I'm plenty upset about that, but it was my own fault, it was Central Park, it was after sundown, only an idiot moron jerk would have been there in the first place.

But see, I wasn't alone. Elsa and I were sitting on a rock after I'd rowed her around awhile 'cause she'd never done it and she'd always wanted to and what the hell, it was a beautiful day, I said terrific and we did it and it was so great we stayed too long on this rock by the lake and then this Limper appears and I'm sitting there and this sonofabitch clubs her and starts dragging her for the bushes and I think I'll fix that bastard, nobody touches my baby—

—and I couldn't stop it. I couldn't do *anything*!—this big guy with shoulders out to here and I swear I'm not making this up, the guy was a pro, he started kicking the shit out of me and I never got hit like that, he knew just where to put his knees, just where to cream me, and I know Elsa's getting the shit beaten out of her and maybe worse and all I want is just one time in this world to be a hero and this guy's going for my wallet and pounding the crap out of me and I'm not even feeling it, it's not the goddamn pain or the goddamn blood so much—

—it's the helplessness—

—the fucking helplessness—

—Doc I wanted to kill him.

I swear, if I had had a knife I would have stabbed him and if I had had a bomb I would have blown him apart, and then I would have gone after the Limper and I would have tried to get him with my hands—

Me, I'm a liberal, an historian, I never once wanted to hurt anybody, I never even wanted Richard Nixon to suffer, and right now I want to kill and it scares me.

I just took five minutes off to go put some cool water on my face, I'm all the hell puffed up and cut and it stung and all I thought was revenge, I want revenge on those guys for making me feel that helpless, nobody should ever be made to feel that way, not in front of a girl who loves him, and I know in her mind she was thinking why doesn't he do something, he's right there, why doesn't he *help me* and shit, I want to take every goddamn Charles Atlas course ever invented and get so strong and then I want those two guys' throats in my hands.

Doc, there's this bunch of juvenile delinquents who seem to live on a stoop a few brownstones down (I don't mean funny juvenile delinquents, these aren't cutesy-pies out of West Side Story, these guys would suck your eyeball for a grape), and when I came home tonight, well, usually they mock me and who cares, they think I'm a creep, so what, and tonight when I walked by I figured with the blood and all, at least I'd get some respect and you know what? One of them said, "Who did it, a midget or a girl?" and they all laughed—because, see, they can take care of themselves, they would have pounded my enemies to shreds and I really think my I.Q. is higher than all of theirs put together and *what good does it do me*?

I'm going to send this, I guess, because I guess I want to ask you, what would Father have said? See, I think he'd have told me that any experience is profitable if you allow it to be, all actions are profitable, no matter how badly you may suffer from them. The true historian never has enough grist. He spends his life in constant searching.

Where's the profit in impotence, Doc, huh?

You tell me.

Babe

# 12

Levy mailed the letter Sunday evening. He was not so swollen, and the cuts in his face were scabbing quickly, but he still felt freakish, so he pulled his peak-billed cap far down across his face and sprinted to the mailbox on the corner at Columbus, then went back to his room to hide.

Monday he was supposed to have the Biesenthal seminar, but he could not go; he looked, as he stared at himself in the morning, unshaven, unappetizing. He had never been one for physical force, and seeing himself cut up and puffed he found strangely unnerving; he had never realized that he had all that much vanity, but evidently he did.

He called Elsa a few times, and she called him a few times, and she wanted to come down—she was, she explained over and over, practically in the medical profession, how much harm could she do?—but he needed not to be seen, to be alone. He played the mugging over in his mind, winning some, losing some, and he tried to read, but more than anything, what he did Monday was study his face in the mirror and hope that it would reform itself into something he found more recognizable.

It did; actually, by Monday night it wasn't the kind of

thing that would cause heads to turn any more. The cuts remained where the big-shouldered man had pounded them, but, with the constant application of cold compresses, the swelling disappeared quicker even than he'd hoped. His back ached from where the mugger had kneed him, but that he could cope with.

Elsa's hysteria proved more troublesome: "*—Did you tell them—I didn't tell them—*"

"Who?—easy . . ." It was Tuesday morning, and she had been pounding on the door until she finally woke him. He knew from her tone, even before he let her in, that she was way into panic.

"—They said they'd come after us—they said they had our names and where we lived, so why did you go when you said you wouldn't—"

"Elsa, what the hell is this—I didn't do a damn thing, I swear—"

"The limper . . ." she began.

"What about him? *Tell me.*"

Her voice was soft now. "When I left my building . . . today when I left . . . this morning now . . . he was there . . . following . . ."

"Are you sure? Did you see his face close up?"

Now she was getting louder again. "You promised you wouldn't tell the police, but you did, you must have, because now the limper comes—"

He tried holding her for a moment, but that didn't work. "I swear I never went. It must have been a mistake or something—did you really *see* this guy?"

"I saw . . . a man outside . . . he was there . . . I started to walk away . . . he came after . . . limping . . . I turned a corner, he turned it after me . . . that was enough, I ran."

"Well, there's only maybe nine million guys who limp in New York, Elsa," Babe began. "I mean, it's world-famous for being gimp heaven—the National Limpers' Association would never think of holding its convention any place besides the Coliseum, I thought everyone knew that," and he kept on, giving her a few lines to keep it lively, putting some water on to boil so they could have a little instant, and pretty soon she began to relax. He had a way with her, it was what made them so terrific. By midmorning she admitted it might have been imagination.

By noon she admitted she was fine.

They took in a Bergman double bill, *Seventh Seal* and *Wild Strawberries*, Babe being a Bergman nut, Elsa totally unfamiliar. Then he bought her a cheapo meal at the local Szechuan—he was a nut for that too. Then he took her to her place, where they touched a little, and after that he headed on home. He was bushed, so sleep came quickly, and he had no idea what time it was when he realized that it hadn't been all imagination on Elsa's part, because, even half awake, he could tell there was someone in the room with him.

Before he had a chance to get afraid, Babe decided to do what Cagney would have done, so in his best *White Heat* voice he said, low and even, "I got a gun, I know how to use it; you make a move, I'll blow your ass to Shanghai."

And from the darkness came his favorite voice in all the world: "Don't kill me, Babe."

Babe practically flipped right out of bed. "Aw, hey, Doc, shit, great."

"Undeniably articulate," Doc said. "But then, the lad has always had a way with words."

Babe let out an actual whoop then, something he didn't do ordinarily, and a good thing too, since it was hardly Emily Post behavior. But what the hell, anything was acceptable on those rare occasions when your own and only good big brother came to town . . .

# PART II

# DOC

# 13

"Lemme get the light," Babe said, and as he flicked it on, Doc went, "Hey?"

"What?"

Doc pointed to the cuts. "Face."

Babe shrugged. "Nothing. I don't want to talk about it, just your garden-variety mugging, nothing worth making a fuss over. Happened Sunday—what's today, Tuesday? I wrote you. When you get back you can read all about it."

"But you're okay?"

Babe nodded. When Doc got to worrying, he could be a real mother hen. "As a matter of fact, do me a favor and when you get back, don't read all about it, just pitch the letter, yes?"

Doc twirled his key chain, which had, among others, Babe's apartment key on it. After a few circles he flipped it high into the air, caught it behind his back without looking. He did it all in one motion, a trick he could do from the time Babe could remember, only in the old days he did it with softballs or marbles. Now, at least when they were together, Doc did it only in times of decision. Babe realized that, though probably Doc didn't; it was ingrained by now. " 'Twill be burned," Doc said. Then, loosening his tie: "I've been off working, and all that was waiting from you upon my return was this, may I say, *obscenely* overwritten piece of purple prose that would have made Rossetti blush—it contained, to be precise, a description of Her Ladyship, and I figured I better quick get my ass down here and meet her before she made her ascension into Heaven."

"Screw," Babe said, "I never went on like that and you know it."

Doc picked up his Gucci bag and plopped it on Babe's desk. "You didn't, huh? You're just lucky I understand you're a mental defective and unaccountable for your actions, or I'd spend the rest of my life blackmailing you. I think you called her 'utopian' at one point. 'Indefectible, utopian and sublime.' Hell, even Annette Funicello was never *that* great."

"Screw," Babe said again, this time barfing out loud, because just once, in a moment of weakness, he had told Doc he thought from certain angles Annette Funicello was "kinda cute" and Doc never forgot anything, especially when you gave him ammo like that to deal with.

Doc looked around Babe's room. It really was crummy. Bare-floored and covered all over with dust. Books piled everywhere, the sofa showing bare springs, the bathroom permanently gray. "You've done wonders," Doc said. He had been down only once before, a week or two after Babe took the place.

"It's not everything it's gonna be," Babe admitted, "but my decorator's so goddamn unreliable. I should fire him, but not many top guys will handle a job this big."

Doc nodded, opening his bag; he took out three bottles of red wine, and looked at them against a bare light bulb by

Babe's desk. "I just hope the sediment's not too stirred up," he said. He looked at Babe. "Corkscrew?"

Babe pointed toward the kitchen, waiting for the lecture to start on the glories of Burgundy wine.

"I'll open the Moulin-à-vent," Doc said. "It's a Beaujolais, but I think you'll be surprised at the power." He concentrated on opening the bottle.

"Terrific," Babe said. He tried a few experimental snores, drooped his eyes shut. "Go on, go on."

Doc was having trouble with the cork. "It's known as the king of Beaujolais—Fleurie's the queen—"

"Fascinating, my God," Babe managed, snoring a little louder now.

Doc ignored him. "This is a splendid year, seventy-one, and the balance is what I want you to pay attention to."

Babe dropped his head limply, began snoring and whistling, snoring and whistling.

"You are a boor and a turd," Doc said, but then he was laughing. "I give, I give, no more wine talk." He paused. "Dammit, I meant to bring glasses down with me."

Now Babe started to laugh. "You bastard, you know I got glasses." He headed toward a cabinet.

"I do not include paper cups," Doc said.

Babe grabbed a glass, handed it over. "Here, goddammit."

Doc started to pour, stopped. "This thing is filthy."

"I never said I had *clean* glasses, asshole," Babe said, and then they said, at precisely the same moment, "Not the shoulders, just the head," and then, again together, they started plotzing out loud, because it was a favorite family story. H.V.

had loved it, about an awkward Brooklyn Dodger, Babe Herman, who got angry one day when a sportswriter said, in print, that Herman was going to get beaned on the head by a fly ball, he was so clumsy in the outfield, and Herman, furious, cornered the sportswriter and called him every name in the book, ending up by saying, "And I'll betcha fifty bucks you're wrong," and the reporter said, "Okay, it's a deal, fifty bucks says you get hit on the head or the shoulders by a fly ball," and Herman thought that one over awhile before concluding, "Nah—nah—not the shoulders, just the head."

Still laughing, Doc went to the sink and turned on the water. "When does it stop being rusty?" he asked after a while.

"If you'd unpack, it'll probably be okay by the time you're finished."

"Might as well wash one for you too," Doc said, and he picked a dirty glass from the sink.

"Just a touch," Babe said. "I'm working up to twenty miles now, and booze is tough on the wind."

"Burgundy is *not* 'booze,' " Doc said, busying himself with the glasses. "I'm sorry I joked about your place," he said, his back turned. "You're a scholar, what the hell do you need with a palace? Live the way you want while you can. Forgiven?"

"I wasn't even sure I'd been insulted."

"Good," Doc said, working away. "It's a crazy world, I tell you, who the hell knows what's gonna happen one minute to the next, I was just reading this morning's *Wall Street Journal* and there's this California firm—you won't believe this but what the hell, they're all nuts in California, I guess, that's how they qualify for citizenship—anyway, this bunch of West

Coast guys have patented a thing they call, lemme get this right now, oh yeah, they call it a 'br—oooo-m'—it's like a long stick with a bunch of hay tied to one end of it, and the *Journal* says they think they'll make a fortune with this thing—they claim with their 'br—oooo-m' you can clean things, floors, for example, just by sweeping."

"Never catch on," Babe said.

Doc whirled from the rusty water. "Jesus, Babe, how can you exist in an armpit of a place like this?"

"Glasses're clean now," Babe said. "Pour the firewater."

Doc poured, giving the bottle a twist to avoid spilling.

Babe took a sip, Doc too. Babe could never remember even seeing his brother high, much less drunk, and the same held true for him. But then, H.V. had more than brought up the old family average. At least during the last days. Last years, actually. Last bad years.

"This expensive?"

"Sort of, why?"

"No reason. Smells it, kind of. Smooth. Whenever I don't have a coughing fit, I figure it's expensive. Oil business must be good."

Doc raised his glass to toasting position. "The oil business is always good." He made a slight religious bow.

"That wasn't east," Babe said.

"I was bowing toward Detroit, jerk—General Motors is more important to this country than Jesus ever was."

"Goddamn polluters and thieves," Babe said. He really hated it that Doc worked at what he worked at. Drilling equipment, selling it all over, contaminating the goddamn world.

"If you give me your ecology lecture now, I swear I'll tell

Irmgaard when I meet her how I caught you pulling your pud when you were twelve."

Babe laughed. "That was a great day for me, really. Up till then, I thought I was the only one in the whole history of the world to do anything that horrible. I thought you'd have to cast me out or put me in the stocks and have the villagers throw rocks at me. When you told me that everybody did it all the time, I remember thinking, 'Those bastard grown-ups, why have they kept it *secret* from me all these years?' "

Doc smiled, pointed to the bed. "Move your debris."

Babe began to. They had a deal: Whenever Doc came calling, he got the bed, Babe took the spring-filled sofa.

While this was going on, Doc said quietly, "Hey? Quit living in a hovel like this, come on down to Washington, I'll set you up in a decent place, we'll be near each other, give it a try, huh, I got the bread, you know that's no problem."

Babe shook his head. "No decent grad schools down there."

"Nothing to compare with the glories of Columbia, is that it?"

"Columbia's not all that great, I'm not saying it is, but it does have a much lower percentage of mouth-breathers than, say, Georgetown."

Suddenly Doc was hollering, *"Jesus, Babe, for Chrissakes, just 'cause Dad did it you don't have to!"*

*"I'm sick of that!"* Babe hollered right back.

Doc stopped short, confused. "Sick of it? I never said it before."

"Professor Biesenthal at Columbia. He did, kind of."

"Wasn't he one of H.V.'s geniuses?"

Babe nodded yes. Then he said, "Look, I like my hovel, thanks for the offer, but I'm staying here, and it's got nothing to do with H.V."

"Bull!"

Babe shrugged, shifted pillows, while Doc continued hanging up the few clothes he'd brought along. "So I'll take you and Etta for dinner, okay? She does need food, doesn't she? Or can she sustain her divinity on pure atmosphere?"

"Wait'll you see her, you'll salivate, I guarantee it."

Doc laughed. "Sonny, you're talking to a guy who was married once and engaged three times before he was twenty-five—it takes a lot to make me lose my spittle."

"What is that, bragging? Four arrests and only one conviction?"

"I haven't had a sincere conviction since I entered the oil game—there's an industry-wide regulation against them." He closed his Gucci bag, shoved it into a corner of Babe's closet. Casually, he said, "Hey, you don't still have that thing, do you?"

Knowing the answer, Babe still said, "What thing?"

"When I let myself in tonight and you were set to blow my ass to Shanghai, you sounded really authentic, very George Raft."

"*Nobody* imitates George Raft for Chrissakes—that was supposed to be Cagney."

"Do you?"

"Loaded." He went to his bottom desk drawer, took out the pistol and the box of bullets. "Here."

"Take those things out, *then* give it to me."

Quickly Babe unloaded the pistol. He was expert with it,

but then, he should have been, considering the hours he'd put in practicing over the years. Doc was the reverse; he'd always hated guns. "Here," Babe said again.

Doc took it, tried handling it as if it didn't panic him. "How can you keep something like this?"

"What do you mean 'how'? You didn't want it."

"*Want* it? Who could possibly want it?"

"Me, obviously."

"Why?"

"No reason. Keepsake. You know damn well why, to get back."

"Babe, Joe McCarthy died a year before Dad killed himself."

"Maybe, maybe not. There's lots of lies have come out of Washington."

"Is Helga sadistic too? Is that one of the things you two cuties have in common? What do you do for fun if there isn't a vampire picture playing in town?" He gave the gun to Babe.

As he reloaded it, Babe said, "You're trying to bait me, you bastard, I know you, because before you called her Irmgaard and I didn't correct you and then you called her Etta and I didn't correct you then either, and just now you said Helga; well, that's also not gonna get a rise out of me, but it's Elsa, *Elsa,* you got that, not Ilse or Ella or Eva, not Hilda or Leila or Lida, not Lily, not Lola."

"I'm sorry," Doc said. "I must be punchy from traveling. I won't get Olga's name wrong again, I swear."

"Olga is nearly it, but Olga is still wrong," Babe said, patiently. "I'm really proud of you for coming so close, anyone who's learned to read as recently as you have would naturally have trouble with two-syllable words, but we're gonna work on Elsa until you get it right, not Portia, Pamela or Paula, not Rhoda either, and it's also not Sara or Stella, Sophia or Shelia."

"Ursula?" Doc tried.

"Closing in on it," Babe said, "give credit where it's due, but it's Elsa, not Vida, Vera or Vanessa or Venetia or Willa or Ysolda. *ELSA!!!*"

"Elsa," Doc said. He sipped his wine, then looked at his kid brother. "Her I got—who the hell are you?"

# 14

Only one road leads past the estate. "Estate" is probably too strong a word; in Palm Springs it would have just been a house, "nothing to be ashamed of." But with the Paraguayan jungle encroaching on the other three sides, the blue house half an hour outside La Cordillera was certainly something close to unique; at the very least, extraordinary.

The peasants in La Cordillera had heard about the blue house, most of them anyway, but not that many had actually seen the place. Because, first of all, it was a half-hour trip even if you knew someone who owned a car, and secondly, the one road was almost dangerously rutted.

And thirdly, the guards.

There were always two, each stationed perhaps a quarter of a mile on either side of the blue house. There was very little traffic, anyway, but whatever came, the guards examined. They never explained what rights they had, where the legal justification came from; they moved with their rifles into the middle of the road and waited for the vehicle to stop. They were not pleasant. They implied, always, menace. Do not return this way unless you must, they seemed to say; we do not like seeing the same faces here.

The only ones they waved through were the ones who

delivered. Every week an ancient open truck arrived with food from La Cordillera. A mail delivery took place every other day. And every afternoon an additional guard would leave the blue house and drive to the nearest village for the laundress.

Always shawled in black, she was a bull-shouldered woman of average height. She would enter the house and, several hours later, leave it; then the same guard would drive her back to the village.

Usually she carried nothing with her, but one late September afternoon she emerged, shawled as always, with a black case perhaps one foot square. She got into the same car she always got into, and the same guard drove her from the blue house. The car looked the same as always, and was, except for in the back seat, under a blanket, where there rested a canvas clothes case. The car left the blue house, turned toward the village, and the guard on the road started to move his right arm into a salute, and probably would have had not the driver waved at him in sudden wild anger. The road guard dropped his arm and stood stiffly, head down a bit, ashamed, hoping that the master of the blue house would not retaliate with cruelty.

The car drove on. The laundress sat quietly, bull-shouldered as always, the black box firmly held in her lap, like some strange security blanket of black leather. Her shawl was pulled perhaps more over her face than usual, but otherwise she looked like the laundress going home.

It was crucial that everything look exactly as everything had always looked, because the master of the blue house knew that although most of the occasional peasants who crept past his estate were just that, peasants, Paraguayan and thick and inconsequential, some of them, not many, but enough to be worrying, were Jews.

The car drove to the laundress's village and straight through it. The driver never spoke. The laundress sat squat and stolid. Both of them perspired. The heat was relentless; unless you were strong, it could kill you. The driver was very strong, the weaker of the two, but filled with power nonetheless.

It was a two-hour drive to the airport at Asunción. The driver got out, began to reach for the canvas case.

"Sit!" the laundress said. The language was Spanish.

The driver whirled back to his place, remained immobile while the laundress took the clothes in one hand, the black leather case in the other.

In Spanish the driver said, "May I ask one question, please?"

The shawled figure nodded.

"What if the laundress causes trouble? How is she to be handled?"

"With great and tender care," the shawled figure replied. "Explain that I shall return in three days at the outside, that she is my guest, that she need do nothing not pleasing to her. Tell her she has been working too hard and I want her to rest."

"She is very stupid," the driver said. "I think she will not understand."

"Then it will be your job to be patient. I want her happy on my return, happy and alive; if she lacks either of those requirements, there will be much suffering, am I being clear? You in particular will be greatly discomforted."

The driver nodded.

"She has an extraordinary natural instinct for ironing work. If I ran this loathsome place I would declare her a national institution. I have not had shirts as crisp since forty-five."

The laundress took the flight from Asunción to Buenos Aires. The Paraguayan Customs men were all insipid fools; there was no passport trouble expected, and none materialized. Argentina, of course, was different, so the "laundress" remained there, and it was a prosperous businessman who headed for the Pan Am counters. A businessman of middle years and totally bald. The baldness was an irritant, of course—he had turned prematurely gray when he was not yet twenty-five, and his hair, curly and white and thick, was his most distinguishing, his most attractive feature. He was terribly proud of his hair; it was one of the things that set him apart from, as well as above, others. "The White Angel" they called him then.

So it had pained him, the day before, back in the blue house, when he had shaved his hair off. Still, he wasn't that unattractive bald. His face showed power. And as soon as he returned to Paraguay, he would of course let it grow back to its former snowy splendor.

He caught the Pan Am flight to JFK. It took more than ten hours nonstop, arriving at New York at a quarter past six the following morning. The following morning would be Tuesday, and he fully planned to get the night flight back for Buenos Aires on Wednesday. Thursday at the outside, but Wednesday, preferably.

Speed was always preferable.

He spent the entire flight awake, the black box in his lap.

Others slept; he, instead, considered contingencies. So many things might go wrong, and he had to be prepared for any and all. His mind had kept him alive so far; he had complete confidence it would not fail him now. His mind plus his black leather box. So long as he had it, anguish was his constant companion. The potential for anguish, at any rate, the very real threat of mind-cracking pain, which was sometimes more effective than the pain itself.

The plane arrived precisely as scheduled, and most of the passengers were bleary through Customs. He pretended to be, though he was, and in fact needed to be, totally acute, because this arrival moment placed him, like some jumbo jet at takeoff, in the time of maximum vulnerability. Not that he was worried about his passport. True, it had been handled quickly, but there were skilled artisans in Asunción who were used to express work. No, the Customs guards would pass him along happily, all would go fine with them, but if there had been an unknown disaster, an unknown informer perhaps, if all had gone wrong and he was to be discovered, the logical time to take him was now.

He retrieved his bag, passed through Customs, moved to the greeting area beyond, looked around. He had never been to this airport before, and its size confused him. Actually, he had never been to this country before, and its size would undoubtedly have confused him too, except that he did not plan on touring it, only the one place, just Manhattan. He stood quite still in the greeting area. Erhard was supposed to meet him. Those had been his instructions, but what if a wire had been silently intercepted, a phone quietly tapped—for a moment, though he would have died before admitting such a thing to anyone, he actually contemplated running. Just flat out bolting toward the nearest exit. Once outside, though, where? Which foolish direction?

Then he saw little Erhard limping toward him through the crowd, followed by big-shouldered Karl, and he realized that if "safe" was a word you could possibly apply to one with his past, not to mention his present, then he was, once again, yet, still, perhaps even permanently, safe . . .

# 15

Doc picked the restaurant for dinner, Lutèce, which Babe had of course heard of but had never been near. Elsa had never even heard of it, but when Babe picked her up and told her it was the most expensive place in town, her already considerable nervousness increased. He taxied down with her—ordinarily they subwayed everywhere, but you didn't subway to Lutèce, not unless you were the dishwasher, anyway—and no matter how he tried, he could not calm her. She looked terrible, her dress was wrong, she hated fancy places, people would stare at her, they would know she didn't belong.

The one thing Babe was sure of was that they'd stare all right. She was in a blue dress, simple and plain, with a single strand of pearls at her glorious throat, and the color of the dress played right into the color of her eyes. "You look illegal," Babe said as they entered the restaurant, which was true, but it did not serve visibly to calm her.

Doc was waiting for them in the tiny back room of the second floor. Just two other tables. If you wanted to be seen, at Lutèce you ate downstairs. If you cared about conversation, you sat in the back room, preferably in the corner.

Doc stood as they walked in. He took a quick look at Elsa, then shook his head. "I thought you said she was pretty," he said to Babe. "Really, Tom, I must talk to you sometime about standards."

"This is Hank," Babe said. That was their way in public. Hank and Tom. No reason for it really. It all started after H.V. died. They needed things to cling to then. Secrets were handy. And cheap. A bridge binding them together. They needed secrets badly after H.V. went; if you didn't have someone to cling to, the currents were too strong; the swirling rumors were enough to knock you down, steal your air, drag you out to sea.

"You're very lovely," Doc told her. "No lovelier than Grace Kelly, but you'll get by."

They sat down. When a captain appeared, Doc asked if they minded if he ordered for them. Babe and Elsa hurriedly said, "Please." Doc spoke French for a while and the captain replied, then disappeared, and Elsa said how well he spoke.

"Thank you, I wish I did—I don't know what I actually said, but what I was *trying* to do was just order some Chablis. Do you know Chablis? It's a Burgundy." He gave Babe a big smile. "The great ones are almost green-eyed; they're the wines that most resemble diamonds," and on "diamonds" he glanced at Elsa, laid his fingertips on her skin, stroked gently.

Gee, Babe thought, he likes her, isn't that terrific?

No, Babe thought, when they were done with the truffle in crust and into the rack of lamb, it isn't so terrific. Dinner, which, at the start, so it seemed, could not have gone better, was now tying him in knots.

Because Doc could not keep his hands off her.

*Stop,* he wanted to scream at Doc.

*Stop him,* he wanted to scream at Elsa.

But you didn't scream at Lutèce. You whispered. You chuckled and you dabbed your napkin across your lips and you nodded when the waiter refilled your wine glass without being asked, and you made pleasant chitchat no matter what was happening inside you; even if your brother was sitting there making a play for your girl, you just sat there amidst the drolleries, even if your girl didn't seem to mind.

Babe put his hands in his lap, clasped his fingers together.

"Some lady," Doc said. They were drinking red Burgundy now, Bonnes Mares '62, and he finished his glass.

Babe nodded as the waiter refilled it.

Doc smiled at Elsa. "You miss being home? Switzerland?"

"I think everybody misses being home sometime. Don't you?"

"I guess," Doc said. "Where is home exactly? I don't know Switzerland all that well. Zurich and Geneva and that's it."

"I'm not from there."

"You must be from somewhere."

"A tiny place. No one has heard of it."

Why's she being so goddamn coy, Babe wondered. She was from outside Lake Constance, she'd told him that, why the hell shouldn't she tell Doc?

"Bet you know skiing," Doc said, changing the subject.

"I'm Swiss, so I must."

"Don't get that," Doc said.

"Oh, it's just a story, I'm not good at telling stories, but there was a Welsh actor, I don't remember his name—he was in some movies though, but I don't remember their names either—"

"You're right, you're not good at telling stories," Doc got in.

They both laughed.

Babe sat there.

"It doesn't matter who, maybe it was Richard Burton, I'll pretend it was Richard Burton, he was the Welsh actor, and he was being asked about a part in a movie, or maybe it was a play, I can't remember, it was one or the other—"

"You're *awful* at telling stories," Doc said this time.

They were both giggling now.

Babe looked at her blue eyes. They had never seemed more lovely. He was very much afraid he was going to do something terrible, just terrible, so he held his hands pressed together in his lap with all his strength.

"—it doesn't matter if it was a movie or a play, the point was he had to sing in the part and the producers or directors, one or the other, maybe it was both, they asked him if he sang and he said, 'I'm Welsh, so I must.' "

"I don't get it," Doc said.

"The Welsh have great pride in being musical," Elsa explained.

"And the Swiss ski, now I get it," Doc said. He emptied his wine glass again, ordered another bottle. "Where did you learn?"

"Lake Constance—that area, a small town nearby, I lived all my life there."

"My *God*," Doc said, getting all excited. "I know where you learned—there's a ski freak works in my company, and he bores the ass—pardon me—he's very dull because all he talks about is his skiing and was the snow powdery in Kitzbuhl and how many feet deep was it at Squaw Valley and what it was like getting helicoptered to the Canadian peaks and coming down through new snow, and if you think the oil-drilling equipment business is dull, you should hear this guy—"

"You're a worse storyteller than I am," Elsa said.

Doc roared. The other two tables glanced surreptitiously in his direction, and he quieted fast, went "Oops, 'scuse me, but there's the point, the be-all and end-all behind my soliloquy, this ski freak's favorite place in all the world is the Lake Constance area, because that's where Mont Rosa is, am I right or am I right, you learned to ski on Mont Rosa, admit it."

"I'm amazed," Elsa said.

"And next to Rosa is Mont Charre, which is great, but just a hair less great than Rosa, am I right or am I right?"

"A hundred per cent," Elsa said.

"I'm making all this up," Doc said.

Elsa went, "What?"

"There isn't any ski freak, there isn't any Mont Rosa near Lake Constance, and there isn't any Mont Charre either, am I right or am I right?"

Elsa said nothing.

Babe just watched them. He didn't know what was going on, but whatever it was, he'd liked it better when Doc was touching her.

"I've done too much business in Switzerland, I know the way they talk, you're not Swiss."

"No."

"What are you?"

"Can't you tell from my accent?"

"German, I'd guess. German, and you're no twenty-five. Thirty?"

"Thirty-two. What else do you want to know?"

"How much longer are your work papers good for?"

Elsa waited before she said, quietly, "Why are you humiliating me?"

"No reason. Just that a lot of foreigners like to marry a lot of Americans—then, when they're all nice and legal here, sometimes the marriages don't work out so well."

"And that's what you think? I'm trapping your brother? Why don't you just come out and ask me?"

"No point," Doc said quietly. "You haven't told the truth about much of anything yet, why should you now?"

"No reason," and as Babe watched, she fled the tiny room, and as Babe started after her, Doc grabbed his wrist and held tight. "Let her go," Doc said.

Babe whirled on him. "Why—because *you* tell me to?"

"This was for your own good—"

"Bullshit—"

"It *was*." Doc held on to him, and Babe couldn't break the grip. Doc was too strong. "I traveled all around, I can spot people, there's a million broads around the world would like to live here, they can't, they'll try all kinds of things—"

"I didn't ask you for approval—"

"You'll thank me. I knew her type the minute she walked in—hell, I knew it when you wrote the goddamn letter, people don't fall all over each other like that unless somebody's after something—"

"You don't know—"

"I do, I *know*, goddammit, believe me—"

"Why should I?—*ever*—pawing the hell out of her and then putting her on a goddamn rack—"

"That's a business tactic, you soften somebody up first, get them off guard, it means nothing—"

"Lying means nothing—"

Doc squeezed harder. It was starting to hurt. There was pain, and they still whispered in the quiet, delicate room. "You never tell the whole truth, you got to withhold things, like when I asked you to come to D.C., I meant that. If I'd told you I'd gotten the mugging note you would have thought I was asking you because I was panicked over you getting hurt, so I held back something—I knew about the mugging—but I wasn't lying—and I'm not lying when I tell you to let this one go, she doesn't love you, forget her—"

"You don't know that—"

"I do, use your head, she's gorgeous, why else would she love you?"

"Because I love *her*," Babe shouted, and he ripped free and took off through the restaurant. He careened into a waiter carrying coffee cups, spun off, kept on, not even pausing when the crash came, down the stairs he went, two, three at a time, stumbling, then past the bar and into the October evening, not stopping until the sidewalk, where he turned one way, the other, then grabbed the nearest cab and raced on up to Elsa's place, buzzed her door hard, again and again, but she wasn't there, she wasn't there. He waited five seconds, buzzed again, no answer, buzzed five seconds after that, nothing, no reply, she wasn't home, maybe he'd beaten her back, maybe he was just too quick. No, it wasn't that, it was obviously not that; she wasn't coming home, not where she'd be a sitting duck for him, because for all she knew, he'd led her into it, let her get destroyed like that. For all she knew, he was just as guilty as Doc, and where she was now was probably walking, just walking, or maybe sitting in some dark flick only not watching the screen. She had a lot to think about, Elsa did.

He loved her. He didn't give a shit if she was Korean, he loved her. She had no way of knowing that, though; no way of knowing how he felt after twenty-five years of awkwardness to suddenly feel graceful when he was by her side.

The thing to do was get back to his place and wait for her to call. Pray for her to call. He could wait by her door, but that was pushy, and he hated pushy Jews. Doc might be back at his place, but not for long. It would take him maybe a minute to pack. They had nothing to say to each other. He had nothing to say to Doc, anyway. Not now. Not now. Babe broke into a run. He went fast, faster than usual, as fast as he could and still sustain the three miles back to his place. Babe tore on through the night. His tooth hurt like crazy . . .

# 16

It was just before eleven when they entered Riverside Park and started toward the boat basin. The bull-shouldered bald man let the one in the black raincoat do the leading. The raincoated one began to say "Careful," but the bull-shouldered one interrupted: "English. Always. Less conspicuous."

"As you wish. But watch your step. It's very dark."

"I do not like meeting in places like this. Even our newspapers report the violence in American parks."

"Scylla set it. The spot and the passwords. He likes parks."

"It was stupid."

"Are *you* frightened?"

"That strikes you as amusing?"

"Yes."

"We all accepted its existence, even when we were winning. Those of us with brains were aware. Once you forget fear, you miss contingencies, and from there it is but a short drop to the grave."

They reached the boat basin at eleven promptly, then began to count uptown, passing the required number of benches. Finally, at perhaps five minutes past, they sat on an empty bench and watched the Hudson. The bull-shouldered man glanced behind him from time to time. Habit. There were trees and brush and shadow, but no movement. "What time is it?" the bull-shouldered man inquired at a quarter past.

The raincoated one said, "Fifteen after. Why didn't you bring a watch?"

"I brought one, I'm wearing one, I just wanted to be sure it was working properly."

A very old woman tottered by, walking quickly home along the Hudson.

"She should not be out by herself," the bull-shouldered man said.

"I don't think she's a she," the raincoated one answered. "Probably a policeman. They do that now."

"America." The bull-shouldered one shook his head.

They sat in silence until the old woman was gone from sight.

"Time!" the bull-shouldered one said.

"Twenty-five past."

"Scylla is late! He's trying to goad me!"

"Scylla is never late" came from behind them.

They whirled.

Scylla's voice came from the dark shadows. "I've been watching your stomachs churn ever since you got here. And, may I add, enjoying it thoroughly."

"Come out here!" the bull-shouldered one said. It was an order.

Not obeyed. "Before the passwords?" Scylla's voice contained astonishment. "Such a breach of etiquette—where is our respect for tradition?"

Angrily, the bull-shouldered man said, "Once they could swim there." He was pointing to the Hudson. "Now, if they try it, they die."

There was the sound of a fingersnap. "Would you believe it," Scylla said, "I've clean forgotten what I'm supposed to answer."

" 'There are many ways of dying'—say it—'there are many ways of dying'—all right, we're done with that, now come down here."

"All right," Scylla said, "but if I'm a fraud, it's your fault."

The bull-shouldered man watched as suddenly a shadow moved away from the trees, down the slight grassy incline toward them.

"Your behavior is very irritating to me, I want you to know that," the bull-shouldered man said, and probably he would have gone on, but Scylla was all over him saying, "Don't give *me* any static about *my* behavior after the shit you've been pulling."

"You know perfectly well why."

"We've had a business relationship, that's what it is, that's what it's been, and what you've been pulling hasn't got a goddamn thing to do with business."

"It has to do with *trust*." The bull-shouldered man stared angrily up at Scylla. "What it comes to is this: *Can I trust you?*"

"You never could, you only had to, and you don't any more—you're the one that hired Chen, aren't you? You already tried to have me killed, so don't give me any innocent shit about 'can I trust you?' "

The bull-shouldered man softened. "What happens to us

now? Surely I cannot fight you; if Chen failed, there wouldn't be much point to me trying, I'm a little too old for hand to hand . . ." He stopped talking then, because the blade had been in his grip since the word "point," which meant there really was no further need for prattle.

To prevent a master technician from performing at peak efficiency, not a great deal has to be done. This surprises most people, but is nonetheless true. To prevent a hook shot by Abdul-Jabbar, you don't have to knock him down. You don't even have to come in contact with his hand. A simple nudge at the elbow is sufficient to make the missile lose target, and just so, the one in the raincoat did not need to do a great deal to Scylla—just hold tight to Scylla's hand for a brief moment; one brief moment, really, and that was enough.

Scylla, of course, saw the blade, saw *something*, at any rate, and he immediately knew the bull-shouldered one was into a supposedly lethal act, but he was not worried. Scylla also knew that he had not paid much attention to the raincoated one, but that was because there was no way the enemy could match him when it came to strength or skill.

He was right, but he was wrong.

The raincoated one had no intention of matching anyone, just a simple movement to delay, holding tight to Scylla's hands for barely a breath intake. But it was enough. Scylla ripped free, of course, and his great arms went quickly to protect his stomach.

But too late. Too late. The knife was home.

*Was* it a knife? Scylla had been stabbed before, but never by anything like this, never by a weapon that went so deep so quickly. He was like a figure sculpted from clotted cream, and the blade or scalpel or whatever it was entered below his navel with such speed and force that Scylla could only grunt and drop his arms in weak surprise.

Then the blade began its journey upward.

Scylla would never have guessed the bull-shouldered man possessed such strength, because no matter how sharp the weapon, flesh and gristle still require power to sever, and the bull-shouldered man moved in close for leverage and lifted the blade straight up through his body.

Scylla began to spurt.

The bull-shouldered man continued his butchering in silence.

Scylla commenced falling.

The bull-shouldered man stepped out of the way. He had a vast acquaintanceship with death, and he pulled his blade free, and before Scylla had hit the ground he was on his way out of the park, knowing the big man was dead or on the verge. The raincoated one followed closely behind.

"That was too bad," the bull-shouldered one said.

"You did what you had to do."

"I know that. But now it starts to get ugly."

The raincoated one knew truth when it was spoken.

Back by the bench, Scylla lay. He was familiar enough with anatomy to know that he was done. Death was a certainty; the only choice remaining was whether to die by the Hudson or not.

It was a filthy fucking place and it smelled in summer and was really good only for rat housing, and that thought, that the rats might get him, served to make him blink. Work on anger, he told himself. Stay with anger, anger might get you going, and he forced the functioning sections of his mind to concentrate on his stupidity in allowing himself to get caught from behind. Wait till the news of his passing hit The Division. The great Scylla, done in by an old fart and an amateur.

*"JESUS!"* Scylla screamed, and while his fury echoed, he was halfway to his feet. He clutched his arms across his body and held himself together as best he could. Then he started to find his way out of the park. It was going to be hard. Probably impossible. No. Nothing was impossible.

He was Scylla the rock, and he had promises to keep.

# 17

Babe paced.

His room was small, his legs long, and he couldn't really get started before he had to stop, spin, turn. What he wanted more than anything was to sprint to the reservoir, just take it all full out and see how many times he could circle the thing before he fell exhausted on the October grass.

He paused, looked at his watch. Still not midnight, but coming up fast on the outside. If Elsa was going to call, it would be soon, because movies would be letting out soon. She must have left the restaurant by half-past 8 at the outside, reservations had been for 7:30, and the whole fiasco couldn't have taken more than an hour.

He had gotten out Doc's Gucci bag, packed it full, which was a stupid gesture, probably—"Never darken my door again"—and he felt like an ass for having done it, but when he'd gotten back to his room and seen Doc's toilet articles in the bathroom, it had gone through him bad, and he'd just grabbed everything and stuffed it in the goddamn Gucci.

Maybe I better unpack it, he decided. It would be more fun than just pacing. He opened the bag, studied it. I'll unpack his stuff, and I'll put it back, but I'll do a crappy job, so that way he'll know I'm not forgiving him but I'm not grudge-holding either.

Babe knew what Doc's line would be—he was just trying to look out for his kid brother. Doc would say that, and probably it was true, because Doc had always looked out for him, ever since H.V. died. He had been ten, Doc twenty, and for the next years, Doc had always been the one to bind up his adolescent wounds. He took out Doc's shirts, dumped them back where they'd been, grabbed the toilet-articles kit and the goddamn Burgundy bottles, and was putting them in their proper places when the phone rang.

Babe swooped down on the thing. "Elsa?" he said.

"He didn't ask me if I loved you. I waited, but he never did."

"Elsa—listen to me—*nothing happened,* you got that?"

She sounded hollow. "What do we do, Tom?" she said; then, after a pause, "now?"

"Forget it, I told you—there's not a damn thing to remember."

"I've been to the movies. Almost two times through I sat there thinking. We can't forget it, because it did happen, it took place, we were both there, and it was all true. Except he never once asked me if I cared."

"Let me run on up and see you, huh? I'll cab, it'll only take a sec."

"No. You would hold me, and I would hold you, and nothing would be spoken. I lied about my age because you looked a child, even younger than you are, and I didn't want to frighten you, and I lied about the German because

Levy is Jewish and many Jews still hate us. I was four when Hitler died, but many Jews think all Germans planned the blitzkrieg."

"Well, *I* don't, so just lemme come up there, I swear we'll just talk, like now."

"There's more. There are other things he did not ask. I've been married and divorced. I almost yelled that at him before I ran away. The only mistake he made was he didn't ask me if I loved you. I let him touch me and pretended to smile because he was your brother and he had that same look so many of your businessmen have, the successful ones, arrogant, this is *mine*, they seem to say, and *that* is mine, I make lots of money so everything my eye sees is *mine*, *you* are mine, and wine was being drunk and I did not want a scene, only that he should like me, that he should approve, he was your brother and you care for him. I want to take today and burn it off the calendar."

"It didn't happen," Babe said. "I told you to forget it a million times already."

"It would fester if we did that. Don't you want to know about my husband?"

"To tell the truth, no, I don't," Babe lied. "Why should I want to know about him? If I told you I'd been married, would you suddenly go to pieces if I didn't describe my wife to you? I haven't been married, nothing like that, but hell, if it makes you feel better to tell me a little about him, I won't stop you or anything. You were probably just a kid, right? You were probably young and he was some jock and gorgeous, only stupid, except, being as you were practically an infant, you didn't really know what a moron he was, and when you did, you ended it, right?"

He could tell she was trying to keep things Teutonic and serious, desperate not to laugh.

"Probably a shot-putter," he went on, "you krauts are big on the weight events, probably grunted on his release—hey, if you're German do you grunt in German? I mean, an American shot-put guy, he goes 'oof' when he lets fly, do your guys go 'ach' or along those lines?"

"You really are impossible," she managed, before she began to laugh.

Hot damn, I did it.

"Babe."

Doc stood in the doorway, arms across himself.

He hung up the phone.

*"BABE!!!"* On that cry, Doc reached his arms out for his brother.

And his stomach began to slip away.

Doc went into his fall.

Babe caught him before he hit, cradled him, hugged him with everything he had till they were bathed in blood. Doc tried to whisper, Babe tried to listen.

It must have been fifty seconds before Doc died.

Long time.

# 18

The cops were acting funny.

Not in the beginning. But before too long, there were crazy things going on.

Babe sat quietly in the corner. Maybe they were acting funny in the beginning too and he just hadn't noticed. He wasn't noticing a whole lot along about then. He had called the police, they had come, two men, quickly, and then, soon after that, three more. They had all five talked to one another in muffled tones—at least they seemed muffled to Babe, but maybe they weren't. He wasn't hearing a whole lot then either. He was just sitting quiet. Quiet in a chair. The chair in a corner. His arms dangling down.

Thinking.

He was the last one left. That's all he was thinking. Just that, putting it through his mind first one way, then another. Once there had been four of them, mother, father, Doc, and Babe. His mother went in a car crash when he was six, and he had no memory of her, except for the couple of pictures H.V. kept around the house on places like the piano or tucked in a bookcase corner.

But it wasn't the car crash that killed her. They just had to put down something for a cause of death, and her car had met a tree and she had been driving, but what really killed her was the scandal, H.V.'s humiliation; that was what had done her in. Sometimes Babe thought she wasn't dead at all, but was down passing the time in Florida with McCarthy and Kennedy and old FDR. Whenever there was a peculiar death, always the rumors had it that the person was alive and in Florida. Why Florida, Babe wondered. Jack Kennedy was a vegetable in Florida, and Roosevelt had been bombed by Stalin and the other commies, but he'd survived, and he was down there too, taking in all that sunshine. Sometimes Babe wondered if it wouldn't be an interesting subject for a paper. If you were a little paranoid and enjoyed tracking suspicion. Like the Bermuda Triangle. That would have been fun to write too.

His father he had found, just like he'd told Biesenthal. And in the fifteen years since, whenever he really wanted to ruin himself a little he'd scream, "It's your fault, *your* fault, if you'd taken the fucking wool paper in to him he never would have done it, you'd have been there in time, *you could have kept him alive*!"

Except, even when he'd told Biesenthal the truth, he wasn't telling the truth. Because he was ten and he could hear H.V. in his bedroom, staggering around, cursing, sometimes falling down, and he was frightened, afraid that if he went in, his own father would do something to him, hit him for interrupting, cause even more pain, a substance nobody needed any more of just then. Simply put, it came to this: If he had been less of a coward, his father wouldn't have died.

Doc had been at classes when the shot came. Doc was always around except for school, where he was a whiz, if you didn't count chem class, which he hated. That was Doc's first reaction when he got home and found H.V. dead and Babe hysterical. "It was chem class," he kept saying. "I was gonna cut the goddamn thing. If I'd just cut the goddamn thing, I could have kept him alive."

It was almost, but not quite, funny, Doc railing how H.V.'s death was his fault while all the time Babe knew that was hot air, it was really his; the wool paper proved it. It would have made a terrific argument, once Babe got old enough to give Doc trouble verbally. Nothing was as much fun as a neat argument, two guys going at it, wham-wham, knocking each other's points to smithereens. God they had had some great times, screaming at each other while Babe was losing in his attempt to cope well with puberty.

No more arguments now.

Babe glanced quickly at the sheet the cops had spread over his brother. Someone was definitely under there, but there was no possibility of its being Doc. Babe didn't think about his own death much, but when he did, it was always going to be Doc who would be there to put him in the ground. Doc was so big and strong and he never got sick, and if there was a flu bug moving through Cincinnati and Babe was in Cleveland, he caught it. No question: When Babe died, Doc would take care of the details, see that it all went right, no goof-ups, all smooth and proper and fine.

The cops were mumbling again; the head cop was saying it couldn't have been robbery because there was still a wallet. Motive—Babe thought for a moment. That must be what they're mumbling about. The head cop went through Doc's wallet, then hurried to the phone.

And that, Babe guessed, was when things started getting funny.

They hadn't asked him anything, in the first place. Oh, a few things, like about who and when, and Babe did his best to speak sentences, but that was hard, so he just nodded or shrugged; he wasn't being difficult, he wanted to explain, it was that he wasn't in any terrific mood for words just then, but he didn't really have to explain that, they seemed to understand, kept the questions to a minimum, and simple ones at that.

The head cop was mumbling on the phone. Babe couldn't make it out exactly. I should really try, he told himself. That's your *brother* they're talking about, *pay attention*.

But he couldn't concentrate on anything until he heard Elsa's voice from the hall. One of the cops was blocking the entrance, and Babe stood, made his way to them, muttered "Please" to the cop, then went into the hallway with Elsa.

"You hung up so without warning, I didn't know what to do. I waited but you didn't call back. I had to know you were all right, so I came."

"Doc's dead," Babe said. There—after all these years, he'd given away the secret, said "Doc" without even realizing it. But that was all right. You needed two for a secret. "My brother's dead, murdered."

She wasn't buying. Not from the way her head shook, side to side and back.

"It's true, believe me, okay? I'm awful tired, Elsa."

"Are you sure?"

Babe began to lose control of his voice. "Am I sure what? Am I sure he's my brother or am I sure he's dead? Yes and yes, Elsa, I'm sure."

"I'm sorry," she said, and took a step away. "I was only worried about you. I'll go now."

Babe nodded.

"How could such a thing happen? Here; what a terrible city. A robbery was it? An accident with a car?"

"That was my mother," Babe answered, and the second the words popped out he saw the look of absolute confusion starting across her splendid face, and right there, within half an hour of the death of his beloved, Babe broke out laughing. It was like a woman he'd heard of who'd lost, in the very same hour, in two separate and totally unrelated accidents, in two entirely different states, a father and a child. The father died first and she went to pieces, and when the call about the child came she heard herself laughing. It wasn't that she didn't care. It was just sometimes you had to laugh or go wiggy.

Once he started laughing Elsa looked *really* confused, and that made it even funnier, and he laughed until it was clear in her face that she thought he might be gone, committable. "I'm fine," Babe said then.

Elsa nodded.

"And I love you. No I don't—I did a little while ago and I will a little while from now, but right at the moment, I'm fresh out."

She came toward him, touched her index finger to her lips, then to his. Then she turned, hurried down the stairs while he went back inside.

Within five minutes, the first crew cut appeared.

The head cop went to him, very respectful.

Babe watched it all from his perch in the corner.

The crew cut went to Doc, pulled the sheet down until he'd uncovered Doc's face, glanced at it, nodded. Then he went to the phone, dialed, and started mumbling.

Pay attention, Babe told himself. *Listen.* And he tried, but all he got from the crew cut were a few respectful "Yes sirs" and a couple of "Commanders" and not much more. Then the phone call ended. Babe gazed at the crew cut. Thirty, probably, in good shape, muscular but not so you'd look at him twice. Just a guy who took care of himself, no one special, not much going on behind the eyes.

The second crew cut, when he got there, was a different story. Older, maybe forty, smaller, but not slight, and not flabby either. But quick eyes, quick and blue, and fair-haired—too blond for a crew cut really, it made him sometimes, when the light was behind him, look bald. But except for that, he resembled nothing so much as a man who should have made a fortune doing Wheaties commercials.

He knelt over Doc, and, unlike the other crew cut, who just glanced at the corpse, this one really did a study. Babe looked away, toward the other corner of his room. There were some terrific cracks in the plaster there, you could get just about any animal you wanted if you worked hard enough, so the next few minutes he only heard.

"They must have ambushed him, Commander," the first crew cut said. Babe recognized the voice from when he made the phone call.

"That or he knew them," the blond crew cut said. It must have been him talking, though Babe couldn't swear to it. But he had that tone of authority you just hated, of being right all the goddamn time.

"What about my men?" This was the head cop.

"You can go," the blond crew cut said, obviously the honcho.

"We'll just move on then," the head cop said.

Babe was about to wonder who could tell the cops what to do like that, but then he found a hippo in the plaster that would be terrific if he could just get it done.

"Ambulance?" the blond crew cut said then.

"I made arrangements before I came," the dark crew cut answered. "It must be waiting outside by now; shall I get them up here?"

"Right now."

Babe glanced over as the first crew cut hurried out. The blond looked briefly at Babe, then went back to his study of Doc. Babe went back to his hippo.

Three guys took Doc away. The first crew cut and two other guys. He couldn't tell from their white jackets which hospital they came from, but that didn't seem to make much difference, when you came right down to it.

Doc was going now.

They had him on a stretcher and the stretcher in the air and the white jackets were doing the heavy work, the first crew cut the leading.

Babe could feel himself losing control.

*No.* Later, fine, but don't you do it now. Not in front of all these bastard strangers.

Gone.

"Want me to wait around?" This from the black-haired crew cut.

Head shake. This from the blond.

Babe watched the first one leave, closing the door; then they were alone. Babe went back to his animals. He found a fantastic owl, you could practically hear it going "Hoooooooo."

"Maybe we might talk; would you mind terribly?"

Babe glanced toward the blond crew cut. The guy was bringing the desk chair over close to where Babe was sitting.

Babe shrugged. He hadn't wanted to talk to Elsa, so why the hell should he feel like shooting the breeze with this arrogant son of a bitch?

"I know what an inopportune time this is—"

"Right!" Babe almost interrupted. "Bingo. Give the genius a box of fucking Mars Bars." Only it wasn't worth the effort, so he just shrugged again.

"I know how close you were to your brother—"

"You do, huh?—you know that, do you?—how do you know that, for Jesus' sakes?—*how do you know anything about anything?*—"

"I don't, I'm sorry, I was just trying to ease into things—"

"What things?—what the hell's going on?—what the hell are you a commander of?—"

The crew cut was really in retreat now. "How do you know I'm a commander of anything?" he tried.

"The flunky with the other crew cut called you that—'commander,' he said, I heard him."

"Oh, that was nothing, Navy talk. I was a commander in

the Navy, it was the top rank I got, and it's the same as a Senator or a Vice President, when they're out of office you still call them that, I don't know, probably out of respect, 'Senator' or 'Good morning, Mr. Vice President.' "

"Bullshit."

There was a long pause. Then the other guy said, "Okay, you're right, no more bullshit, but look, we're not hitting it off any too well, I'd say, and it's important that we do. Forget the Commander stuff. I'll explain it all. My name's Peter Janeway." He held out his hand and made a dazzling smile. "But call me Janey. All my friends do."

# PART III

# PULP

# 19

"I'm not your friend," Babe said, not even starting to make a move toward taking Janeway's hand, just letting it hang there, awkwardly, in space.

"I know that, believe me. But it's not important now. Only one thing is important and that's this: You and I have *got* to talk." He pulled his hand back, clearly embarrassed.

I should have shaken with him, Babe thought; it wouldn't have killed me or anything, a quick shake, what the hell's that, nothing. But even while his mind was working in that direction, his words were headed elsewhere. "Everything's important with you, isn't it? It's 'important' that we hit it off, it's 'important' that we talk. If you've got a list of other things that are going to be 'important,' I wish you'd tell me now."

"And I wish you'd stop being difficult," Janeway said.

"I haven't started being difficult," Babe replied, kind of liking the sound of his answer even as he spoke it. Bogart might have said something just like that. Not in any of the great ones like *African Queen* or *Casablanca*, but it was a decent-enough comeback for most of those crummy B pictures Warners was always sticking him in.

Janeway sighed. He mimed pouring a drink. "Do you have anything?"

Babe shrugged, nodded toward the sink area.

Janeway got up, found a bottle of red Burgundy, opened it quickly. "Want some?" he asked as he poured some wine into the closest remotely clean glass.

Babe shook his head, no, wondering why he was acting so crummy toward Janeway. He seemed a decent-enough guy, well-spoken, tactful. He reminded Babe of . . . Babe rooted around a moment before he had it: Gatsby—if Janeway would lose a couple years and let his hair grow, he'd be a ringer for Gatsby, and you *love* Gatsby, so why take it out on Janeway? It wasn't Janeway, he realized then; it was the presence of Janeway that was so ruffling.

Because I need to be alone, Babe thought; I want my chance to mourn.

His mother he'd been too young to remember, and when it came H.V.'s turn, he and Doc had keened together. "I shoulda gone in sooner, Doc, I shoulda shown him the paper on wool." "Shut up, you don't know anything, it was me, it was my fault, all of it my fault, that goddamn chem class." And then they would go silent, because all their bickering wouldn't make the old man move.

And now it was Doc done with moving, and Babe would have to be sure the event didn't pass unnoticed. It didn't matter so much if he shed tears. But they had laughed a lot together, and those times needed to be remembered.

Janeway downed the first glass of wine in a gulp, poured another, smaller portion. Then he came back to Babe, sat.

"Do you think you might try to be helpful?"

Babe said nothing.

"Look: I'm not about to get trapped into any wit-matching

contest with any semi-genius historian, so if you want to prove you're smarter than I am, you've proved it, that game's over, I give, you win."

"Who told you about me? How'd you know what I was studying?"

"Later; later I'll explain everything, but first it's important that you tell me a couple of things, okay?"

"No, it isn't okay, because when you say 'it's important that we talk' you don't mean 'it's important that *we* talk,' you mean it's important that *I* talk and you listen. Well I'm probably being inconsiderate as hell, but my brother was just murdered and I'm not feeling all that chatty, if you don't mind."

Janeway swirled the wine around in the glass, sniffed it. "Go change," he said softly. "Shower if you like; then we'll try again."

"Change?" Babe said, all confused. Then he said, "Oh," because he was still in the same clothes as when Doc died, blue shirt and gray pants, and both were layered with drying blood. He touched the blood with his fingertips. I must always save this shirt, he reminded himself. I'll fold H.V.'s pistol up in it. The pistol and the extra bullets, all wrapped up together. It was too bad he had nothing of his mother, a piece of tree bark maybe. Babe began to blink. Tree bark? Where was I? Oh yes. Keep the bloody clothes.

"You all right?" Janeway asked.

Babe kept on blinking, lightheaded. "Fine," he said, louder than he meant to.

"I'm looking for a motive," Janeway said then. "Believe me, I'm just as anxious to find whoever did it as you are."

"*Quit making those stupid overstatements.* He was my

*brother*, my *father* practically, he brought me up, and I never once heard your name, so I'm more anxious, wouldn't you agree?"

Janeway hesitated a long time. "Well, of course," he answered finally.

But his tone was odd. Babe looked at him, waiting.

"We were both in the same business, you see; we knew each other quite well for quite some time."

"I don't believe you're an oil man."

"I don't care what you believe except this—*I want who did it.*"

"It hadda be some nut—this is New York, nuts are slaughtering people every moonrise—some addict tried getting his money and he wasn't quick enough handing it over and you know the rest."

"I don't think that's even close," Janeway said. "I think it was political. At least, that's the assumption I'm going on till proven otherwise. And I wish you'd do what you could to help me."

"Political?" Babe shook his head. "My God, why?"

"Because it makes some kind of sense. Considering what your brother did. And, of course, your father."

"What about my father?"

Janeway sipped his wine. "Why are you determined to make this so unnecessarily difficult?"

*"What about my father?"*

"He was H. V. Levy, for Chrissakes."

"And he was innocent!"

"I never said he wasn't."

"You did—you did, goddamn it, you implied it."

"Well, he was convicted, wasn't he? That's a helluva lot more than implying, that's *fact*."

"He was *not*!—he was in no way convicted—" Babe's voice was out of control. "Do you know that in four years, McCarthy never offered legal support for one single charge—it was all the court of public opinion—did you know he was a Nazi, a fucking Nazi, and he had the country scared pissless. My father was an historian, a great historian, and Acheson asked him down to Washington and he went, like Schlesinger and Galbraith went later, and he was there when McCarthy hit. Two guys suffered worst from it all—Hiss went to jail but at least he's alive, selling stationery, and my father. He tried defending himself but he didn't have a chance against that Nazi son of a bitch—it was a Senate hearing and my father was just cut to shit—every time he tried to establish a point McCarthy made it funny. My father talked in long rambling sentences and McCarthy made jokes out of it. It didn't matter that he had no real facts, McCarthy killed him. He killed his ego, and when you're like H. V. Levy and kids start laughing at you, it's over. I was five in fifty-three, that was when they had the hearing, and Dad quit Columbia and began to write a book about the whole thing, to clear his name and get it all together again, but he couldn't do it—my mother died the next year, and that left just the three of us, and Dad was drinking bad by then. He lasted till fifty-eight. Five years on the bottle, staggering around. Those years I remember, and that's a shame because he was nothing then, he was garbage then, but what I'd give to have known him before. I read every book he ever wrote and they were great, and I read every speech he ever gave and they were great, but I never met that guy, not so I remember, just this husk is all I have for memories, and you can keep all your goddamn stupid implications about my father, just you wait, wait till I finish, it's all gonna be down in black and white, right there in my doctorate and—and—"

And *stop*, Babe told himself. Right now. He doesn't care.

"And?" Janeway said. He sat impassive, watching.

Why is everybody staring at me nowadays? Everybody's got such great eyes nowadays, and they're all the time staring at me. Biesenthal, Elsa, now this one. Babe wondered, for a moment, about the early symptoms of paranoia. Make a note, he told himself. Check it out.

"And?" Janeway said again.

"Don't stare at me any more."

"I'm sorry. It's only because I was interested."

"Don't humor me."

"Then finish up."

"Huh?"

"I want this bubble out of you. I mentioned your father, I touched a nerve, something burst. All that talk of yours was simply a draining process. We'll never get to what's important until you're done. So finish your father."

"Nothing more to say."

"Fine," Janeway said. "We'll leave his guilt in abeyance and get on to other things, if that's what you prefer."

Babe couldn't believe it. "You didn't hear one thing I said," he started, again unable to control either pitch or volume or timbre. "*There was no guilt.* That's the whole point to my doctorate, and I'm gonna get my dissertation published, the whole story, I got it all in my head, I been researching it and researching it, I got boxes of notes, *facts*, not newspaper gossip, not public opinion; *I'm clearing my father with truth*, just that, nothing else but, but it'll do the job, you'll see, you'll see . . ." Babe was almost panting now. "Hey," he said, after a time.

Janeway looked at him.

"You made that happen, that last part, about the publishing. I was done except you got me to go on, didn't you? That was the bubble you were talking about."

Janeway shrugged. "I suppose."

Babe looked back into the quick blue eyes. "Maybe you're not as dumb as I figured you were."

"I probably am," Janeway assured him. He flashed a quick white smile.

Even his goddamn teeth are even, Babe thought. He probably never had a pimple all through adolescence. And then he remembered asking Doc once about pimples and masturbation and if you did the one, did you get the other, because some goon named Weaver had said it was so and Babe had said baloney and Weaver replied, "Yeah, well I never had pimples till I started jerking off, argue with that," and Babe couldn't. He couldn't even whip a meatball like Weaver in intellectual debate, and that night he tried to casually get the subject about to acne and onanism and was there maybe some connection, and when he finally managed to do it, which wasn't easy, Doc was serious and reflective before saying, "*Newsweek* published a study on that, now what the hell were those statistics?" and he closed his eyes and Babe said, "Go on, it doesn't have to be exact, just kind of a general idea," and Doc said, "There is absolutely no causal relationship between blackheads and beating your meat, and it also doesn't cause feeblemindedness," and Babe said, "I knew Weaver was full of it," and Doc said, "The odd thing they found was that excess lying lengthens the nose," and Babe was halfway through an empathetic nod before he realized that Doc had nailed him again, skewered him, taking advantage of Babe's unending supply of gullibility, except that when Doc did it, you couldn't get mad; no, you could, but you had to laugh first.

Babe could feel himself starting to lose control. I hope this guy goes, he thought. Soon. He got up and poured himself some Burgundy.

From across the room, Janeway said, "I'm still looking for a motive. A specific. Why was tonight different from any other night?"

Babe came back and sat down, thinking that Janeway was far from a dummy, because that was a Jewish expression he'd just used, a paraphrase of one of the questions in the Passover service.

"Why don't you start and tell me what happened this evening?"

"I was home. He came in. He died. The police came. You came." He swirled and sniffed the wine, thinking how Doc would have described the nose and he would have faked a snore.

Janeway leaned toward him. "That's everything? You couldn't possibly have left out any minor details or along those lines?"

"I'm a demon on details."

"You mean you want me to do some explaining now, is that it?"

"I think it's important," Babe said.

Janeway sighed.

Babe just sat there.

"You have no idea how much I've been dreading this," Janeway said. "You have every right to know, but it's still embarrassing; I hate it, it all gets so goddamned never-never land." He took a breath, plunged in. "You don't really think your brother was in the oil business, do you?"

" 'Course he was, for years, how the hell do you think he earned his living?"

"I know *exactly* how he earned his kopeks, and believe me, the closest he came to the oil business was when he filled up at his friendly Standard station." Janeway shook his head. "You're amazing, you know that? He always said you were gullible, but *this* gullible I never dreamed."

Janeway was full of it.

"He wouldn't lie to me. We never lied to each other—oh sure, maybe fibs, like that, but hell, everybody fibs once in a while."

"All right, where did he live?"

"Washington."

"And what's Washington the center of?"

"Everything: the government."

"Okay. Now are you aware just how much each part of the government hates each other part? Example, the military: The Army hates the Navy and the Navy hates the Air Force. Why? Because once upon a time the Army was *it*, and then the world changed and the Navy became the glamor branch, and then flip, another change, and now the Air Force gets everything it requests while the admirals and the Army generals eat it. Think of what's going on down there today—it's on TV all day long, plain and crappy. The FBI hates the CIA, and they both hate the Secret Service. They're squabbling and whining, continual internecine rivalry, and the whining gets loudest when you get close to the limits of their powers. The edges are sharp, and between those edges are crevices.

"We live in the crevices," Janeway said, after pausing, taking a swallow, giving it a paragraph for emphasis.

He's really a fantastic liar, Babe thought.

"We were formed when the crevices widened. Date it after the Bay of Pigs, if you like. Now, when the gap gets too large between what the FBI can manage effectively and what the Secret Service, say, can bring off, more than likely, we're called in."

"And you're who?"

"This is where it gets embarrassing if you've the least intelligence. I'm a Dartmouth graduate, honors, and all the code names and passwords are enough to make you scream. We're The Division. That's all. Capital T, capital D. Which is a totally inaccurate name, since we exist only because of the divisions between other groups."

"What do you do?"

"Provide. That is how we're referred to. I was a Provider until I more or less got promoted into the executive end; if I live long enough and don't behave too stupidly, I've got as good a chance as anyone of running things. Finding your brother's killer wouldn't be unhelpful to my cause. He was a Provider when he died."

"What did he provide?"

"Anything that was necessary."

"That's kind of vague."

"Yes, isn't it."

"When you say anything, you don't mean *anything*?"

No reply.

"I mean, you don't mean, well, not bad things."

"Isn't that a fairly simplistic way for an historian to view the present world struggle for ultimate power? 'Good things. Bad things. Meanies.' "

"He wouldn't ever hurt anybody. I'm positive of that. I don't care what you say."

"Do you know who Scylla was?"

" 'Course, but Scylla wasn't a 'who,' Scylla was a 'what,' a giant rock off the coast of Italy."

"Scylla was your brother's code name."

Babe shook his head. He wanted fresh air, except he didn't, not really, but he did want something. Doc, I guess, Babe thought. I want Doc back.

"Shake your head all you want, it's true."

"You're telling me my brother was a spy—I'm sorry, Provider—and I never even had a notion."

"I'm telling you your brother was a *top* Provider *because* you never even had a notion. He always drank Scotch, except with you it was wine. There wasn't a hand gun made he hadn't mastered, except with you he always pretended to panic at a

BB pistol. I think the single thing that frightened him most was that someday you'd confront him with all this."

"Why?"

"He dreaded your disapproval."

"*Why?* I used to copy him. If he started using an expression, I'd pick it up. The way he walked, facial expressions, I used to love it when I could wear his hand-me-down clothes. I . . ." He lacked the energy to go on. He was tired and dirty, and the news rocked him, and even before that he'd been exhausted; the outburst about his father had taken a lot out of him. Defending was always so hard. How great life must be if all you ever did was attack. Wouldn't it be terrific to wake up one morning and find yourself Attila the Hun?

"I'm sorry," Janeway said, his voice gentle.

"Is that it? Do I know everything now?"

"You know nothing, maybe a particle, at the most. I promise you, Dave's death will not be written up in the *Daily News*, that's all been taken care of."

The blows were coming at him from all angles now, and he was helpless to stop them. "Dave . . . ?" Babe blinked. "Dave . . . ?"

"We all called him that, he wanted us to. Obviously, you know it's his middle name, Henry David Levy."

Babe leaned back and closed his eyes. "All my life we were together, and I never once called him that. 'Hank' in public, and 'Doc' was our name. From *I Love a Mystery*. That was his favorite. He was always going on about Jack, Doc and Reggie, and for a while I called him Reggie, but he said, 'No, I'd rather be Doc,' so that was it. And when I was eight he took me to a little-league game and I was pitching, H.V. was supposed to bring me but he was too bombed, so Doc did, and I hit a homer. My very first real one. I mean actually hitting it over the outfielder's head. They were playing me in, I guess, seeing as I was the pitcher and pitchers aren't supposed to be much with the bat, and it was such a thrill that when we walked home I said, 'Doc, I'm giving up pitching, I'm not gonna be any big-league pitcher, that's kid stuff, I'm goin' for the long ball, Doc, I think I've got a shot at Babe Ruth's record,' and from then on I was Babe, except when there were strangers around," and then, his eyes still closed, the cry "I don't *know* anybody" broke across the room. After a moment, Babe said, "I'm sorry, I'm fine now."

Janeway stood and started moving around the room. He opened his eyes. "Dinner," he said. "Begin there."

"Dinner was fine, dinner was terrific; no—wait a second, it wasn't, that's right, dinner was awful; it seems so long ago, what time is it?"

"Almost one o'clock."

"That's *all*?"

"Dinner was awful," Janeway was saying, moving quietly now, here, there, always gracefully moving. "Can you be a little more specific?"

"It was at Lutèce and there was me and Doc—me and Dave, you'd say—and my girl, Elsa, you want her full name?"

Nod.

"Elsa Opel, she lives up around Columbia, four one one West One hundred thirteenth, phone number four two seven four oh oh one—" Babe stopped. "Why aren't you taking notes if it's all so important?"

"Because we're trained to put nothing down, it's best that

way." Then he rattled off "Elsa Opel—four one one West One one three—four two seven four oh oh one." He sipped lightly at his wine. "I assure you I'm paying attention. Go on."

"Well, it . . . the first hour, maybe, Doc couldn't keep his hands off her, she's gorgeous, and he was pawing her like he was in heat."

Janeway took a longer drink.

"Then it turned out he was just getting her guard down, and when she was all softened up he got her to admit she'd been lying to me about her age, and where she was from, a lot of things, and she was humiliated and ran out, and Doc and I had words, and then I ran out and looked for her and couldn't find her and came back here hoping she'd call. She did, but then Doc arrived, and the rest you know."

"Okay, push this now, really go back over it all in your mind. Let's try and re-create a little—there's blood all over the stairs, so clearly he wanted desperately to get here. Was it just to see you? Could there have been any other reason? Anything at all?"

"Like what?"

"I don't know, but did he ever leave anything here, keep anything here, send himself mail here—along those lines?"

"Never. No sir." Babe shook his head, trying to remember. "I mean, you can go through his suitcase if you want, but I think it's just a few clothes, toilet articles; you can examine it all you want."

"I'll take it with me when I leave, if you don't mind. We'll run some checks, for the hell of it, but it probably won't come to anything."

"He appeared in the doorway suddenly—leaning against it—he said my name, then again, loud, 'BABE'—and then he crumpled and I caught him and held him till he died. Maybe I rocked him a little."

Janeway rubbed his eyes. "Not a bad beginning, I suppose."

"I don't get you—'beginning'? What comes next?"

"I can't say for sure, because this is a situation where we can only counterpunch, which we'll do. But I can guess that whoever killed Scylla wouldn't have risked it if some situation somewhere wasn't coming to a head. It's also not unreasonable to assume they thought he knew something. And since he lived here when he was in town, and since he died here, if I were in their position I'd feel justified in assuming you knew something too. Or might. People do, it's known, say strange things when they're dying. Conclusion: If I were whoever killed him, I'd sure as hell like to ask you a few questions."

"But I'm *ignorant*—I'm not even involved, not in anything."

"I know that and you know that, but tell me, how can they know that?"

Babe was a little short of answers.

"Tom?"

"Yes sir?"

"I'm going to say something just rotten to you now, for two reasons. First, because I believe it's possible, and second, because I want to scare the shit out of you so you'll do exactly what I tell you."

"Listen, Mr. Janeway—hold it a sec. I'm not gonna disobey you, I promise. I'm edgy enough as it is."

Janeway nodded, began packing up Doc's belongings.

"Fine. I was just going to tell you what I think's going to happen to you."

"I'm not so sure I want to hear that," Babe said, and then he said, "What *do* you think's gonna happen to me?"

Janeway looked over from his packing. "I think they're going to try to capture you, and then I think they're going to try to torture you, and then I think they're going to try to kill you . . ."

# 20

Janeway finished packing in silence. "You still there?" he asked after a while.

Babe nodded.

"That really was only a guess, but after a while, you develop a sense for these things, a feel for the way other minds operate. And in our business, whenever anyone in our immediate family's damaged, we automatically assume it wasn't accidental. Dave told me about your mugging and why he was coming—to try to get you down to D.C. for a while." He started fastening the suitcase. "He left some extra stuff here, I think, for when he ran short."

"Quit trying to trick me—you asked me that already, did he leave anything, and I told you already, no."

Return of the quick smile. "I guess you weren't your brother's brother for nothing."

Babe started with Janeway toward the door.

"I'm at the Carlyle—we oil types live well—it's just a quick shoot across the Park, call me whenever you want—seven four four one six oh oh, Room Two one oh one." He reached for the doorknob. "Now listen to me—we won't have our own surveillance working on you till morning, the police will handle things till then, and I haven't got unbounded faith in New York's finest. So what you do is this: You stay locked in here overnight, okay?"

"*Surveillance,* for Chrissakes?"

Janeway spun on Babe. "I'm not telling you to turn hermit, I'm just saying stay inside till I have faith in the personnel."

"And then what? I get to go through life with some crew-cut jerk sneaking around after me?"

"For you, as a special treat, nothing but intellectuals and longhairs. Now look—I worked alongside Dave a long time, we were very close, believe that, and we'll meet in hell, and I've got plenty to answer for, but I'm not about to let him chew my ass off for not watching after you. So do what I say and shut up."

"If you're so worried about my health, why are you leaving me alone, then?"

Janeway put the bag down. "I thought it was obvious. How are we going to find who killed him if they don't come after you? You think we're dealing with morons? You think they'll break in here and say 'Shucks, he's moved out' and then we'll jump them from the closets and say 'Put 'em up, you dirty guys?' If you're not here, they'll know it, and they won't come. If you are here, they probably won't come anyway. It's risky, they know how our minds work, they'll guess surveillance. But if they're desperate, and I think they are, then they'll come."

"In other words, you want to watch after me, but you also want to use me for bait."

For the first time, Janeway looked really tired. "I want to catch who killed him. I've got no better notions. If you do, tell me. If you want to come with me to the Carlyle, for Christ's sakes, say so. I'll get you a room, I'll take you down to D.C., we'll keep you hidden till whatever this is is over. Anything you want, I swear, please, just tell me."

Babe didn't even hesitate. Bogart wouldn't have hesitated. "I wasn't upset, Mr. Janeway, I swear, it was just curiosity; now that I know, I think it's terrific. I mean, historians don't get much chance to have adventures, it's kind of a sedentary profession, you know what I mean? Sit on your tail all day, read, read, read. Besides, I hadn't planned on going out till the afternoon, so what you're asking me to do is what I was going to do anyway, only without police protection." Babe could tell that Janeway was watching him closely, trying to fathom if he was telling the truth or not. But that didn't bother him, because he was. He wondered if he would have been quite so confident if he wasn't a dead shot with a loaded pistol in the bottom drawer of his desk, but that was all academic. He had the pistol, he could use it like a bastard.

And how wonderful, if only Janeway turned out to be right in his guesswork, to be able to have revenge so quickly. If only Doc's killers would come and he could blast away and watch them fall. He ran his hands across Doc's blood on his shirt.

"All right," Janeway said finally. "I'll go, you stay. How can you reach me?"

"Carlyle—seven four four one six oh oh—Two one oh one."

Janeway was reasonably impressed.

"I wasn't my brother's brother for nothing," Babe said.

"Lock it behind me," Janeway ordered. He took the suitcase and left.

Babe locked it behind him.

All of them were gone now.

Everything was gone now.

Doc most of all.

Mourning time.

Babe went to his chair in the corner and sat. Now there was no one left to butt in, no reason to dam up his heart. He sat very still, alone, the sole survivor of the union between H. V. and Rebekkah Levy.

He really was alone now, whatever that dread word meant. There was no old family homestead to return to. This horrid student's room was, as much as any place, the family homestead now, and that by itself was almost cause for mourning. An aging rectangle of a place, a single crummy closet, a single crummy sink, rusty water, a tiny windowless bathroom with a tiny tub, and practically hidden off in a corner one nearly cracked window with a mildewing frame that never brought in any breeze or—

—*Christ!*—the window—the goddamn window, was it locked, had he locked it, because if he hadn't there was a fire escape and that's how they'd come for him, up the fire escape, hide in the darkness, get out their rifles with the silencers, burst in, torture him, kill him, and gone.

Babe ran to the window, checked it.

Of course, it was locked.

Jerk, he told himself. Working yourself up over a stupid thing like that. When there were important deeds to be done, there was mourning to be done "and only I am left alone to tell you."

Babe went back to his chair in the corner and sat. He cleared his mind to mourn.

No chance.

"Doc," he said out loud. "You're gonna have to give me a raincheck." Because the truth was, the terrible and very strange truth was, simply that in all his adult life, he had never had an adventure before, and the thrill of it swept all possibility of thinking far, far away. Bogie and Cagney, they had adventures every day of their lives. Edward G. too. And now it was his turn.

T. Babington Levy was maybe, hopefully, in danger.

Fantastic.

Let the stoop kids try to call him a creep now. Let *anybody*. Maybe what I'll do, Levy decided, is get my gun and stick it sort of in my pocket but not all the way, and then just kind of walk past the stoop kids and let them see the heater, really scare the pee out of the bastards, and maybe the head of the gang might get up the nerve to whisper, ". . . hey, sir, is that a . . . a you know?" and he, Levy, would turn and give his best Alan Ladd look and maybe say, "I don't know; why don't you mess with me and find out?"

You need a better answer, Levy told himself. A real clock-stopper of a retort. Lemme think . . .

Don't bother, Levy told himself. Janeway said you can't show your head till noon.

Screw Janeway. He wasn't any kid.

"I'm not any kid," Levy said. He was an historian and historians had freedom of choice unless they were Marxists, and he didn't work that side of the street. He was free and he could go and come when he so desired, just as he'd done ever since he'd rented his pit.

Hadn't he survived an entire summer on West 95th Street in New York City without a single incident, not counting the mugging, and that took place in the park? And if you could make it through a summer on West 95th, if you could live through August without air conditioning, you didn't need any crew-cutted Provider to tell you what was safe and what wasn't.

He was sitting there, genuinely calm, until he heard them starting to force his window.

All things considered, later, Babe thought he reacted rather well. He didn't panic, didn't scream or run. Instead he just dove across the room toward his desk, ripped the bottom drawer open, and then the gun was in his hand, and as he stood he cocked it, and as he cocked it he aimed and moved dead at the window.

Obviously, there was no one there.

It had just been a creak, old buildings did that, this one more than most, and the rest had been his imagination. Babe stood still, the weapon in his hands, and he didn't feel stupid and he didn't feel proud.

He felt frightened.

He remembered the precise moment the fear entered him: It was when he grabbed the gun. Because that was reality, and reality was a brother murdered and maybe him standing somewhere in that same line.

Babe began to sweat.

Jesus, he wanted air. He started toward the window,

stopped. That wasn't air outside. It was just floating dirt. And besides, it was very dark by the fire escape, a killer could hide by the fire escape.

Perspiration was pouring off him now. His tongue felt dry and what would have really tasted good would have been an egg cream, cool and relaxing—stomach-settling too. Probably the old egg-cream guy on the corner would be closed now, but maybe not, maybe on hot nights he stayed open as long as business stayed good. But even if he was shut, it would be better than staying alone, panic building, pointing a pistol at sounds. So, carefully concealing his weapon deep in his windbreaker pocket, Babe took out his wallet and key and left his room.

Heart, goddammit, pounding.

Cagney wouldn't have even thought twice, Bogie would have gone unarmed after the egg cream, and here he was, panicked as he crept down the reasonably well lit stairs in what he knew was a fruitless quest for a mixture of chocolate and cold milk and club soda.

Babe moved at a slow pace down toward the main floor. Every half dozen or so steps, he brought himself to a sudden stop and whirled around, watching and listening, making good and damn sure no one could sneak up behind him.

He continued down, continued his eccentric halts and spins, his right hand deep in his windbreaker pocket, glued to the gun.

God, the swings of fear, Babe thought.

Just a few moments before, joy at adventure.

No more.

He reached the landing of his brownstone, hesitated, peering through the doors toward the street, trying to spot the police.

He saw nobody.

Carefully, heart still pounding, ready to fire, he stepped outside into the night. It was Indian Summer gone berserk; no wind, nothing to help it along.

"Hey, Melendez," one of the stoop kids said, "it's the creep."

"Hey, creep, past your bedtime," Babe heard, and he turned, fighting the temptation to point his pistol in his windbreaker pocket, because he knew it was the stoop gang. There were four of them drinking beer and smoking on their steps. A couple of girls, one pretty. Probably marijuana in the vicinity.

The one who mentioned his bedtime, their leader, evidently Melendez, sat bare-chested and jeaned in the awesome heat. "Hey, creepy, ain'tcha scared you might catch cold with just that little jacket," he called to Babe. "Wanna borrow my parka awhile?" The others laughed.

That Melendez is cleverer than I am, Babe thought. He dwelled on that awhile, because it took his mind off the stupidity of his situation, looking for an egg cream after one in the morning with a pistol cocked and ready in his pocket. A sixteen-year-old delinquent shouldn't be able to outwit me, Babe decided. He did his best to sound unruffled, casual: "Where's the nearest egg-cream place, I wonder?"

"You mean the nearest *open* egg-cream place, don'tcha?" Melendez replied. "You can probably break into the one down around the corner if you're really desperate—that's how most of the other egg-cream addicts handle things." The gang hooted again.

Humiliated, Babe backed inside. What a wipeout—totaled by a Spanish Milton Berle. Babe bolted back up the stairs, ran to his room, unlocked it, stepped carefully inside, locked it behind him securely. Then, gun clear of pocket, he checked the window to see that it was still locked, the bathroom to see that it was still empty. He jerked open the closet door, made sure no one was hiding behind his sport coats, quickly, foolishness growing, dropped to one knee, making certain no one was scrunched up under his bed. After that he crossed the room, dialed the Carlyle, asked for 2101, and before the second ring there came Janeway's voice, urgent and loud: "*What?*"

Babe felt embarrassed. "It's just me."

"Yes, Tom, what? Go on."

"Nothing. Nothing crucial or anything."

"Tom—you called me, remember? You must have had something on your mind."

"I just . . . I was about to take a bath and hit the sack, and I wanted you to know everything was fine."

"Lie."

Babe could almost see the quick blue eyes boring in at him. "After you left, I was terrifically excited, but that didn't last—I got scared, Mr. Janeway, and I wanted to talk, that's all. To anybody. You qualify . . ." Babe waited, but there was only silence from the other end. "That was supposed to be a joke," Babe said.

"Are you still frightened?"

"No, I would never have called until I had control and everything, I wouldn't want to come out a jerk."

"Lie."

"I'm a lot better. I don't want you to think I'm walking around here giggling to myself, but I'm definitely on the road to recovery. True."

"Do you want me to come over?"

"No sir."

"Do you want me to come get you and bring you back over here?"

"No, really."

"I'm not offering charity, you understand."

"I do, yes sir, but if you came here, they'd know I wasn't alone, and if I came there, they'd know my place was empty. Let's just leave things like they are, it's best."

"They probably won't move tonight anyway—they don't even know that Scylla's gone—if they went back to where they got him, they'd find he wasn't there. They'll have to check around to see, and that takes time. You wouldn't be ruining anything if you came here, and I'll be honest, I don't like the way you're sounding."

"Maybe that's because I'm a little bothered on account of the real reason I called was to tell you there isn't any surveillance outside, Mr. Janeway. The police never showed."

Silence from Janeway.

"I checked very carefully; I'm really right."

"You went outside," Janeway said, and Babe could hear his anger building. "The one thing I said don't do, you did."

"Only for a second, in and out, like that."

"Levy?"

"Yes sir?"

"You're not *supposed* to be able to see surveillance. I've got four men from Division on the first shuttle down in the morning. Do you think when they take over, they're going to wear sweatshirts saying, 'Do not disturb, I'm on surveillance'?"

"You don't have to humor me, I just had some information I thought you ought to know."

"I'm not humoring you, if I had you here I'd kick your ass across the Carlyle. When I left tonight, there was a cop there. He wasn't in uniform but he was there, with nice long hair and pretending to be stoned." He paused a moment. "I don't like the way you're acting or sounding. Give me a few hours' rack time, I'll be there by six. Set your alarm for a quarter of, because when I get there, if coffee isn't ready, your life will *really* be in danger."

"Thank you, Mr. Janeway."

"*De nada.* I was a friend of your brother's."

They hung up, and then, at last, Babe started to undress, taking the bloody clothes from his thin body. He went to the bathroom, turned on both spigots till the water stopped being rusty, drained the tub, turned the spigots back on again. He continued undressing, pondering whether or not to take his gun in with him while he bathed. He was so jumpy, he'd probably shoot his thing off reaching for the soap. "Rhodes Scholar Emasculates Self in Tub," the *Daily News* might headline "Thought He Heard Meanies."

Babe shoved the weapon into its proper place in his bottom desk drawer, went back in, turned off the water, then padded out again for something to read. He did a lot of his best work in the tub; you couldn't beat warm water when it came to ruminating, going over notes, or rereading history books. But which to study now? He looked around his place; it was starkly lit, with just four cheap unshaded lamps set in strategic places, one by his bed, two flanking his desk, one by his reading chair in the corner.

He decided on Cowles's *1913*, because even though she was not a noted historian, she had selected an interesting year worldwide, because there were points and minutiae you had to comprehend fully before you could really grasp not just the war that followed, but the twenties that followed the war. He grabbed a pair of clean pajamas and entered the bathroom.

What about locking the door?

Babe put the pajamas over the towel rack and pondered. He could begin to feel his heart again. Why should he lock it? He never had before, and he wasn't about to be stampeded into it now. Shut it, sure; that was okay, even though in the past he had not made it a blind habit. Still, nothing wrong with shutting it, it didn't mean you were chicken.

He started to get in the tub, testing it with his big toe; it was too hot. He spun the "cold" spigot, but it made too much noise, he thought suddenly, because what better time to sneak in than behind the curtain of water thundering down? Thundering? His crummy trickle of a cold-water spigot and he was calling it "thundering"? Babe waited foolishly by the filling tub for the temperature to make itself bearable, and when it did he got in, expertly flicked off the "cold" spigot with his big toe again, and began thumbing through the book. Then he took the book, closed it, held it between his hands, shut his eyes.

That was his way, often, of finalizing facts. He would almost command a book to obey him. Once he had read it carefully and gone back through it again, he would hold it tightly and then by force of will order the facts to file into his brain. The summer in London had been hot. Deaths from the heat wave. Carpentier knocked out Bomber Wells in mere seconds, a Frenchman annihilating an Englishman. The suffragettes were building, and one of them threw herself under the king's horse at the Derby and was killed for her gesture. The tango was the dance sensation. Babe paused a moment, because even though he didn't dance, he was quite sure there was something basic in the enterprise, that somewhere there was a paper in it, minor, to be sure, but worthwhile, comparing an era's chosen dances with its morals, perhaps not its politics, but certainly its lust for sex and blood and—

—and *click.*

*Jesus Christ what was that?* Babe lay frozen, except for his eyes, and they would not stop blinking, because he had heard it, had heard it!—heard what?—what the hell was that sound, that click—it came from outside, from his empty room, so *what could it be*?

Nothing, he told himself. Just like all the other sounds tonight have been nothing. It was a creak from an old rotting cripple of a building, *and that's all*!

Except it didn't sound like that. It was different, it sounded sort of like a lamp being clicked off. No, not "sort of"; it sounded exactly like a lamp being clicked off.

Babe leaned out of the tub, trying to get a glimpse under the door to see if the room beyond seemed darker, but he couldn't tell a damn thing. So what, he was big enough to handle himself, especially when there was nothing to take care of.

Nothing.

Now, he had four lamps out there, so if there were four sounds like that, four clicks, then you might have a situation on your hands. But you don't, so forget it.

Back to *1913*.

Germany was having a bitch of a time getting their Zeppelins to work right. Benz was already a thriving car company, and the Krupps were already richer than anybody, all this even before things started heating up, before munitions became an A-number-one priority or—

—or *click*.

Babe half dove out of the tub, locked the bathroom door. In doing so, he created a small wave and considerable splashing, so it was hard to hear for a bit, but once he was back in the water, things quieted, and he shut his eyes, trying desperately to listen.

No sound.

Two of his four lamps could have been clicked off, or it could have been two creaks. He remained very still, and even though he was undeniably concerned, he was also more than a little pleased with the fact that his panic was not growing. Better, his mind was functioning, logic was his, and logic said that if there were people outside turning off lights, they wouldn't stop with two or three, they'd need total darkness, which meant don't sweat it till you've heard the big fourth, and if that happened, well then—

—then *click*.

*1913,* Babe commanded, the book clenched all he had in his thin hands. Russia. He shut his eyes tight. Russia. The Sleeping Giant. Nicholas was still running things, but Rasputin was coming up fast on the outside, his hold on Alexandra stronger by the month, each time he cured another of her son's hemophilia fights while the doctors stood around helpless. Lenin was humping the cause of restlessness when and where he could, making headway. And in America? Money. M-o-n-e-y, thazzall. The Vanderbilts gave a little soiree with not just Franz Lehar himself doing the orchestra conducting, and not just Kreisler *and* Elman sawing away on their fiddles; no, for the capper they had Caruso entertaining the guests with his tenoring. How about that? The world sliding down the tubes, and over here you just didn't count unless you could have old Enrico himself belting his lungs out for the entertainment pleasure of you and your four hundred intimates. Amazing. How could we have been so out of things? Is it any wonder that it all exploded, that finally—

—finally *click.*

Babe was ready for it. He just calmly put the book down and said to himself, There will be a fifth click. And if there is, that means all the clicks weren't clicks at all, they were creaks, and my four lights still burn, and all is well with the union.

There will be a fifth click, he repeated.

I have complete confidence that the fifth click will come, because logic dictates that it will, and if you've put your life in logic's hands, you don't say "So long" at the first sign of a little uncertainty.

His position was simple: All he had to do was just wait around for the fifth click and, when it came, go back to hitting the books.

And if it didn't come?

Still simple. Just wait inside, locked safe and sound, because they built buildings solid when they built his pit, so let them try and break the door, what they'd get for their troubles would be shoulder separations, and screw, what they got they deserved.

Unless they were giants. Giants could splinter the door in pretty quick. Maybe they hired a specialist, a door cruncher, and if they had a guy like that, he'd be in for a few sweaty moments.

"Help," Babe said, experimentally at first, because he had never called that word before, not and really meant it; oh, as a kid sure, everybody called for help all the time, but then it meant "Make this bee quit chasing me," not *SAVE ME SAVE MY LIFE!—*

*—click.*

Babe lay back in the tub and thanked God that the walls were thick, and so he didn't have to get out, humiliated and dripping, to explain to some unknown neighbor that there must have been some mistake, he hadn't been the one that yelled for help, why would he go and do a thing like that? No, Babe decided, that would make the neighbor angry, and the neighbor had, after all, done a good deed, so what he would do is say, "Oh, you heard that yell for help too, so did I, it came from outside in the street, maybe those stoop kids are mugging somebody, wait just a sec till I get dressed and we'll go investigate." That would be a good, reasonable thing to say to a neighbor in the middle of the night, except, of course, since the fifth click, it didn't matter all that much now—

—now *scratch.*

Babe held his breath. That was what the fifth sound had been, not a click but something that sounded like it, a scratch, and here it was coming again—

—again *scratch.*

*Scratch.*

Someone was taking off the hinges of his bathroom door.

"Help!" Babe hollered, but not loud enough, so he did it again. *"Help!"* and he was really working into it now, his lungs loosening up fine, but just before he was about to really start to scream it out, he heard something that scared him. Worse than anything.

Rock music was blasting from his room now, blaring out, his radio turned up full, covering even the loudest cry.

*Scratch.*

*Scratch.*

*Scratch.*

*Scratch.*

Babe got the hell out of the tub and stared around for something to attack with. They were coming in to get him, and son of a bitch, why did he use an electric razor? His father had used a straight razor, and Babe had loved to watch him with it, scraping the whiskers, and if only he'd copied H.V. that way too, then he'd have a straight razor clenched and ready so that when they came in he'd just calmly swipe the shit out of them, and when they were helpless he'd call the cops and wouldn't that be something—

No it wouldn't—quit this now—because you don't have a straight razor.

But he did have the gun.

The problem was getting to it. Babe stood in a corner of the room, naked, desperately trying to figure what the hell to do, but all he could come up with was to get dressed. It would be too humiliating if they roared in and he was naked—you couldn't fight your best if you didn't have any clothes on, that was just giving them too much of your vulnerability to aim at—so he quickly got dressed, pajama tops and bottoms, the bottoms tied tight, the top buttoned all the way up.

There, Babe thought. That's a lot better.

*Better?* Better, you asshole, they're coming to get you and you're feeling like a big deal 'cause you've got pajamas on? *think* of something!

And he did.

"Save me," Babe shouted. "Save me, help, hellllp," and they turned the rock music on even louder, which he figured they would, and that was fine with him, because they had to know he was helpless and cringing and ready to fold the way he was calling out "Hellllp for Chrissakes, somebody save me" and that was what he wanted them to think, because as long as they thought that, the last thing they'd expect is that *he'd* attack *them*, unlock the door and yank it full open and dive into the darkness, falling toward his desk, and once he got his hands on the gun he'd fire the fucker, he wouldn't aim it, just fire it, because once they knew he was armed it was all his, every ad point worked his way, because they'd be in a room with an armed man, armed and deadly and ready to kill.

"Save me," Babe screamed, creeping toward the door. "Help please Jesus!" he hollered, his fingers edging toward the lock. "Omigod won't somebody please do *something*," he shrieked, and when he had both hands ready, one on the knob, one on the lock, he let go one final begging *"Pleeeeeeeease!"* and then he unlocked the door and threw it open and was all set for his dive and roll toward the desk.

Babe was candy.

The Limper blocked his dive, and then the big-shouldered guy was all over him, slamming him back into the bathroom, and as Babe spun he thought Jesus, they're going to beat me to a pulp again, and he tried some feeble defense, but it was garbage, the big-shouldered man was forcing him down, and then the bathroom lights went out and there was nothing but the sound of the rock music as Babe went into the tub again, his legs kicking and splashing, his head going steadily under water, so he knew it wasn't a beating this time at all; this time it was drowning they intended.

No air. Even the rock sounds were gone now. Nothing in the world but giant hands keeping you down, even if you kicked, even if you tried with all you had to thrash and flail and find an opening. His kicking got weaker, less frequent. He wanted to go out as well as he could, because Janeway had said these were probably the guys who'd killed Doc and Janeway had been right about everything else so far, and the memory of Doc sent a new surge of strength through him, not much, but enough to get his head out of the water, and for an instant he heard again the blare of rock.

But only for an instant. The giant hands were firm now.

No way to sway them. Nothing to do. So this is what it's like to die, Babe thought. Underwater, he kept his eyes closed. It really isn't all that bad, he decided; not as bad as you'd think.

But then he had to cough and his mouth opened and the water poured in, and the big hands held him down. No, Babe realized then. He was wrong about death not being as bad. All wrong. It was worse.

# 21

Damp, drained, pajamaed, in a room, in a chair, tied, Babe awoke, alone and—hey how about that—alive.

He blinked, trying to sort out impressions. Nothing special about the room—plain-walled, small, but brightly lit—maybe unusually so. Nothing special about the chair either—except, he realized as he leaned back slightly, that it was kind of a recliner. He could adjust his angle within reason, although doing it didn't greatly add to his comfort, because he was bound too tightly, hand and foot, for anything resembling ease. It must have been a while since they attacked, but it couldn't have been too long, or his clothes would have been dryer. There were no windows in the room, but he was willing to bet it was still night, probably not much after three or in that vicinity. Summing up, he was uncomfortable, completely captive, undoubtedly the helpless victim of relentless sadistic destroyers.

But who gave a shit, he was breathing.

My God, Babe thought, what an underrated function—we ought to declare a National Breathing Week, pick some time of year, maybe late autumn, when the air quality was pretty decent, and just let the public go around inhaling the ozone.

He was getting giddy, not proper behavior for historians—where would the world be today if Carlyle had gone giddy doing his rewrites?—but he couldn't help it, he was there, present, the earth was turning and he was spinning too; he had no cause whatsoever for complaint.

From behind him a voice said, "He's awake." The Limper came into view, staring down at him.

There were more footsteps, and the big-shouldered man was on the other side of the chair, watching him too. He was carrying an armload of clean white towels, beautifully folded.

"Give me," the Limper said.

The towels were handed across.

"Keep his head still, that's the most important," the Limper said, his voice suddenly going into whisper.

Because behind them now: quick footsteps.

Babe watched as the men stiffened slightly, almost as the police and the first crew cut had stiffened back in his room when Janeway had first made his appearance.

But this man now wasn't Janeway. He was completely bald, powerfully built, bull-shouldered. And blue-eyed—bright, brighter even than Biesenthal's. A squat bull of a man, but Babe had seen enough around campuses to be able to spitball that this one was not and never had been, anything less than brilliant. He carried a rolled-up towel in one hand. And a black leather bag in the other. He indicated that he wanted a lamp to be brought closer to the chair. When the Limper hurriedly did that, the bull-shouldered man spoke. Quietly: "Is it safe?" he said.

Babe wasn't ready for the question. "Huh?"

"Is it safe?"

"What?"

"Is it safe?"

"Is *what* safe?"

As patiently as ever: "Is it safe?"

"I don't know what you're talking about."

No change in tone: "Is it safe?"

Babe's voice was starting to rise: "I can't tell you if something's safe or not unless I know what you're asking, so ask me specifically and I'll tell you if I can."

"Is it safe?" the bull-shouldered man said, steady as a rock.

*"I can't answer that."*

"Is it safe?"

"I don't know—*don't you hear me?*—I do not know—tell me what the 'it' refers to."

"Is it safe?" Like a machine.

It was getting to be the Chinese water torture. "Yes," Babe said. "It's very safe. It's so safe you wouldn't believe it. There. Now you know."

"Is it safe?"

"You don't like 'yes,' I'll give you 'no,' it isn't safe—very dangerous. Be careful."

It was still said with infinite patience, but this time there came a finality into the tone: "Is it safe?" so when Babe quietly answered back, "I really really don't know what you want me to tell you," he was not surprised when the bull-shouldered man started to move to begin effecting changes. He gestured toward the big man, and immediately Babe felt the giant hands pressing in against the sides of his head, holding it tight and steady. The Limper brought the lamp closer still.

While the bull-shouldered man put down his black

leather bag, he opened the towel, and Babe could see a bunch of slender shining tools. It was hot in the room, and as the bald man selected a tool he was perspiring lightly, and without a word the Limper reached across with a small clean towel, wiped the forehead dry. The big man's hand shifted, forcing Babe's mouth open. The bull-shouldered man took out a clean, angeled dental mirror, then picked up another tool with a kind of rounded end. Concentrating totally, his blue eyes unwavering, he began to work.

My God, Babe thought, he's cleaning my teeth.

Madness. The guy moved his tools around quickly in Babe's mouth, light taps here, gentle probes there, all very deft. I wonder if I should ask him how bad my cavity is, Babe thought. Then he wondered what the guy's fees were because what the hell, as long as they were all together, the guy could at least put in a temporary filling for a few bucks. For the briefest moment, Babe wanted to laugh.

Only, of course, he didn't, because it wasn't funny.

Because, of course, it was frightening. Dentists were frightening, no matter how much music they piped into their offices or the number of Novocain shots they offered. It was all very primitive. It went beyond pain.

The dentist meant fear, just like in *Psycho*, in the shower scene, that meant fear. There was something unconsciously terrifying about taking a shower with a curtain drawn, and it was the same with a dentist. You never knew what might happen next.

Christ I'm scared, Babe thought, I must try and keep that from him. He stared back into the blue eyes, thinking, I shouldn't be, though. He's not coming close to hurting me and he could have, he spotted my cavity first thing. Now he was back to it, using the spoon excavator, but with such caution it still didn't hurt, and Babe was a terrific patient anyway, if anyone could be—he usually went through most stuff without Novocain because he hated the needles and the hours of numbness worse than the few minutes of actual discomfort. The bald guy was scraping gently, quickly away at the cavity, getting the decay out. The tooth was one of the four front ones, upper incisors, and as he sat there in the midst of his lunatic dental appointment, Babe didn't know a lot of things, but one fact he was sure of: the bald guy was one hell of a craftsman.

His fingers were strong, sure, lightning fast: They moved with almost unnerving speed as they cleaned out the decay. Babe, pinioned, could watch the bright blue eyes, and the concentration was incredible. Not a flicker; nothing distracted them. The scraping just went on and on and on. After several minutes, the bull-shouldered man stopped, took up another tool, looked for a long moment at the cavity. "Is it safe?" he said, his voice still as it had always been, patient, calm, seeming capable of enduring any wait until the sought-after answer was achieved, but Babe could only come back with "I told you before and I'm telling you now, I swear I don't know." That would have been his answer anyway; but before he got halfway through it, the bull-shouldered man took the new tool, a needle-pointed explorer, and shoved it up through the cavity into the live nerve.

The top of Babe's head came off.

He had never experienced such sudden suffering and his scream was almost instantaneous with the attack, except the bald guy pulled the explorer tool out and the big guy covered Babe's mouth with his hand, so the scream was nothing really: a little muffled thing, a child's whimper.

"Is it safe?" the bull-shouldered man said again, patiently, his voice almost more gentle now.

There were tears in Babe's eyes—he couldn't stop them, they were a reaction, they were there. "I don't—" he began, but again came an interruption, this time the big man forcing his mouth to stay open while the bull-shouldered man pushed the sharp explorer back up, deeper into the nerve.

Babe began to black out, but just before he could, the tool was pulled away again, and he could not reach unconsciousness. The bald guy looked at him now, gentle concern in the blue eyes. He understood pain, this one; he knew just how far you could push in, just when to pull out. He reached out again toward the towel, and then there was a small bottle in his hands. "Oil of cloves," he said, the first time he had varied, and he put some on his finger, and the big guy forced Babe's mouth open again as the bald one put his finger on the tooth.

Oh Jesus, Babe thought, the son of a bitch is gonna kill me.

Nothing like that happened.

The bald man gently rubbed the cavity with the liquid, and as he did it, the pain began to magically go away. "Is it not remarkable?" the bald man said. "Just simple oil of cloves and how amazing the results."

Babe licked at the finger, ran his tongue across his cavity.

The dentist smiled, took some more oil of cloves, rubbed it over the cavity again, expertly, soothingly, making the pain disappear.

Babe began breathing regularly again.

"Life can be, if only we will allow it, so simple," the dentist said, pausing for the Limper to reach out, remove the least sign of perspiration. He held up the oil of cloves: "Relief." He held up the explorer: "Anguish." He took the towel from the Limper and dabbed at Babe's features. "You seem a bright young man, able to distinguish light from darkness, heat from freezing cold. Surely you must prefer anything to my brand of torment, so I ask you, and *please* take your time before answering: Is it safe?"

"Jesus, lis—"

"You did not take your time, you rushed. I will not repeat the question; surely by now you know what it is and also its implications. When you are ready, reply."

After a moment, Babe said, "I . . ."

The blue eyes waited.

Babe shook his head. ". . . can't satisfy . . . what you want . . . because . . . I don't . . ." and then he said, ". . . please, aw please, don't—don't Jesus don't" because the big guy was holding his mouth open again and the bald bull-shouldered dentist was moving in with the sharp-pointed explorer, into his mouth, into the cavity, up, higher, higher than it had ever gone—

—Christ! Babe thought, he's going to push it through my brain! and then his senses at last gave out on him and he sagged, semiconscious, and as the straps were taken off he heard the dentist's instructions being given: "Karl, take him to the spare room—take the cloves with you, and some smelling salts—get him ready, and be quick."

"You think he knows?" the Limper asked.

"Of course he knows," the dentist said. "But he's being very stubborn." Then there was a long pause. Then Babe heard the worst words of his life: *"Next time I'm afraid I'm going to really have to hurt him."*

The big-shouldered guy, Karl, lifted him then. Babe blinked as Karl carried him out of the bright room and down a long hall in what must have been a railroad-car type apartment, and at the far end of the hall Karl pushed a door open and dropped Babe on a bed in the far corner and shoved some smelling salts in his face, and Babe blinked, coughed, coughed again, he couldn't stop coughing, so he tried to turn away, but Karl wouldn't let him, he could not escape the smelling salts, and when he was finally able to keep his eyes open, Karl said, "Take this," and shoved the oil of cloves bottle at him and poured some on Babe's finger, and Babe groggily pushed the finger against the wounded tooth, trying to make the pain go away again, and he licked the tooth too, the warm covering of his tongue helping some, and then he held out his finger again for more of the oil of cloves, and as Karl poured, Babe was somehow able to force a single thought through his unclear head, and that thought concerned life and how uneven it was, what a jagged craggy thing, peaks naturally following valleys as you moved along, because no more than a few minutes earlier he had heard with his very own ears the worst words of his existence, the news that the bull-shouldered dentist was going to really hurt him soon, that the agony he had lived through up till now was just a warm-up, the prelims, kid stuff, and here, not many minutes later, he was able to see with his very own eyes the most glorious vision he had ever been privileged to behold in all his troubled years, because behind Karl now, moving silently, slowly, through the door, came Janeway, with just the most beautiful knife held tight in his hand . . .

# 22

Babe realized that he had to keep his eyes away, not just from Janeway but from Karl too, because if the big man ever saw them, he would know that something was ten feet behind him, and if he turned in time, Janeway would be finished, because even though he had a knife, Karl had cornered the market on brute power. ". . . Please . . . more . . ." Babe muttered staring hard at the mattress he was sprawled across. ". . . More . . ." and he held out a trembling finger for the oil of cloves.

Instead, Karl shoved the smelling salts full into his face, and the strength and surprise of that sent Babe falling full out on the mattress, gagging and coughing again, and it was rotten, sure, but it got him a chance to shoot a look toward Janeway, to see how he was doing on his wonderful errand of mercy.

Eight feet to go. Maybe seven.

Silently, Janeway was coming on.

*Look away!* Babe commanded, immediately obeying himself, forcing his body back onto one elbow. ". . . The other . . . please . . . the other . . . for the pain . . ." and this time Karl did allow him the oil of cloves, pouring it on Babe's finger, and Babe raced the finger to his mouth, rubbing and rubbing the damaged tooth, and whatever the stuff was, whatever was in it, it was amazing because the ache in his mouth was diminishing rapidly, but he had to keep that bit of news from Karl too, lest the big man start to drag him back to the chair, and anyway, where the hell was Janeway, *what was keeping him*?

Unable to help himself, Babe risked the glance, one fast eye flick, and Janeway was close now, not close enough for an accurate strike, but he had traversed most of the distance, and more than that, he hadn't made a sound. He must be part Indian, Babe decided, to cross a room in total quiet, and he dropped his eyes and began to rub his tooth and tongue it, and make weak appreciative sounds.

Three feet to go.

And coming. Aaaaaaannnd coming.

". . . Please just a little more . . ." Babe said, but he said it either too fast or too loud or perhaps it was the combination of the two coupled with the glance he'd made toward Janeway.

It didn't really matter what his specific mistakes were; the conclusion was the bad thing, because, without preparation, Karl turned, saw Janeway, began to give a cry of warning as he stood with surprising speed, his great killing arms already in position to slaughter Janeway.

Karl was candy.

Babe never saw anyone move like Janeway moved, nowhere near that quick, because in one single blurred motion he stepped inside the bigger man's arms, spun him, threw his left arm around Karl's throat, lifted Karl slightly off the ground, using his left hip for leverage.

And then Janeway's right hand moved.

Babe saw it all. He was staring into Karl's peasant face as the right hand thudded home. Karl screamed like a baby, then pitched forward across the bed, Janeway's knife sticking out of him, and if you made an X on a man's back opposite from where the heart would be, that was where the handle held.

Janeway grabbed Babe, pulled him up, yanked him out of the room, down the railroad-flat corridor, grabbed a door open, revealing the flight of steps to the street and cried *"Go!"* to Babe as the Limper appeared at the end of the hall, gun in hand. But Janeway outclassed him, because now there was a gun in his hand too, and he fired and fired again, and Babe did his best with the stairs, holding tight to the banister with both hands as behind him he heard the Limper's shrieks, and they went on until Janeway fired a third time, and that was that as Janeway ran down after Babe, catching him easily, leading him the rest of the way to the street. It was dark and empty, and Babe didn't know where the hell he was; the house they'd left was a boarded-up slum place next to a warehouse, but that was all Babe could make out, because Janeway was yanking him, not caring if Babe stumbled, and then throwing a car door open, shouting, "Get in—no, goddammit, the back—get in the back and lie down," and Babe tried to obey, but not quick enough for Janeway, who shoved him hard, ordering "Down—*down*—get on the floor and stay still!" and once Babe did Janeway slammed the door shut, turned the ignition, gunning the car with all he had as they roared into the night.

"Okay, it's all starting to come together, now listen to me

and don't interrupt," Janeway began, until Babe said, "Can I get up?—is it all right now?—what time is it?—where are we?—what's happening, you just saved my life, that was really nice, thank you."

"You just interrupted me, which is the one thing I asked you not to do—"

"I wasn't trying to be rude, but nobody ever saved my life before and I wanted you to be sure to know I was grateful—"

"You just did it *again*," Janeway said. "Now, if I answer your questions, will you just goddammit listen till I'm finished?"

"I'll try very hard; I will."

"Okay—about getting up, the answer is no, it isn't all right, I don't know what kind of total operation they're running, and the less your head is visible, the longer it's liable to stay attached to your shoulders, and where we are is the West Fifties, way west, near the Hudson, warehouses, deserted mostly except during the day, trucking then, meat storage, and it's probably four o'clock or a little before, and I know I saved you, I was there when it happened, and what I want in return isn't your thanks but your silence, your silence, Levy, understand me?—what I'm saying is shut *up*, think you can handle that?"

"Yes sir," Babe said quickly from the back seat, lying almost doubled over on the floor. He wasn't really that bad a guy, Janeway, once you got to know him a little. Oh, probably he was spoiled about getting his own way all the time, but when people went around rescuing you from anguish and death, you could learn to overlook little things pretty fast.

Janeway took a corner on what seemed like two wheels, the tires screaming in the darkness. "Okay. That first guy, the big one, was named Franz Karl, and he was a human pimple, that's probably the nicest thing you could say about him. He thought he was a big ass-man, and he liked making people suffer—women were a specialty. He should have been a prison guard in some Southern jail—he hated blacks. That probably would have been his idea of heaven, just sitting around swilling beer and clubbing nigras whenever he got bored. Not much of a specimen, God knows.

"The guy I shot was Peter Erhard. He was Karl's cousin and boss. A higher-type pimple is all. That place we just left, they lived there. It wasn't theirs, they didn't own it, but they were told to live in it, so they lived in it. Tell them something simple enough to do and you could consider it done. That was their greatest achievement, they could follow simple instructions, and they served a purpose."

"What purpose?"

"Shut up—ever hear of Josef Mengele or Christian Szell?"

Silence from the back seat.

"Goddammit, Levy, answer me."

"I'm sorry, Mr. Janeway, I'm getting everything all wrong, I thought you just said to shut up."

"I did, but that was a direct question." Janeway took another corner, and again the wheels protested.

"Mengele or Szell? No."

"Jesus," Janeway exploded, "I thought you were supposed to be this self-proclaimed hotshot historian, haven't you heard of any Germans except Hitler? You have heard of Hitler?"

"Martin Bormann?" Babe tried.

"Bormann's dead, most likely—oh I know, I know, it's always in the papers how he's on the loose in Bogotá or running the singles program up at Grossinger's, but most of the top Nazi hunters think he's dead, and they've got a pretty good batting average, I wouldn't want to argue with them. Szell and Mengele, though, everyone agrees they're still with us. They ran the experimental block at Auschwitz. And they're the two biggest Germans left alive."

Babe tried getting comfortable in the back seat, but the floor was too hard and too narrow, and his mouth was starting to throb now. Every time Janeway hit a bump, it hit his mouth like a fist.

"The reason they've survived is very simple: They were smarter than anybody. They were always referred to as the 'angel twins.' Mengele they called the 'Angel of Death,' and Szell was the 'White Angel,' because he had this incredible head of beautiful prematurely gray hair. Mengele had a Ph.D. *plus* an M.D., and he was considered the dummy of the two." He hit a pothole going top speed, and the car bucked.

Babe cried out involuntarily.

"What?"

"Nothing, nothing, go on—what're you saying, the ones you just killed, they worked for these 'twin' guys?"

"No. Just Szell. And they were only part of the payroll, believe me. Don't you know how rich the big Nazis were?"

"No. Millionaires?"

"I guess you could say that without being accused of exaggeration, because, for example, in August of forty-four, when they figured things were going badly, a few of the top fellas got together and paid out five hundred million to

Argentina in exchange for identity cards. *These guys raped a continent.* When Göring killed himself in forty-five—you know he stole paintings from the Jews—well, when he died, his collection was worth two hundred million dollars. That's two hundred million *then*. Think what's happened to the art market and think what's happened to the dollar and you're talking about at least a billion today."

The car hit another bump.

"Jesus," Babe said.

"It really is incredible," Janeway went on. "Mengele was born big rich, but Szell had to work for his. He was Mengele's protégé, partly because he was so brilliant and partly because of his looks. See, Mengele hated *his* looks—he thought he looked like a Jew or a gypsy, and the thing was, he did. Half the crap he did was because somehow he was desperate to change his appearance, but why he grafted tits on men or tried to grow arms out of other people's backs, no one knows."

"He didn't do that," Babe said.

"You're right, he didn't succeed, but he sure as hell tried. Okay, that's Mengele, now forget Mengele, because Szell's the point of all this. I said he was poor going in, and naturally he started with gold, but then the word spread around Auschwitz that he was buyable, that you could escape if you paid enough to Christian Szell, and in the beginning he actually did let a few people out, just enough to keep the rumor alive. And these poor fucking Jews, well, they tried to keep anything they had of any value on their person, up their asses mostly, like any other convicts. And they'd come to Szell, or try to, and the richest ones he'd see, and make a deal with them, and once they'd given him everything they had, all their diamonds, whatever, he had them killed.

"Both he and Mengele had life-and-death power in the experimental block, and with the things Mengele was doing to people, you couldn't blame anyone for trusting Szell. They had to take the risk, what with goddamn Mengele raving around, convinced that if he just worked at it long enough, he could breed blue-eyed people." Janeway took a long breath then. "Okay, Tom, that's most of the back story. Is it clear?"

"So far. Except, how does it get back to me?"

"Szell's father died accidentally within the last couple weeks."

"So?"

"Remember I said Szell started on gold? Well, pretty soon he went into diamonds. He traded everything for diamonds. No paintings, no cash, just every diamond he could steal or get his hands on. No one ever knew how much he had, but in early forty-five he managed to fake his father out of Germany, and the old man came here."

"To America?"

"To New York. He had a sister in Yorkville, and he lived with her under a phony name. Eventually she died, but he stayed on. He stayed and they stayed."

" 'They'?"

"Szell's diamonds. Szell gave his father every goddamn one except what he figured he'd need to make it alive to South America. He lived in Argentina till Peron got canned, and then he quick beat it to Paraguay. The diamonds stayed here, because Szell wanted it just that way, so that in case he ever got caught, his fortune would be safe and he could use it to buy his freedom with. His father kept a safe-deposit box, and whenever Szell needed money, he'd get word to the old man, and they had a courier system set up. The diamonds would eventually wind up wherever the diamond market was highest at the time—sometimes Switzerland, sometimes West Germany—and then Szell would exchange whatever the top currency was for Paraguayan money and life would go on till he needed more. It all worked perfectly until the old man got totaled in the car crash. See, not anybody can use a safe-deposit box, just the renter and an alternate; they only have the alternate in case of this kind of thing, unexpected death. Szell was his father's alternate, and what's going on now is that his people are trying to figure out how dangerous it would be to try and sneak him into America for a day or two. Would the safety factor be too high? That's their problem. Personally, I think he's got to come, he hasn't got a choice, he can't let his fortune rot."

Safety factor, Babe was thinking, safe factor, and then he said, "Before, you said that Szell 'naturally' started off with gold. Why the 'naturally'?"

"Obvious reasons—he was famous for it—he'd knock it out of the Jews' teeth, they never found much gold in the Auschwitz ovens. Szell was a dentist."

Babe stuck his head up over the seat then. "He's not coming to America, Mr. Janeway. He's come already. He's here."

Janeway turned around and looked at Babe a moment. Then he went back to his driving. "No," he said after a while. "We'd have heard something." A while later he said, "And put your head back down." And a while after that: "What makes you think so?"

"Because it was a dentist damn near killed me, not Karl and Erhard."

"Go on." There was an excitement starting now in Janeway's voice. Babe could sense it rising.

"He just kept saying the same thing to me over and over: 'Is it safe? Is it safe?' "

"What did he look like—did he have blue eyes?—did he have the gray hair?—"

"Oh God, the eyes yes, they were incredibly blue, but he was bald, totally bald, except that—"

"Except that doesn't mean a damn thing, he could have shaved it off! *Go on.*"

"He was just so good. He was so incredibly experienced when it came to hurting me—he knew just when I'd pass out, he could tell exactly what I was going to do right before I did it."

"Then the 'is it safe' business—that meant, 'Is it safe for me to get the diamonds—is it safe for me, Christian Szell, in America, to go to the bank?' because once he picks up those diamonds, anybody robs him is going to pick up a lot of money, fifty million, maybe five times fifty million, and you don't pay taxes on it," and then he was going on in triumph, "Son of a bitch, the bastard's here and scared shitless about making his move!" Janeway was almost shouting now. "I'd be scared shitless too, because once he leaves the bank with that goddamn fortune, he's helpless—he can't very well go to the cops and tell them he was robbed!"

"I still don't get where I fit in."

"Obviously, the son of a bitch must think your brother told you something before he died."

"You're saying Doc was involved with Szell?"

"All our work cuts both ways—sometimes we sell secrets to other countries—no sweat, because we know they know our secrets. Szell stayed alive by ratting on other Nazis. So when there'd be raids to get him, he'd have word in advance and get out in time. Over a thousand of them have been brought to trial, and I'd guess Szell's responsible for anywhere between twenty-five and fifty. Your brother was Szell's contact. Erhard would get the diamonds from Szell's father and he'd take them to your brother and he'd get them to Europe on one of his trips. To Edinburgh. There was a guy there, in antiques—he was the one always did the selling. There were rumors for years that he was ripping off Szell—you know, selling something for a half a million, turning over four hundred fifty thousand, like that, but he was so good at knowing where the market was strongest, he kept the job. Anyway, like I said, it was only rumors about the rip-off. Then he'd give the cash to a courier and it would go down to Paraguay and Szell. That was more or less the operation." Janeway turned another corner, picked up speed. "Tom, I'm going to ask you something now, and please, you're going to have to tell me the truth, I don't care how hard it is."

"Anything."

"*Stop protecting your brother*—it's clear you must be—he should have been dead when he got torn apart, I know about wounds, remember that, and I examined the body, remember that too. He must have wanted to see you so much he stayed alive for just one reason, to tell you something, something incredibly important. He wouldn't have done what he did just to shout 'Babe' a couple of times and then keel over. Okay. Now's the time. Let it out, it's crucial: What did he say?"

Babe lay quietly on the floor in the back. "I've told you everything important that happened, I swear."

"Maybe something unimportant, then—he's dead, he doesn't need your protection any more, and nothing you can say is going to shock me, people say terrible things in my business, I've heard about how dangerous he was, how he was a double agent, how he was a thief, a raving homosexual, you name it I've heard it about him, and I'll bet he heard worse about me, but we're dealing with a fucking Nazi now, we could try swimming through all the blood he's spilled and never make it all the way across to the other side, so for Christ's sake, *what did he tell you*?"

"Nothing . . ."

"Shit," Janeway said, and he slammed down on the brakes till the car stopped.

Babe stuck his head up.

They were back where they'd started, by the boarded-up house, and both Karl and Erhard were waiting. "I couldn't make him talk," Janeway said, getting out of the car. "He's Szell's now."

*"No,"* Babe screamed. *"You killed them!"*

"You're much too trusting," Janeway said, "and it's going to cause you grief someday." Again the quick smile. "Welcome to someday."

Karl reached in for Babe. Babe had nothing left to fight with. Three minutes later he was strapped back in the chair.

# PART IV

# DEATH OF A MARATHON MAN

# 23

"Hurry it up," Janeway said as Karl and Erhard finished strapping Babe into immobility. "One of you go get Szell."

Karl looked at Janeway. "You do not give me orders."

"Oh, come on, come on," Erhard said, limping off. "We've no time." Karl followed him.

Babe just stared up at Janeway. "It was all lies, wasn't it, all a lot of crap about you being this buddy of Doc." Janeway said nothing for a moment, and as he watched him, Babe couldn't catch much Gatsby resemblance any more. What Janeway really looked like was the Nixon lawyer Dean—a pilot fish they called him. A thing that hung around the biggest shark for power.

"Scylla was a romantic fool, it killed him eventually. He was always trying to overpower his love objects with the breadth of his passion. Every lover he ever had was unfaithful to him. He was never as friendly with me as he thought—business before pleasure, didn't someone once say something like that?" The dazzling smile again, and now Gatsby was back. "Who do you think got him involved with Szell?"

Again, the footsteps in the hall.

And just as Karl and Erhard had stiffened at their sound, so did Janeway now. Gatsby gone, the pilot fish returned.

"I'll leave you," Janeway said, and then Babe and Szell were alone in the room. Otherwise, things were much the same: bright lamps, clean towels, the black leather case resting close. Szell stood at the sink, washing his hands. Done, he shook them, dried them with a towel. Then he brought them under the brightest lamp and examined them carefully. Evidently, something displeased him, because he went back to the sink and scrubbed again, harder than before. This time, when he was finished, he brought his hands back under the light and started talking. "You must pardon me, I am terribly fastidious, it is, you could say, my fetish. Where I live, I have my own laundress each and every day. She is greatly gifted." He took another towel, dried his hands, turned to Babe now. "So you are Scylla's brother."

Babe didn't answer.

"Oh please—now is our time for conversation; pain is in great part mental, and believe me, there will be plenty of that coming up for you. But now, I think it would be pleasant if we talked. Would you like to know how you were taken in? The bullets were blanks, the knife had a retractable blade, only effective if you don't look too long or too closely, but if you don't, most effective indeed, wouldn't you agree?"

Babe said nothing.

Szell walked over to him. " 'Thomas Babington,' Janeway reports. After, of course, the great British historian. What do people call you? 'Tom,' I expect."

Babe closed his eyes.

"I tell you something: I understand your having a certain aversion to me, but you see, *I* want to chat and *I* am in command just now, but I would never force my presence on someone who did not want it. Therefore, if you do not wish to speak to me, fine, if that pleases you; but if I wish to excavate more deeply into your cavity, then also fine, if that pleases me."

Very quickly Babe opened his eyes and said, "Why do you have so little accent? I know about languages, and it's very hard to hide the German."

Szell almost smiled. "Janeway alerted me that you were smart, but even I did not expect such an opening foray. 'What are you going to do with me?' would have been expected. Perhaps some queries concerning your brother. But you have found my pride first shot, and for that I salute you."

"I'm just interested in languages, that's all, it's part of social history," Babe said. Then: "What *are* you going to do to me?"

"Bad things," Szell promised, and, going on without a pause, he said, "I had alexia as a child, which is a disease—"

"I know about alexia, it's where you can't understand written speech."

"Very impressive," Szell said.

"No, it's just I kind of don't mind studying so I do it a lot, English and psychology I minored in actually, it's all related to history. What bad things, couldn't you just tell me now, I'm not all that crazy about surprises."

"We were speaking of alexia and my childhood problems, and I would never change such a subject, since, first of all, you asked the question, and, second and more important, your fear is growing as we talk, you are already anticipating pain, and I would guess your cavity is aching worse than two minutes before. Don't bother answering."

"It is," Babe said.

"It was very hard for me—I don't expect sympathy from a Jew, but you can clearly understand that my childhood was not a particularly pleasant time, since here I was, brilliant, I *knew* I was brilliant, I was positive, but everyone around me thought me backward, if not actually retarded. At any rate, I have always hated written speech—my penmanship, you would call it, is still in the scrawl stage, I loathe etymology, philology, but morphology I find fascinating. I assume you know what that is too."

Babe nodded.

"Well then, there you have it. Inflections fascinate me. I love the vernacular. Plus one more thing."

"What's that?"

"I've spent the last quarter century and more in South America, and there isn't much to do down there. If you're not a revolutionary, it's a very dull place. So I speak German, naturally, and naturally, Spanish, and also French and British and American. I am at the present time learning to speak Italian, and then, alas for me, it will all be over, I am too old to start Chinese."

"Russian," Babe said.

"You betray your youth," Szell said. "As an historian you have gaps that need filling. After what we did to the Russians, I might just as profitably learn Hebrew." Szell shook his head. "I was surrounded by madmen." He looked at Babe and started laughing. "That must strike you as being humorous, since I'm quite sure you consider *me* a madman."

"I really don't, no," Babe said. "Listen, we all have our little quirks, you say you're innocent, that's good enough for me." He nodded as reassuringly as he thought feasible, considering the circumstances.

"I have not been innocent since I was twelve years old and had my way with a chambermaid. I never said I was innocent. I merely say that I was never involved in any lunatic fancies. Whichever T.P. came under my care was there for a sound, viable reason."

"T.P.?"

"Test person. We called them that in the experimental block. How is your tooth, hurting very badly?"

Babe nodded.

"Are you hoping someone will rescue you?"

Babe nodded again.

"Possible but doubtful. Never lose hope. My father owned this building, and Erhard and Karl are the sole tenants. Next door the warehouse is unused. Keep hoping, please. It makes the pain expand. Once one stops aspiring, one becomes sluggish, a derelict. It is very difficult to force the truth from such a person."

"I've *told* you the truth," Babe said. "I've told you and I've told Janeway. A hundred times. I don't know anything."

"I paid your brother very well, top commission for bringing the diamonds to Scotland. I trusted him for such an exercise; Jews are only to be trusted when it comes to money. You may have different feelings, fine, I do not choose to argue. But they can only be trusted with limited amounts. Scylla worked for me for years, but once my father died, it was a different thing. I think your brother planned to kill me after I left the bank and take my diamonds, what do you think?"

"I don't know anything about anything," Babe said.

"You see, I do not believe you. Your brother was trustworthy because he loved money. He was, after all, an American, and that is something of a national trait; an exaggeration, certainly, but not totally without foundation. Scylla was a courier for me, and a splendid one, powerful, armed, alert, all but impossible to rob. He received for his services much money, but always bit by bit over the years. Some now, more then. But the day of thousands is done; we have quantum jumped. Now we are into millions beyond dreaming. Now we are dealing with a different Scylla, and he cared, I am led to believe, for you, and he died, I am led to believe, in your arms, and so therefore it must not be overlooked that you would perhaps know something, perhaps only a little, perhaps a great deal, perhaps all—was he, for example, planning anything, and if he was, was he planning to do it alone, and if not, who else had he gone into business with, and since he is no longer with us, will they stop *or does the plan stay in effect regardless*, am I going to be robbed when I leave the bank—perhaps you could clarify some of these questions for me."

Babe's cavity was steady with pain now; he could tell the talk would be ending soon. "I don't know."

"For the last and final and, I promise you, ultimate time: *Is it safe to get my diamonds?*"

There was nothing Babe could say.

Szell opened the black leather case.

And took out a portable hand drill.

"Probably you have been thinking," Szell said, busying himself with the equipment, "that you have been running in bad luck, having a cavity already sore for me to pick at. It would not be unreasonable for such a thought to have crossed your mind. If it has, let me tell you that, in point of fact, you were lucky, not the other way around."

Babe's heart would not stay in place. He remembered a bird from his childhood. It had gotten so excited when a cat came to its cage that it fluttered and screeched for a wild moment and then toppled, dead, its poor heart unable to stand the menace.

Babe wondered about his own heart, because this menace was very clearly growing. Szell plugged in the drill, switched it on experimentally, then quickly off once he determined it was working. He reached into the leather case again and removed what looked like a good-sized nail. He put the sharp end into the drill, locked it in place, called for Karl.

"His head," Szell indicated quietly when Karl was in the room and the door shut again. "Very steady. It must be *very* steady this time, Karl, no movement at all, yes?"

Karl took Babe's head between his big hands and exerted really a tremendous amount of pressure. Babe was helpless. No, he had been helpless all this while, he was only more helpless now. But was that possible? He tried forcing his good brain into concentrating on that particular subject.

No good.

His mind was not his to control now. He could only stare at the drill and the nailheadlike object sticking out of it.

Szell saw his fascination. "A diamond stone," he said, indicating the nailhead. "A portable hand drill, obtainable at, I should think, any first-class hardware store, and an ordinary diamond stone, an absolutely standard dental tool. That is the beauty of it all, *the ease of availability*. Back at the camp, I tried getting that point across, but Mengele was so obsessed with his lunatic notion of breeding a race of blue-eyes that he ignored the implications of what I was trying to get through—but then, I told you he was a madman, what could any one expect? But, you see, throughout combat over the centuries, a captured spy was of value only if he spoke the truth, and you know about iron maidens in the Middle Ages and testicle shock in more modern times, but they don't work—they have no *build* to them. You're feeling fine, then you're in agony, and if they keep it up you die, and if they stop the pain eases, and it really could have all been so simply solved if Mengele had listened. You see, *anyone* can do to you what I'm about to do to you—a few days of training is more than enough, and if Mengele had listened, there would not have been a captive able to resist us, because a newly cut nerve is much more sensitive than the one I touched in your cavity before—that nerve was already in the act of dying before I began."

"You're going to cut a nerve?"

"A live nerve, yes, a healthy one. I'll just drill straight into a perfectly healthy tooth and in no time at all I'll reach the pulp."

Pulp. Babe registered the word.

"The inner substance of your teeth," Szell said. "With a young person like yourself, the pulp is easily reachable. It shouldn't take me more than a minute. Drilling into a healthy tooth isn't all that dreadful, except in this case the drill will cause a good bit of heat, and of course that won't help you much, but until we reach the pulp it should be more or less bearable. The pulp is where the nerves are. It's really a complex of blood vessels and nerve fibers, veins and arteries and lymphatic tissue all intertwined—don't worry, though, there won't be a lot of bleeding—oh, I'm not saying there won't be a drop or two, but no more," and with that he started drilling straight into the front of Babe's biggest tooth, the upper left incisor in the center of his mouth.

Babe stood it.

Szell kept on drilling.

A little heat from the drill now.

More heat.

Szell bent closer.

Babe wanted to scream, but wouldn't give Szell the satisfaction.

Szell kept at it.

Babe screamed.

"I told you the heat would be uncomfortable," Szell explained. "Just a few more seconds and we should be through to the pulp."

*"I don't know what you want—Christ wouldn't I tell you if I knew?"*

"Your brother was very strong. Strength is an inherited trait. No. I'm sorry, but I'm afraid we won't know the extent of your knowledge until we're well into the pulp. You'll tell me everything then."

"I've *told* you everything."

"Quite so." He went back to his drilling.

Babe was tensed to scream again, but it wasn't that bad this time, the heat hadn't developed to a point beyond bearing. And then, surprisingly, no more than a few seconds after he had begun, Szell turned the drill off.

"We're at the edge of the pulp now," Szell said. "You told

me before you didn't like surprises, and I was just being helpful. Now, in just a moment you'll understand how right I was when I said that a nerve in an existing cavity is infinitely duller than a good fresh one. I don't think there's anything to equal a good fresh one, especially in a young person like yourself. Tell me if you think I'm right."

He drilled into the pulp.

Babe started to cry. It wasn't something he had any control over. There were suddenly tears of affliction criss-crossing down, and Szell seemed not at all surprised, only nodded and kept going deeper into the pulp.

Babe was half unconscious when Szell stopped.

"Care to see a nerve?" he asked Karl. "It's all right, he needs a moment, let his head alone."

Karl took his hands away, allowing Babe's head to go limp. Gently, Szell took Babe's face and opened his mouth. "That red is a nerve," Szell said softly. "Didn't know that, did you?"

Karl made a negative sound.

Without the drilling the pain was considerably less. Babe lay quietly, head limp. It was important to keep that from Szell.

Only Szell knew, because at that exact moment he said, "All right, back to it," and again Karl stationed the head, and again Szell drilled, and again Babe cried. This time when Szell stopped, he did not allow Karl to release his grip; this time Babe's respite was shorter.

In the silence, Babe managed, ". . . How . . . how can . . . you do this? . . ."

"*How?* Shall I give you one old Jew's answer? A wise

man. He said this: 'We were not for them the same.' You are not quite, for me, human."

After the third session, Babe begged, ". . . Kill me . . ."

"A Jew cannot die when *he* will, only when *we* will" was all Szell answered. Then they went back to it.

After the seventh session, Szell shouted for Erhard and Janeway. "He didn't know—he told me nothing—if he had known, he would have told me, we've wasted time, get rid of him."

Babe was only barely conscious in the chair.

"Kill him, you mean?" Karl asked, making sure.

"How would you like it to happen?" from Erhard.

*"Do once something right without me!"* Szell thundered, patient no more.

# 24

Almost before Szell had slammed the door, they started bickering. "Unstrap him," Janeway said.

Erhard limped to the chair and started to work, but Karl did not move. He stared at Janeway. "I have told you already, I do not tell you a third time: Keep your orders."

Janeway stared right back at the bigger man. "You pick him up, and don't give me any goddamned static."

"Oh come on, come on," Erhard said, releasing the last of the straps. "Karl, you're the strongest, you handle the boy; it would be no trouble for you, not with your power." Karl liked to be reminded of his might; Erhard did it as often as necessary.

Karl grabbed one of Babe's arms, pulled it around his thick neck, dragged Babe from the chair. Babe was dead weight. "Walk!" Karl said, and Babe tried to make his feet move. Karl was still doing the bulk of the work, but every so often Babe was able to take a half step on his own.

Janeway opened the door and Erhard hurried on ahead, limping along the corridor, holding the door that led down the stairs. As they approached it, Babe was able to walk a little on his own, but the stairs were too much for him; he stumbled, almost fell, surely would have if Karl had ever let him go. "Banister!" Karl said, and Babe reached out, took it with his free hand, and by the time they got to the bottom, he could almost keep his balance.

Erhard was the first to the street, Janeway following, Karl and Babe the last. "We'll use my car," Erhard said, and he gestured toward the corner. "Come on, come on," and he limped ahead. He liked to do that, Janeway noted, take the lead. Whenever they were going anyplace and Erhard knew the destination, he was always first. "Come on, come on," he liked to say, and Janeway never objected; let Erhard have his little triumphs, it hurt nothing.

Karl, though, was a different matter. Back upstairs when Erhard had said that Karl was the strongest, it had nettled Janeway. Not that in a pure weightlifting contest Karl wouldn't have been victor, but put them in a darkened alleyway and Janeway knew Karl wouldn't have survived half a minute. Probably that was ego talking—he hadn't been an active Provider for several years now, and desk work took a certain amount away from you. Karl might have survived fifty seconds with him now, he had probably slowed that much. Why did he loathe Karl so? Probably a natural contempt any species has for a lower form, coupled with vast differences in tastes, entertainment, lusts.

They turned the corner and entered the dark side street. "Come on, come on," Erhard said from up ahead.

"Did you park in Jersey, for Chrissakes?" Janeway said, angry at even having been ordered to go along. Surely these two failures could have finished the boy. Szell must have been particularly furious that his methods hadn't worked; otherwise he would never have humiliated Janeway by forcing him to go along on something as trivial as this.

"It's just a little more, come on, come on."

"You take him now, your turn," Karl said.

Janeway ignored him.

Karl muttered something then, probably "fag" in German.

Janeway decided not to hear that too.

Karl's irritation was growing; he pushed Babe. "Walk—you can walk."

Babe did his best. At first he slipped, but then he got the hang of it, managed tiny steps, didn't fall again, as he had almost done coming down the stairs.

"Here we are," Erhard said, "just one second more and we'll be ready to go." The car was an old Ford, and Erhard took a bunch of keys from his pocket, searched around in the darkness to find the right one.

"You *locked* this thing?" Janeway said incredulously.

"Here is a terrible neighborhood," Erhard tried to explain. "Everyone always steals everything, and this is a wonderful car, never one moment's trouble, not once in now twelve years."

"If it's so goddamn wonderful, why can't you Jesus Christ get it open?" Not necessary. Nothing gained insulting a cretin like Erhard; if you must insult a cretin, insult Karl, who was standing stupidly watching by the hood of the car, which Babe lay silently sprawled across.

"Here, here, I've got it now, no need for trouble," Erhard said, and he put the key into the lock, jiggled it.

"Don't force it," Karl said, "—last time you forced it it was the trunk key—don't do that again—"

"Nothing is being forced," Erhard said, and then, a second later, "Dammit," and Janeway angrily moved to him, saying, "Give it to me, just let me have it, I'll open the stupid thing," but Karl said, "You don't know this car, I've ridden in it, I've driven it, I know how to open it," and he grabbed the keys from Erhard as Babe rolled off the car hood and tried to stagger away, but Janeway saw him immediately and said to Karl, "You were supposed to stay with the boy, go get him," but Karl said, "I'm doing the keys and from you, no orders," so Erhard said, "Oh I'll do it, just get the door open," and he went limping to retrieve Babe.

"Outrun by a cripple," Babe thought, reeling like a Bowery drunk along the dark street; that's some finish for a marathon man, all right, the perfect epitaph. "Here lies Thomas Babington Levy, 1948–1973, Caught by a Cripple."

Well, of course, there were circumstances. Obviously Erhard wouldn't have had a chance if he'd been in shape, but it had been a while since he'd slept, and what Szell had done to him didn't help his cause any either, and now as he tried to make his inept way, the pain was with him, because every time he tried to inhale, the night air hit the holes in his teeth and attacked the open nerves, and, of course, the street was hard and filled with sharp dark things and he didn't have shoes on to protect him, he was still in his pajamas, a helpless creep just like the stoop gang always said, staggering along with a cripple closing the gap behind him—something jammed into his foot then, something that hurt enough to penetrate into his brain deeper than the air against the nerves, and Babe hoped it wasn't broken glass but only maybe a rock that would hurt like crazy but not lay his foot open to even more serious pain. He should stop, he knew, he really should, because then he could tell himself, "Hell, he never woulda caught me, I stopped, no cripple catches a marathon man," but then he wasn't a marathon man, what kind of a marathon man would go around barefoot?

*Bikila!*

Abebe Bikila, the great Ethiopian cop who ran the Olympics in Japan, and in the documentary of that Olympics Babe had cried, because the Russians were the favorites with all their power and their doctors and their special diets, and the Germans were right up there too, and everybody ignored the black Ethiopian, or if they didn't, they laughed, because not only was he alone, he didn't even have shoes, he was going to try to run the whole damn 26 miles 385 yards barefoot, *barefoot* in the twentieth century, for God's sake, and the race started and the Russians were tough, but the Germans were no pushovers, and then after maybe ten miles they tried their moves, but the Russians weren't *just* tough, they were *too* tough, and the Germans fell back, and now the Russians had it all and it was only a matter of jockeying it correctly so that the right man finished first and the right man finished second, because they were very big on that in sports, the Russians, if you put in your years, you got your victory, even if a younger man was better, because his time would come, and then from way back there was this little noise, this kind of murmur, no louder than that, because you didn't have big crowds at marathon runs, at the start yes, at the end yes, because they were both in the stadium, but during the race there were always only just a few people standing around watching the nuts sweat, because you had to be a nut to flog your body into that kind of effort, and fifteen miles along the third Russian began to realize that something kind of odd was taking place and he glanced around and here came this skinny black guy *with no shoes* and moving up fast and the third Russian picked up his speed and then all three Russians were in this kind of conference as they ran along and the news was being passed, there was this *thing* back there, this really weird kind of happening was taking place back there, on account of this barefoot guy was *gaining* on them, so the Russians picked up the pace, made it matchless, they could do that, they had trained to do that, they had run right and eaten right and the right doctors had done the right things and when they had to crush you, you were crushed, and after twenty miles this barefoot guy passed the third Russian and now there were only two to go and the Russians had to do something, so they let it out full, six miles to go, and they turned it on, everything, and whoever was behind them had to fall back or burn himself out, and that's what happened to all the runners except this black guy, who didn't even have shoes, because what he did when the Russians turned it on full was something no one had ever done before, *he* turned it on fuller, and the Russians were standing still, they weren't even snails as this barefoot guy they'd all been mocking two hours before went by, sailed by, zoomed by, jetted by, triumphed by, and when he hit the main stadium the crowd started screaming like they hadn't screamed for a marathon man since Nurmi, and now there were two in the pantheon, two legends, Nurmi and the barefoot genius from Ethiopia, the great Bikila, and . . . and "Screw it," Babe thought, "I'm not getting caught by no cripple." So what if his foot hurt and his teeth caused constant pain? When you were a real marathon man, you did whatever needed doing.

At great cost, Babe picked up his pace just a little.

From behind him Erhard shouted, "I can't catch him."

Janeway glanced up from the car and saw the boy running perhaps half a block away, heading toward the river and the West Side Highway. "You!" he said to Karl. "You give me those goddamn keys and *get him*!"

Janeway's words echoed along the dark street, and Babe knew it was the brute after him now, big Karl. Well, Karl was strong, strong like the Russians had been, but Bikila had beaten the Russians, and Babe knew that if just his teeth would stop destroying him, he could put Karl away easy, because Karl seemed like an arm man, big through the chest and shoulders, sure, but not in the legs, no power, no endurance, and Babe took his right hand and put it over his mouth, because if he could keep the night air from hitting the open nerves directly, he could cut the pain—

—bad idea—

—because it also threw him off balance, and he had run all these years to get that right, that was all running was really, proper balance so you didn't tire, you learned to protect your body from fatigue by using it correctly, and the arms were the key to balance, and when he put his right hand over his mouth his balance went, his left arm had nothing on the other side to set up the countering rhythm, and Babe could hear Karl's heavy footsteps gaining on him as he did his best to run with less pain, but no balance either.

Karl was closing.

Forget the pain, Babe thought, and he shoved his tongue up over his front teeth and that was some warmth, some protection, and pumping with his arms, he held Karl's footsteps even.

Then he picked up the pace a little bit more, and Karl's sounds grew softer.

"Help!" Karl called out, panting.

"Shit," Janeway said, and then he left the car and started to run.

And could he move.

Babe could tell from the quickness of the footsteps that this was it. He had the lead, sure, but could he hold it, and for how long?

Ahead now was the Hudson, and Babe turned his corner and hesitated a moment, not sure at first whether to try to go uptown or down, where was salvation, and of course it wasn't anyplace, but he chose uptown, because no more than a couple of blocks away in the dark night was an entrance to the West Side Highway, a steep incline, a hill, and Babe was always good at hills, if he could just beat Janeway to the incline he knew he could hold him off, because in college when he ran cross-country he did great on hills, not so sensational on the flat, because he didn't have natural speed, but other guys panicked when they saw a rise coming.

Not Babe.

Janeway had already cut his lead deeply. He glanced back,

and Karl had passed Erhard, but Janeway had already passed Karl, and there they all were, his three Fates. Babe ducked his head and started pumping his arms with all he had, because Janeway was just slaughtering him. Janeway was faster, no question about that, but there was one thing nobody knew, and that was could Janeway go the distance, could he take it when his lungs were burning? Probably not, Babe thought, he doesn't look like a marathon man to me, he looks like a sprinter, a guy who'll kill you for a while, but if you can just hold him off until it starts hurting, you got him, and Babe was only a block from the incline entrance now but Janeway was less than half that behind Babe, and gaining as Babe saw Nurmi up ahead shaking his head at him, and that wasn't fair, Nurmi shouldn't judge him off tonight's performance, when he was in shape he could run with anybody, and Bikila was jogging barefooted alongside Nurmi and he was shaking his head too and starting to laugh and that *really* wasn't fair, Bikila should know better than to humiliate a fellow marathon man because he had been mocked at Tokyo but he had shown them and all right you bastard, Babe thought, go on, laugh at me, I'll show you, and he picked up the pace as much as he possibly could and then went a notch even over that.

But he couldn't shake Janeway.

How far behind? Eighty feet? Sixty now? The incline too far ahead. He's too fast for me, I can't handle him, and then Bikila dropped back beside him, saying, "Of course you can," and Babe said, "You shouldn't have laughed at me," and Bikila said, "I would never laugh at a marathon man, I was laughing at them, thinking they could beat one of us with a sprinter," and Babe felt better when he heard that, but not enough to keep Janeway from sprinting closer still, and the test of the heart was coming now, and ordinarily Babe would have relished it, but not now, not in this pain, and he did what he could to hold Janeway even until Nurmi came alongside him, he and Bikila flanking Babe now, and Nurmi said, "In Finland once I broke a bone in my foot but I never let on, I would have died before I limped, no one knows what's in your heart, only you, your heart and your brain, that's all we have to battle Time," and Babe said, "I can't think, the air hurts so, I don't know how to act, what to do," so Nurmi said, "Slow down, begin to lose your rhythm, do that and do it now," so Babe slowed for a few steps and then Nurmi said, "Fly," and Babe took off for as long as he could and Bikila said, "He doesn't know what you're doing now, sprinters have no brains, God gave them speed but they cannot think, once you get them thinking they're done," and perhaps it was true, because now Janeway's footsteps for the first time started to recede and Babe said, "I beat him, I did it," but Nurmi said, "Not yet, he'll try his burst, he'll give whatever he has," and Bikila said, "If you hold him off he's done, but you must do that, we cannot do it for you," and Babe said, "Will you at least stay with me?" and Bikila said, "Of course, we are all marathon men, only we understand pain," and Nurmi said, "He's coming!"

And he was.

With every step, Janeway closed, and Babe said, "I'm sorry, I can't, but please, don't leave me, I'm done," and then Bikila was shouting at him, "He's starting to wobble—listen—his rhythm is going—keep on, keep *on*," but Babe replied, "It hurts too much, I'm burning up inside," and that made Nurmi angry, "Of course you're burning up inside, you're supposed to burn up inside, and you keep going, you burst through the pain barrier, I did it, that's why I was the greatest runner," and Babe said, "I would have beaten you, it's true, if I'd had the chance to live long enough, I would have brought you down—"

—Janeway brought Babe down then.

With one final desperate dive at the start of the incline, he launched himself across the night and barely grazed Babe's ankle, but it was enough to send them both sprawling groggily.

"Up, man!" Bikila cried. "Up and be quick about it, he's a sprinter and that was all he had, he's done, he'll never catch you if you start to move," and Babe was on all fours, dizzy, as Nurmi said, "I thought you were supposed to be so wonderful with inclines, well, here's an incline, run it, or would you rather just stay here and listen to him gasp?"—

—it was true—Janeway was gasping, pulling the night air deep into his lungs as he tried to rise.

Babe hobbled to his feet. His ankle hurt like hell and his face had scraped along the pavement, but he knew the sound of a beaten runner when he heard it, and that was all Janeway was now, an also-ran, and so what if the incline was steep, Babe had beaten hills with twice the angle, and behind him he could hear Janeway calling, "Get the car—the car!" but by that time Babe was halfway up the incline and increasing his speed, something both Bikila and Nurmi noted, and don't think that didn't give Babe a shot in the arm; I'm a marathon man, he thought, a real one, and you better not mess with us because if you do you'll get in nothing but big trouble.

Then *Jesus*, Babe thought suddenly—*they're coming for me in the car.*

They'll be roaring up the incline at ninety miles an hour and what the hell am I gonna do? He ran along the right edge of the West Side Highway going uptown, trying to think of some way to escape them, because once they got the car they had him, so do something, *do something*—but what?

In the end, what he did was altogether brilliant.

Oh, not brilliant like Einstein or Sir Isaac or Orville and Wilbur, but still, considering the fact that he didn't have all year to noodle ideas around, he had no cause for taking a back seat to anybody.

What he did was, without warning, simply hurry across the elevated highway, step over the yard-high divider, and start running in just the opposite direction, downtown.

He had entered the highway uptown at 57th Street, and the first downtown exit was quite handy, 56th Street; actually, it couldn't have been much handier.

It was three minutes before Janeway and the others drove onto the incline heading uptown. Babe watched them from the downtown incline, standing deep in shadow.

He wasn't all that sure, but he thought the first exit they could possibly take if they figured out what he'd done was all the way up to either 72nd or 79th.

The exit was, in point of fact, at 72nd Street, but by the time they had passed 66th Janeway had realized what Babe must have done. Realizing it and acting on the realization were not quite the same thing. There was nothing for Janeway to do but mutter "Shit!" so frequently as to make it sound like a Druid incantation while he waited in wild frustration for 72nd Street to put in its appearance. When it did, he wheeled off the Highway going uptown, made several sharp turns, got back on the Highway heading downtown. He raced along it until he came to the 56th Street exit, which he assumed Babe must have taken. And so did he.

But by that time Babe was heading safely, at least for the moment, away. He was sweating and his teeth hurt and his ankle was throbbing, but he had, at least for the moment, and at their own game, beaten them.

He wasn't his brother's brother for nothing.

# 25

On the seventh ring, she answered. "Yes?"

"Elsa—"

"Who?—"

"Listen—"

"Tom?—"

"Yes, but you gotta listen, there's no time—"

"You're all right?—at least tell me that—"

"Yes, fine, and I know it isn't even five and I woke you, but you gotta do something for me, Elsa, I *need* you, you're the only shot I have."

"Of course."

"Get a car."

"A motorcar, you mean? To go someplace?"

"Elsa, please wake up—yes, a motorcar, yes, to go someplace, I don't know where, but I have to buy some time, I have to think, bad, I'm in trouble and I want to get where it's quiet."

"I'll get one. Somehow. Where should I meet you?"

Babe looked across the large living room, then, as Biesenthal, in his Liberty robe, entered carrying a tray with two steaming cups of instant coffee. "There's an all-night pharmacy, Kaufman's—Forty-ninth and Lex, I think, in that area—it'll still be dark, so keep your doors locked, I don't want anyone trying anything on you. Six o'clock. That's about an hour. Got it all?"

"Kaufman's. Forty-ninth and Lex. Six o'clock. Do you care for me?"

"What?" Biesenthal was watching him closely.

"When I came to see you before, you said you didn't but you would again. Do you again? If you do, say it, or I don't get the car."

"I care for you, I care for you, g'bye." He hung up. "Sorry if it got a little mushy toward the end there," Babe said, crossing toward Biesenthal and the coffee tray.

Biesenthal sat on the sofa, holding his cup in his lap. "A man in my position doesn't get exposed to a great deal of mush. I don't find it unpalatable, in small doses, just be sure that—"

"Father?"

Babe turned. A stunning Jewish Princess stood in the doorway, robed and lovely, large-eyed, the proper olive skin, the long, dark hair.

"Is everything all right?"

Biesenthal looked at her. "Do you mean am I in dire physical peril? I don't think Tom's out to hurt me." He stood, made the quick introduction. "My daughter Melissa, Tom Levy."

"Father's spoken of you," she said. Then, turning, "Excuse me." Then she was gone.

"Bright child, senior at Barnard, she'll be Phi Bete barring a complete collapse. She wants to be an archaeologist, but then, she also wanted to go to Bryn Mawr. I stopped that,

I'll stop this—she should be more than contented looking after *my* bones in my dotage, don't you think that's fair? I tell you, the poets are always declaiming on the power of love, but for sheer brute strength, it's incest all the way."

Levy wasn't listening. Everything was changing too fast. Once he would have stammered a greeting to that girl; now he didn't even bother with a nod. Once he would have savored the fact that Biesenthal had actually mentioned him to his family; now he only reached for his coffee and took a sip, but the steaming liquid attacked the holes in his teeth, hit his nerves, and he cried out, managed to get the cup back to the tray without spilling too much of it. He put his tongue over his wounds, helping the soothing process along. "Sorry," he muttered finally.

"And you still won't let me be of help, you won't speak to me of your trouble?"

"I never said there was trouble. I never told you I was in any."

Biesenthal put down his cup and began to stalk the large room. "Oh, come now, sir, we are neither of us chowderheads, there is a distinct shortage of horses' asses in the immediate area, so I should like to think you would at least give me the credit of knowing distress when it brushes me before five o'clock in the morning. Consider: I am awakened by my wife, who has been awakened by the night doorman, who has, I'm sure, been awakened by your pounding on the locked door of the building. Message? A young creature clad solely in pajamas cannot pay his taxi, would I mind taking care of that? I inquire after the pajamaed loony's name, find him to be a student of mine as well as the son of a dear, dear friend; now, when faced with that decision, who needs a few hours' sleep or a few dollars? Down I go, pay the driver, up we come, I inquire, 'What is all this, what's wrong?' and you reply, 'Nothing, nothing, can I please use your phone?' Note, Levy, that I always give credit where it's due: You *did* say please."

"I'm sorry, and I did come here for a reason, but telling you my situation sure wasn't it. And neither was the money, but I did have to go someplace where I could get the guy paid—he was sort of cruising half asleep on Twelfth Avenue by the docks and I ran in front of his car or he never would have stopped—I don't think he knew the word 'apparition,' but he figured that's what I was so he said, 'Yes sir, yes sir,' when I gave your address, and did we make time. I came here because there were other circumstances involved, but you've been terrific, putting up with me like you have, and I really thank you."

"There's nothing else I can do?"

"I'd love some money—ten dollars for taxis and stuff, twenty if you have it."

"My wallet's still in my robe." He took it out and handed over twenty. Levy nodded thank you. "Is that the end?"

"No, I'd sure love an old raincoat or something, Professor Biesenthal, I feel like such a jerk moving around town in these pajamas."

"There's a raincoat in the foyer closet, yours when needed. Is that the end?"

"Yes sir."

"All right then; why did you really come here?"

"Why did I come here?" Levy said softly; then he shook his head, stopped dead silent.

"Pretend it's for your orals," Biesenthal said after a time, "make believe you have to answer *some*thing."

"Yes sir," Levy said, and he got up, moved to the window, looked out over Riverside Park. "I bet you can get a great view from here," he said.

"Particularly when the sun is up," Biesenthal replied.

Levy whirled on him: "I'm really smart, Professor Biesenthal; you may never get the chance to find if that's true, and I know I sound like an idiot, but I promise you, you never had anybody better when it comes to hitting the books, and what I'm about to say doesn't make sense, and when you're supposedly strong in the brain department as I am, it bugs you when you can't sort things out straight, but here's the thing, before my Dad died, *I* was the family dunce—I was only ten, but every teacher I had, I knew they felt I wasn't near what Doc was—"

"Doc?"

"Henry David—my brother—his first three years at Yale he led his class, no one had marks as good as Doc's in a decade, he was that smart, and he was getting better, he was going to be this genius lawyer, this defender of the downtrodden, demolishing tyrants whenever they had the guts to face him, and he was twenty when Dad died, and his senior year, well, naturally things slipped for him, it's shitty when your father kills himself, and somehow, without meaning to, *I* became the defender of the faith and *he* became the money grubber—I think, goddammit I *know*, we were both reacting to the same event, the shooting, and this guy who knew Doc, he said to me earlier tonight, 'Your father was guilty, wasn't he?' and I blasted him pretty good, lemme tell you, I set him straight, but now I know he must have gotten that from Doc, it's what Doc must have thought too, he went one way because of what he thought and I went the other, and I have to know something you can tell me, and that's, was he innocent, my old man?"

Biesenthal closed his eyes. "The guilt still lingers after all these years." He shook his head. "You know, the ecologists warn us that plastic takes hundreds of years before it disappears, decomposes. I think that's nothing, compared to guilt. Down it comes through the generations like an uncounted gene." He opened his eyes, looked at Babe. "But this isn't answering your question, is it, sir? You want to know was your father, the noted H. V. Levy, a commie-pinko-fellow-traveling-radical-red-filthy-bolshevik-bomb-thrower?" Biesenthal almost smiled, but sadly. "He was the perfect patsy, that's all he ever was: brighter than anyone had any right to be, and he seemed arrogant, and he *was* impatient, he never learned to suffer fools, and he tended to appear patronizing if you didn't realize that was just his insecurity being blanketed away, and he was the head of the History Department at a capital letters Eastern Establishment Ivy League University, and he had been invited to Washington by the Opposition Party, and he had a funny name, and he was Jewish. My God, half a dozen H. V. Levys and Joe McCarthy might have made President." Again the bright eyes closed. "How did Keats put it in the poem about Chapman's Homer? Cortez was Keats's image, when he first sees the Pacific. Your father was as innocent of charges as Cortez was of the Pacific's existence the moment before he found out it existed." The eyes opened, watched. "Sufficient?"

Babe nodded, went toward the foyer for the raincoat. It was too small, but not so much that you'd stop traffic with it.

Biesenthal followed. "Please let me help."

"You already have, you must know that."

"At least call the police. Or if you won't, let me do it for you."

"Police?" Babe blinked. "Police? Why would I call them, what good would that do?" He buttoned the raincoat. "I don't want justice, are you kidding, screw justice, we're way past justice, it's blood now. . . ."

He took a cab outside Biesenthal's building, took it to 96th and Amsterdam, got out, paid, hurried to the deepest shadows, and moved through them down to 95th. All of 95th was dark, the whole of it from Amsterdam to Columbus; with the delinquents that lived on this block, what chance did a light bulb have? Still, he stayed close to the building line as he crept toward his brownstone. Every so often, when he'd forget to keep his teeth covered, the night air would attack the nerves so he felt like crying out, but he kept control, simply sliding his tongue up over the injuries or covering his whole mouth with his hand, moving silently on. He had to get back into his apartment, if only for a minute; he needed to get there, everything hinged on that, but there was a good chance it was the single most monumentally stupid thing he could do, because New York was the Apple, a lot of places to hide, and the only place Janeway knew about was his apartment, so if Janeway was going to try to head him off, it would be there, at his place, in case he was dumb enough to try getting back, but there were risks you had to take, stupid or not, and *dammitall—*

—a car was double-parked several houses down from his building. It was too far yet to see if it was empty or not, and maybe it was just some drunken Spaniard who couldn't find a hydrant to sleep it off in front of, so he just passed out when he'd gone as far as he could.

Please be a drunken Spaniard, Babe thought as he took another few quiet steps. He never realized he could be so silent under pressure, and that was about to give him the kind of bucking-up-fear-banishing pride he needed a few bottles of right about then, until he realized it was pretty hard to be noisy when you were barefooted, and that's what he still was, a shoeless weirdo creeping down 95th Street in the night toward . . .

. . . toward what? Babe stood by a building, trying to tell as precisely as he could about the double-parked car. It was still too far and it was still too dark to be very specific, but this much was sure: There was a man inside. And he wasn't passed out, he was sitting there. A big man, probably. Maybe even as big as Karl.

And if it was Karl, he wouldn't be alone, Janeway would never have allowed something important to be Karl's job alone, so that meant Erhard too. Somewhere. In his mind now, through remembered pain, Babe vaguely heard Szell screaming at the three of them, '*Do once something right without me!*' so Janeway had to be around too, all of them in different darknesses, waiting.

Babe crept forward. A little more. A little more.

He stopped when he was as close as he dared, waiting for his eyes to get as accustomed as they could to their surroundings, and New York had millions of big guys, monsters like Karl, lumbering around, snorting hello to each other as they shouldered past the common folk into the subways each morning.

So this wasn't Karl. The odds were just too strong.

Babe stared. He froze his body and concentrated as much attention as he had left on the vehicle.

It was Karl all right.

Waiting.

Without a pause, Babe moved to the next brownstone, slipped silently up the steps and into the foyer, and began pushing the Melendez button as hard as he could. First there was nothing, no reply, so he kept at it, working the button with his thumb, jabbing at it, holding it down for a while, then jabbing again, stab, stab, stab, then hold, then stab, stab—

—suddenly this Spanish woman was screaming at him over the intercom.

"Listen . . ." Babe whispered, ". . . I can't talk loud, but if this is Mrs. Melendez I'm really sorry to bother you, but . . ."

Her scream built in insistence.

". . . I need your boy, your son . . ." His knowledge of Spanish was next to nil; beyond "Sangria" he was in deep trouble, but he had never had cause to regret his ignorance till now. ". . . Child," Babe said, "the young man, the . . . the . . ." what the hell else should he try, "bairn"? "urchin"? "scion"?

It didn't matter. With a final vituperative burst, she hung up.

Babe pushed again. He just jammed his thumb against the Melendez buzzer and kept it there.

This time when she came back she was really in full voice, screaming steadily, and all his "Please you've got to understands" and "I'm terribly sorry but this is important" couldn't wedge their way through, so before she had a chance to hang up on him again he pushed the buzzer really hard, until suddenly another Spanish voice was forcing its way through the mother's, and then the stoop kid was saying into the intercom, "You wanna lose your finger, keep buzzing."

"It's me," Babe whispered, taking his finger quickly away. "Me, you know—"

"—just one more buzz and it's coming off—"

"Melendez," Babe said, louder than he wanted to, "don't you recognize me, listen, listen for Chrissakes, it's me. Me." Hating himself, Babe said it: "The creep."

There was a pause. Then: "Creepy? That you?"

"Sure."

"What you want?"

"Talk."

"Okay."

"Private," Babe said, and when Melendez pushed the button from upstairs, the foyer door opened. They met a moment later on the first landing, by Melendez's place.

"What?" from Melendez.

Babe took a deep breath. "I want you to rob my apartment," he said.

Melendez just looked at him funny.

"Right now; you have to do it. If you won't do it now, it's

no deal. You can't do it alone, you'll need as many of the others from the stoop as you can get, and if any of you have weapons, you better tell them to bring them along."

"You kidding? Who don't have a weapon?" Then, "Why?"

"That's a little hard to explain without getting detailed, but there are some people who are kind of after me and if I go myself they'd have me and I don't much want that and I don't think they'll be as anxious to try anything with you."

Melendez couldn't help smiling. "That's some swell-looking raincoat, Creepy, but isn't it a little big for you?" and then he said, "Hey, are those pajamas?" and started to laugh.

"Just tell me yes or no, I don't need your shit," Babe said.

That stopped the laughter for a while. "What's in it for me?"

"Well, I got a radio and a black-and-white TV that's not too bad and a ton of books you're welcome to sell, probably you'd do best at the bookstores around Columbia, they do a real business on used stuff, and of course any of my clothes you want, and hell, I don't care, whatever you can carry you can have, and if you're caught I'll tell the cops I told you you could have it all so they won't be a factor."

"I'm all relieved," Melendez said, "I'm sure glad the cops won't be no factor." Then: "What's in it for you?"

"Well, I'd like my Adidas shoes, they're probably in the middle of the floor someplace—"

Melendez started laughing again.

Babe told him what else he wanted.

Melendez cut the laughter.

"The door's probably locked," Babe said, "I was going to try and find the super but—"

"Doors aren't no problem," Melendez said. Then, "What's the catch?"

"The catch is it's dangerous."

"That's not the catch," Melendez said. "That's the fun." Smiling.

Karl smiled rarely. Many times people thought that was because he didn't have a sense of humor, but he knew that was wrong; the truth was things just didn't strike him funny very often. What he felt inside most often was restlessness. He looked ponderous, with his great muscled arms, but what he needed to keep him in any kind of decent spirits at all was activity. He liked little jobs, lots of them, one piled on the next. That was pleasure.

Sitting was no pleasure.

Karl sat in the car, his hands around the steering wheel, his head still, his eyes moving from a glance through the windshield to another into the rear-view mirror. Those had been his instructions from Janeway, and he was going to fulfill them perfectly, because Janeway was trouble: If Karl ever made a mistake, Janeway would tell. It was ridiculous—the street was so dark it didn't matter which way he looked, there was nothing to see, no Jew, and so confident was he of his inability to spot anything that when the half dozen niggers suddenly appeared, coming toward him from behind, Karl came as close as he ever did to being startled.

No. Not niggers, he realized, spics. Half a dozen or more,

perhaps even seven, dressed strangely, hardly dressed at all, none of them with socks, all moving in a group behind one leader.

I hope they come for me, Karl thought. I hope they see a man alone in a car and try to steal it. He glanced quickly at the doors, making sure they were unlocked. He had a knife only, but he did not think he would need it for spics. Just grab the first by the arm, swing him into the others, keep that up until the sound of the arm eventually snapping would send them into desperate flight.

The group came to a stop before the Jew's building. For a moment he thought of getting out and making sure they kept on going. Give them a good scare; with his size, in this darkness, they would flee.

But, of course, those had not been Janeway's rules. Janeway had said wait for Levy, and if he came, take him. If he comes, I'll do that, Karl decided. In the meantime, let Erhard worry about the spics . . .

Erhard, from his position at the rear of the main floor, saw the gang halt in front of the building, and he felt immediate panic. If he had been better at violence, he would have enjoyed it more. But, tilted as he was, unbalanced as he always stood, he was forced to enter any fight at too great a disadvantage. Perhaps if he had overcompensated as a child, had whipped his misshapen body into always doing more than it happily could, had spent his nights with barbells for company, well, perhaps then he would have grown into a terror.

But he had been too smart. That was his flaw. He was too smart for strength and not smart enough to overcome the unpleasantness of his appearance. You saw him, you thought, "freight elevator operator," or you envisioned some night person, a man who came out after sundown, did his job, got his pay, and then was back inside before the sun grew too bright.

The gang was starting into the foyer of the building now.

Erhard moved as far back in the hallway corner as he dared. Probably he should somehow alert Janeway or maybe go to Janeway and tell him, but they had no signals for this kind of thing—who would dream of signals for this kind of thing?—and there was nothing to tell Janeway yet. Just a bunch of Spanish teen-agers in the foyer of a building; perhaps they lived there, the Puerto Ricans had enough children, maybe they were all from one brood mare of a mother, dark and pendulous and—

One of the gang was working at the foyer door.

I should tell Janeway, Erhard thought. But how? In order to get to Janeway, he would have to move to the stairs, and the stairs were by the foyer door, and what if he got there at the same time they managed to open it and there he was, alone, at the mercy of all those venomous Spanish?

"It's not my job," Erhard whispered, half aloud. His job was to stay silent watching the fire escape in the rear, and if Levy tried to get to his apartment using the fire escape, then he was to act, stop Levy, kill him perhaps, if required. Erhard had a gun. He was not good at shooting it, it made so much noise and he hated noise, but close up he could hit Levy, he could kill a Jew if he had to, especially if such a thing would please Szell. Szell rewarded when he was pleased. When he was not pleased, he could crucify, but that was his right, he was Christian Szell, alive and breathing in the 1970s, a marvel; different rules applied to him than to cripples.

The foyer door opened.

"My God, what if they come for me?" Erhard thought. He could shoot them. Some of them he could shoot. But not enough. And what would the others do to him then? He was afraid of Puerto Ricans when he rode the subway by himself; the idea of four or five avenging their dead brothers, kicking his crippled body to pieces, was too much for Erhard. Janeway. Janeway. He filled his mind with the name. This was Janeway's operation, Janeway would know what to do.

The gang started silently up the stairs.

Erhard wiped the sudden sweat from his face, listening to the footsteps rise. Thank God, decisive action was up to him no longer. It was Janeway's problem now . . .

Janeway, standing in the darkness at the far end of the corridor from Levy's room, thought the footsteps belonged to the police, and he was not at all upset. Levy leading police perhaps; even that didn't much bother him. First, he was with Division, and could easily prove it. Second, a Division man had been retired tonight, in this very place, so why shouldn't he be there, waiting, lurking, doing whatever he damn well felt like to avenge a fellow worker, the police were noted for always doing just exactly that too. And if Levy had made melodramatic charges, well, why shouldn't he, the boy had been through hell, a brother had died in his arms, could any of us truthfully know how sanely we would react on such a night?

The footsteps kept on coming.

Six, Janeway thought, listening. Then he heard a slightly different pattern and, from experience, correctly adjusted the number to seven. And clearly not police. Seven policemen couldn't move that silently if their graft depended on it.

Seven what, then?

It was a bit disturbing, because Janeway had as quick a mind as any, and quicker than most in crisis; no one in Division could react to sudden change with greater speed than Janeway.

Seven *what*?

The floor below him now.

And rising.

It was very bloody irritating was what it was, Janeway thought, aware that his anger was greatly his own frustration, more that than any danger in his present situation. After all, the present situation wasn't something he'd had all year to think about. Besides, there had been no other place to look for Levy. It was logical that Levy would come home, get whatever debris he needed. It might not be bright behavior, but it was not illogical, and he had been in bad shape anyway, beaten and cut; no one expected clear thinking from him at this point.

Seven what, goddammit?

Janeway gaped as they reached his floor.

Seven *children*?

He looked again. No, not children, not at all children, just small, probably anywhere from fourteen to eighteen, PRs, a gang of PRs, now what the hell would they be doing here?

The leader, as if in answer, immediately began jimmying Levy's door.

Janeway watched for a moment, immediately realizing that conclusions were beyond him; even a computer had to have the proper data fed it, and there was much too much he simply did not know. He took a step toward them along the corridor, softly, because he wanted surprise to help compensate for their numbers; he had no thought in mind, really, other than to send them packing.

"All right," he said, and he took his pistol out clearly, gave them a good look at it, "right now, *move*."

The group spun toward him, all but the leader. He was the one Janeway watched, because that was who you needed in a struggle: Get the bosses edgy, the drones run.

The leader turned slowly toward Janeway from his work on the door. He looked at Janeway, then at the gun, then dead into Janeway's eyes again.

"Blow it out your ass, motherfucker," the leader said.

*Well!* Janeway admitted that wasn't quite the answer they prepared you for at leadership school. He continued watching as the leader went back to working on the door. It was almost a scornful ignoring on his part, returning to his rightful labors after this interruption that could only be called trivial.

And now two of the others had heat in their hands. Oh, not real power, nothing like his pistol, Saturday-night specials only, but it seemed pointless to try to prove anything just at the moment. He was outnumbered seven to one, and they weren't afraid of him, not remotely. Then the leader forced the door open, and they all slipped into Levy's apartment.

Janeway sped past the door and down the stairs. It was clearly a waste remaining here any longer. They would have to finish Levy at the lake. Not an ideal situation, perhaps, because it would be light by then, and death was always best accompanied by darkness. Still, you could do only so much, and he had tried whatever was available. So the lake it would have to be. Now it was up to Elsa to get Levy there.

# 26

Babe hesitated before entering Kaufman's. It had to be close to six now; things were starting to lighten up just the least bit, making everything more visible, especially him. He glanced along 49th Street, then along Lex, trying to be sure it was safe to enter.

*Paranoid!*

That's just how he was acting, sneaking around the city near dawn in an undersized raincoat and running shoes. Nobody attacked you in Kaufman's, for Chrissakes, it was a legendary place, they understood about darkness, you didn't get kidnapped in Kaufman's every day of the week. Babe took a deep breath, trying to get his head on straight, but the air hurt his tooth like crazy. It wasn't really that he was paranoid so much as beat. He hadn't really slept since Doc had put in his appearance, and when was that, was it—?

My God, could it have only been about twenty-four hours since his brother first appeared from the darkness with the words "Don't kill me, Babe"; was it possible it was only six since he died?

There was a clock in Kaufman's window, reading 5:51, time enough for him to go in, get the oil of cloves he'd come for, pay for it, wait outside for Elsa. Babe walked into the pharmacy and was halfway back to the drug department before stopping cold.

What if you needed a prescription?

Babe hesitated by the food counter that ran along one wall of the store. Was he being paranoid again? No. No, because whatever the hell was in oil of cloves numbed you and whatever numbed you was a drug and drugs were *verboten* unless you had a prescription—the strong ones were, anyway. And oil of cloves was strong, it had nearly dammed up his pain, so you knew you weren't dealing with Aspergum.

I better have a good story for the pharmacist, Babe thought, something solid; lemmesee, I've got a prescription but like a fool I left it in my wallet and I left my wallet back home.

No good. "Go get it," the pharmacist would say.

All right, I was mugged. There. Terrific. I *had* the prescription but a couple addicts jumped me on my way and they took it along with my typewriter and color TV.

Now that *was* good. Don't embellish it, though, forget the TV and the typewriter. You were mugged, period. Hell, I'd believe a story like that, and I just made it up.

Confident, Babe made his way to the pharmaceutical section, and he was all the way there when he realized that it didn't matter what story he told, the drug man was going to know it was a lie, because as he drew close Babe could see the guy waiting for him with a smile you could only call strange, and then the guy started walking and Babe saw, too too late, the limp.

Erhard was waiting for him.

Babe whirled, ready to try one final dash to the street, but Karl moved out from the paperback racks, blocking his path.

It was over. It was over. Babe sagged against the counter.

". . . seems to be the trouble?" Erhard said.

Babe glanced up as the speaker limped around the counter toward him. It wasn't Erhard's voice, and that made sense because it wasn't Erhard, just another member of the maimed legion, a poor, tiny night man who limped like Erhard and talked exactly like W. C. Fields. Babe turned toward the book racks where Karl had blocked him. A fat old guy was examining the books. Big, sure, but he looked as much like Karl as Cuddles Sakall resembled Argentina Rocca. I *am* going paranoid, Babe thought. No. I'm not going, I've reached it, I'm there.

He breathed in sharply, forcing the air into his front teeth, and the quick pain brought him to his senses fast. The pain lingered, and he tried to blink it away. The pain was all he had for now to bring perspective. "I'd like some oil of cloves, please."

"Oil of cloves, oil of cloves," the W. C. Fields man said, "now why should you want that little pipsqueak of a cure?"

"Tooth," Babe said.

"I didn't think you'd want to paint your bidet, m'boy; my point is, there's better on the market."

"Just the oil of cloves, please," Babe said. It was 5:56 now.

The druggist limped back behind the counter. "Now here before your very eyes I plant some Red Cross Tooth Drops," and he placed a container on the counter. "Far superior ointment, in this humble burgher's opinion."

"Just the oil of cloves, please," Babe said.

"Ah, you see, this little item *contains* oil of cloves, plus other magic ingredients, *plus,* mind you, tooth picks and cotton swabs, so all you have to do is push the pick into the cotton, the cotton into the elixir, the dampened lump into your cavity, and *voilà*, your pain is diminished as if by legerdemain."

"Just the oil of cloves, please," Babe said, beginning to wonder if that was to be his ultimate fate, repeating "just the oil of cloves, please" to a little limping man who tried to make his life bearable by sounding like W. C. Fields.

"Have you considered oil of cloves?" the druggist said, "some people seem to like it, very devoted following," and he put a small bottle on the counter.

Babe took it, paid, went to the front of the store, looked out.

Elsa was parked at a bus stop across the street, motor running. She wore the same black shiny raincoat as when they'd first met.

Babe opened the oil of cloves, dipped it onto his index finger, rubbed and rubbed, poured more on, rubbed again, and then, when the deadening began to happen, he closed the bottle, pocketed it, and ran out of the store. She saw him coming, and her arms reached out for him through the window by the driver's side, and in a moment he was embracing her on the street. Then he broke it, tore around the car, got in, and this time they clung to each other until from behind them there came a bus honking, so Elsa reluctantly let him go, put her hands to the wheel of the car, and started driving.

"Come closer," she said softly. "Rest."

He moved toward her, put his head on the shoulder of her black raincoat. "I am tired," Babe said.

"Soon it doesn't matter any more, because we're going to be so happy, I know."

"I could sure use a dose of that along about now."

"Do you like the car? I had to sell practically my body for it, I hope you like it."

"It's very nice," Babe said, eyes half closing.

"There is a man above me in my building who finds me most attractive—at least he used to, I don't know what his opinion is now, since after you called I could only think to wake him and say I needed his car, could he do me that favor."

"What favor did he want?"

"The obvious. I believe he did, I'm not quite sure, since we were both very tactful and neither very awake. You see, the reason I could only think to bother this man was because you said over the telephone that you wanted a quiet place, a place to think, and the same man who owns this car, he also has such a place, and I thought we might go there, it's by a lake."

"Lake?"

"Yes, he owns a little house about an hour out. There are a few other houses and docks, and it is very beautiful. He invited me there one weekend, and it was like living in a subway car, with all the motorboats and water-skiers, but that was summer. Once September begins, it becomes, almost overnight, deserted. On the weekends a few people still come, but in the middle of the week, like now, there is no one. Why don't we try it?"

" 'Kay," Babe muttered, eyes fluttering.

"Rest," Elsa whispered.

His head against her shoulder, Babe closed his eyes, and for just a moment he really thought he was going to be able to obey her soft command, "Rest," but then there began the knotting in his stomach, tension and sadness intertwining, and even before it happened, he knew that although he might have chosen a better moment, a lonelier place, still, when your mourning time came you took it, and suddenly his body went into spasm and the tears literally burst from his weary eyes, splattering his raincoat, hers, and for a while he was blinded.

Then, as suddenly as it had come, it left him, with just the sharp intake of breath as a memory that it once had been. But it *had* been. He had mourned. Unsatisfactorily. God knows insufficiently. Elsa was looking at him, almost, Babe thought, with fear.

"You are all right?"

He made a nod.

"Yes?"

He nodded again.

"Nothing is wrong then?"

"Tired."

"Yes."

She brought an arm around him, drew him close. "Comes soon the lake. And all will be lovely . . ."

It really was lovely. They reached it not much after seven, and the sun was already hitting the water at a strong angle; as they took the road around, Babe could tell how quiet the place was. He saw no activity. Nothing but the dust rising behind them as they drove along. He rolled down his window. The air brought nature sounds into the car, the kind of thing he hadn't really heard since he'd hit Manhattan months ago.

Elsa drove into a run-down driveway and stopped the car. "I think this is his house," she said, getting out. "I hope it is. I know where he keeps his key." She went up the porch steps and around to a drainpipe and bent down. "I think half the lake keeps their keys in their drainpipes," she said, laughing, and Babe smiled back at her. She opened the front door with little difficulty and stepped inside, then quickly out. "Musty," she said.

Babe got out of the car. "Leave it open, let it air a little," he said, "let's walk down to the water."

She nodded, came down the steps, held out her hand to him, and together they headed for the lake. The sun was growing brighter now. The breeze had died, and the nature sounds were louder. Elsa smiled, and glanced off in the direction they'd come from. They stepped out onto the small dock. Babe pointed back to the house. "Szell's?" he asked.

"Zells?" she said, her head tilted, as if she had not heard the name.

"Oh, come on," Babe said. "You're in on it. I don't understand what you do exactly, what service you perform, but you're in on it."

Elsa shook her head, smiled again.

"I don't really *know* you're in on it, I just *know* you're in on it, if you understand me—you didn't do anything wrong, no mistake or like that—it's kind of like Janeway said once: After a while you get a feel of the way the other guy operates, you get a sense of his mind."

Now she said, "Janeway?" She had not heard that name either.

"I'm talking," Babe shouted, "about two very famous people, George Szell and Elizabeth Janeway, and nobody who hopes to win my heart can be a functional illiterate, so quit acting like one."

"I'm sorry," she said, and she held his hand very tightly and looked at him adoringly with her eyes. "You're very tired and very funny and I care for you."

"My brother loved me," Babe said.

"I know. You've been through a terrible time."

"He really did, he loved me plenty, no more than me him, y'understand. We fucking cared for each other, and after you tore out of Lutèce, you know what he said? He said I should forget you because you didn't love me, you were just using me, and I said bullshit, how can you tell, and his answer to that, *his answer*—and remember, we would have died for each other—his answer was that you were gorgeous so you must have been using me because *why else would someone love me?*—

"—Can you imagine how that hurt? I mean, I knew I wasn't in Tyrone Power's league, but can you conceive what it's like when someone that loves you says a thing like that to you? It just racked me so bad until I realized I was wrong, he *didn't* love me, because no one who loved anyone would say such a crippler, anything that cruel . . . and then when he died—when he bled away in my arms—I knew I'd been right the first time, that he did care, and when he said why else would someone love me, he *knew* you were using me, somehow he knew, and that was a shorthand, a code kind of, and I thought back to all the things, like your lying about being

German and Szell being German and the funny way you stood up in the park just before the mugging and how you happened to find a guy with a car and a deserted place on short notice, and none of it means anything, no court would call it evidence, but you're in on it, I know it and Doc knew it, so I'm asking you again, is this Szell's house or not?"

"George Szell? I don't think so. Someone would have mentioned it, don't you think?"

"What did you do for Szell?"

Elsa sighed. "It isn't charming any more, Tom; stop it."

"Where's Janeway?"

She just shook her head.

"Was this Szell's house?"

"Tom, I can't tell you things I don't know, believe me, please."

"When are they getting here?"

Elsa only shook her head.

"What did you do for Szell?"

*"Nothing."*

"When are they due?"

She must have known then that he wasn't going to stop, because softly she said, "Soon."

"Oh," Babe said. "Good. Right." And they stood there, alone, close together on the tiny dock with the sun getting warm, the truths at last spoken, not all of them by any means, but enough, the crucial ones, and Babe could only think of Gatsby, Gatsby at last at Daisy's house, just before they all took off for their deadly trip into and out of the city, when she looked at him in front of Tom her husband and said, "Ah, you look so cool, you always look so cool," and Tom knew then and they all knew then that she loved him, Daisy loved Gatsby, his tortured trip from Shafter's to the blue lawn had not been so in vain.

They started walking slowly up to the deserted house with the door open, a Wyeth place, ghosts abounding. "It was the sister's," Elsa said, gesturing toward the house. "Then, when she died, Szell's father kept the house himself; he would come here weekends. For whatever reasons, it reminded him of home, the lake." She glanced off toward the distance again.

"What's keeping them, do you suppose?"

Elsa shrugged. "Just making sure there were no police following after you."

Babe had to smile. No one understood that what he wanted was just one thing: the final class reunion. He wanted his very own try at that, and afterward, fail or not, it ended how it ended. "No police," he told her. They continued on up, approaching the house. "What did you do for him?"

"Courier work, mostly. The diamonds went from the bank to the capital and then to Scotland, and a fat antiques man did the barter. I took the money down to Paraguay, made whatever currency changes were necessary, gave the money to Christian."

"Kind of a glamor job, sounds like: easy hours, lots of travel."

"It had to be done."

"Did Szell kill my brother?"

She shrugged.

"Yes, you mean."

She said nothing.

They entered the house, walked into the living room, looked out. Far in the distance now, a car. "Them?" Babe asked.

"I should think yes."

Babe nodded.

The car was coming steadily closer.

Babe's teeth were hurting now. Sudden, severe pain. He reached his hands toward his raincoat pockets for reassurance. In the left, the box of bullets, in the right, his father's gun, loaded and ready, and he was a good shot—no, he was a great shot, he was a goddamn Daniel Boone with his father's pistol, and he damn well should have been, the hours he put in when he was old enough, firing it and firing it, all out of some neurotic hope for revenge.

And now revenge was coming steadily closer down the road; all of his wishes were coming true; Christian Szell was coming toward him down the road, and in a little while Christian Szell was going to die, if Babe just had the guts to make it happen. He didn't care if he made it out himself, he didn't even think much about making it out himself, just so Szell didn't make it out too, that would make things more than even-steven, thank you, because Szell had killed them both, H.V. and Doc, no matter what anyone said; he had killed H.V. even though they were continents and quarter centuries apart, a Nazi was a Nazi, you couldn't ask for better if you needed a bad guy, and he had to have killed Doc, Babe wanted that so badly it just had to be true, it couldn't have been assholes like Karl or Erhard, Doc would have whipped them without breaking stride. Babe stood very still, watching the car's approach, realizing that at blessed last all his wishes were coming true, and on this perfect day, he could feel himself starting to fold.

He couldn't help himself, he was crumbling.

Babe could practically hear his wild heart because so what if he was deadly with the gun, so what if he could rip the bull's-eye out of any target you could hang, he had never fired at *flesh* before, and suddenly he knew that with Szell and Janeway and Erhard and Karl and Elsa standing around him, what he would do would be just what he always did under pressure, make an ass of himself, just like the coward he was—if he hadn't been a coward, if he'd only gone in with the goddamn wool paper, H.V. would still be breathing and—

*—dear dear God, this one time, please don't let me think too much, I'm going on an animal hunt, let me be an animal, I never asked it before, there's not gonna be a chance at asking it again, so this once, this one time, please . . .*

The tooth pain was horrid now, and he reached into his pocket and pulled out the oil of cloves and with all his strength hurled it smashing against the nearest wall.

Elsa jumped, frightened by the sound, confused by the sight of broken glass and spreading liquid.

"Painkiller," Babe started to explain, and then he thought, "Save your breath, let her think you're crazy," and then he thought, "Forget about her, just inhale, *inhale*," and he pulled the air in sharply, forcing it against the open nerves, his tight gasping the only sound in the room. Babe kept right on inhaling and oh, but it hurt, Christ it was terrible, but it was necessary. If he was ever going to do what he had to do, he needed all the pain he could get.

# 27

The car was in no hurry. It just moved along at sightseeing speed. Elsa watched Babe but said nothing, just stared into his frightened face.

Then the car stopped, parked behind Elsa's car in the run-down driveway. For a moment there was nothing inside. No movement. Then the doors opened. And Karl got out and Erhard got out and Janeway and Babe whirled on Elsa, grabbing her hard, saying "*Where's Szell?*—there's only the three of them, where *is* he?"

Elsa shrugged.

Babe stared at the car, waiting, praying for Szell to move into the sunshine, but the car was empty now and it was all going to be for nothing, because Szell hadn't come, but where could he be, he couldn't be getting the diamonds yet, because no bank was open, and anyway, he'd never *get* the goddamn diamonds, because once there was a death, safe deposit boxes were sealed until after the law had its chance for examination; they'd gone through all that when H.V. died and they couldn't get into his safe deposit box, nobody was allowed to touch anything for a long time, not that there was anything there much worth touching. "Is Szell waiting at the bank, *what bank*?"

"I know nothing," she was about to finish, but Babe took his gun out then, and that stopped her. "I'm not afraid," she said.

"You will be," Babe told her, and he gestured her out toward the porch. She moved quickly, and he followed her, his gun hand already damp.

"Morning," Janeway called. He stood between Karl and Erhard, and his smile had rarely been more dazzling.

Babe just watched him.

"Perhaps we might come up and have a chat," Janeway said, and Babe could only think again of Gatsby, and the whole thing was a house party, fun and games and tea sandwiches when the time came.

"He is armed," Elsa said. "He has a pistol."

"Can't be too safe nowadays, I suppose," Janeway said, the smile still there.

"Say, 'Old Sport,' why don't you?" Babe said.

Janeway started toward the porch. Slowly, but his direction was absolutely clear. "My favorite novel, yours too?" he said. Karl and Erhard followed.

Babe let them come. When they were close enough, he said, "Stop."

Janeway obeyed immediately, the others too.

Babe hesitated.

"We're awaiting further instructions," Janeway told him. "Do we take three giant steps—what?" He did his smile again.

Babe didn't know what to do; it wasn't his turf, he didn't understand the boundaries. He could try firing now, and perhaps get one, but that left two free to roam, with him trapped inside an unfamiliar place, and maybe that was the thing to do anyway, just fire like a madman, but he wasn't sure. He had a hostage, and that was probably good, but what for? Should he try a move that way, using the girl? Could he? Would they buy it if he tried?

"Surely there must be more fruitful ways of passing time," Janeway said then.

"I like waiting," Babe said, which was a lie—ordinarily he hated it—but there was something bothering Janeway, the standing around was getting to him, so that made it just fine as far as Babe was concerned.

Karl muttered something; Janeway shook him off.

"Tell Karl not to get upset," Babe said. "They'll be here inside five minutes." And before they could ask after the "they" he supplied an answer: "The cops." Babe was really very proud of himself for that. They all suspected the cops were coming, why not let them have their suspicions? Any pressure you could add to the enemy burden was a blessing—that had to be true, he wasn't his brother's brother for nothing.

"He said there were no police," Elsa said.

"And I was telling the truth too," Babe said. "Probably."

Erhard began twisting his body around, staring along the road. Again Karl muttered something, moving straight to Janeway, but again Janeway shook him off.

"I haven't got my watch, anybody know the exact time?" Babe asked.

"I don't believe the police are coming," Janeway said.

Babe nodded. "We agree on something, neither do I." He gave Janeway his smile, hoping it was dazzling.

Then came the crucial pause. Because after it was over, Janeway said, "All right, how much? And can we please discuss terms inside?" He moved his hands away from his body, so that if he was armed, he would be at a distinct disadvantage in getting to it quickly. The other two followed his gesture.

"That supposed to imply trust?" Babe asked.

"Along those lines."

Babe gestured with the pistol, and backed into the living room, bringing Elsa with him. He continued on until he stood in a corner of the room, no windows close, nothing. Janeway came in first, arms still away from his body. Karl followed, Erhard shut the door.

"You understand, of course," Janeway began, "that I'm only authorized to go to a certain limit; even if I want to go higher, it's entirely out of my control, only Szell can give—"

"Oh cut it, there are no terms," Babe said, "you only wanted to get inside so you could finish me easier."

"Then why did you let us?" Janeway said.

"Because you're all in my killing range now," Babe said, and he pushed Elsa away from him, his father's gun ready.

Janeway examined him awhile. "I'm sorry," he said finally, "but you're just not good casting for the part, I rather have my doubts."

"I'm a crack shot," Babe said, but he knew they weren't buying, and his gun hand was really sweating now, his heart going wild again, and he could almost begin to sense that he was paling, going lightheaded. "I am!" he said, too loud for belief, much too loud, and he knew it but he couldn't take the words back.

"There are no police," Janeway said. "If there were, he wouldn't be panicking."

"They're *coming*," Babe said, "and you're going to be one stunned son of a bitch when they take you, and then Szell goes, you're all going." He was panting from his speech.

Janeway took a short step away. "We'll all just wait here," he said, very softly, "and we're none of us about to do anything, are we, Erhard, because we don't have to, isn't that right, Karl, we're just going to watch, and, Elsa, move away a bit please, I think the boy could use a bit of breathing room."

Tall, skinny, Babe leaned into the corner. It was terrible, but he was losing it all; he had the gun, the weapon was his, but everything was drifting from him. He knew it, they knew it. There were few secrets in the room. "I'll tell you my terms," he said, making his voice loud but not too loud, he didn't want that mistake again.

"Yes, by all means," Janeway urged. His blue eyes hit Babe's.

He *knows*, Babe thought. He knows the difference between shooting targets and shooting bone, he knows about tearing pulp and scarring flesh. He knows about screaming and dying and he knows I don't. "My terms are Szell, that's what I want, just tell me when and where he's going after the diamonds and give me an hour's head start."

"Oh, we accept," Janeway said right off. "Those are certainly equitable terms, but I'm a bit confused as to how we can insure your head start—how can we make that work? What if you take one car and deflate the tires in the other, that should do it, we'd be at least an hour getting after you, and that way we'd all be happy, what do you think?"

"I think—" Babe began, but then Janeway was screaming "*No!*" because Karl was making his move, Karl was going for capture, it was going to belong to him, all of it, not Janeway with his talk, not Erhard with his whining, and as he roared toward the skinny figure trying to back still farther into the corner, Karl reached out his giant hands for Babe's throat, fingers ready and spread, and he was within a yard of triumph when Babe shot his eye out and Karl screamed, careening into the wall and down, and as he did, Babe went into a roll because Janeway was going for his weapon now, and as Babe's once gawky body moved he was aware of something new and different and that was grace, he felt it, he didn't feel like a creep now, he felt like a fucking menace now, and there was death in his hands and enemies all around him and Erhard was going for the door when Babe squeezed off a shot and Erhard screamed like Karl had done and fell, leaving Janeway, and that was tough because Janeway was on the move too, a gun in his hands now almost ready for shooting, not pointed yet, but there, and did you try for the wrist or the heart, did you try to hit the weapon like the Lone Ranger or did you rearrange the brain, and in that indecision Babe fired and hit, but the stomach only, not a good-enough shot to stop Janeway, so he fired again and this time Janeway fell, his weapon sliding across the floor, but still Janeway wasn't done, and Babe was beginning to wonder what you had to do to stop him, and he got off one more shot before he realized that Erhard was moving, and he fired again in that direction, hoping to Christ he was sharp because Elsa was going for Janeway's gun and he had to beat her to it because he needed to reload now, but there wasn't time, and she had the lead except she was a girl and he was a marathon man and his legs got him there and he kicked the gun out of her reach and then went for it, grabbed it, pointed it at her face and started to squeeze as she cried out, *"No—no—Jesus—"* and Babe said, "The bank—Szell's bank—" and she said, "—I don't know—" and Erhard was groaning, groaning, and his crippled leg was twitching out of control, and Janeway was pouring blood as Babe said, "You lying bitch, you do know, you know and you're going to tell me, you're going to tell me or I'll kill you," and she screamed, "You're going to kill me anyway," and he screamed right back at her, "You're fucking right I'm going to kill you but *you're still going to tell me*," and her face wasn't so lovely now because she was panicked and she managed to get out "Madison—Madison and Ninety-first" and that might have been wonderful news for Babe, ordinarily it would have been triumphant information, but not any more, because Janeway was alive and Janeway's hands gripped his ankles and Babe could feel his balance starting to go and as he began firing into Janeway's body he saw that crippled Erhard was crawling toward him too, and he kept on firing but there were no more miracles, this was it, this was the end, all his corpses were coming for him, and he wondered where the rest were, where were Doc and old H.V., one with the bloody temple, the other with the split up his insides, why weren't they reaching out for him too, everybody else was, the universe was bleeding, the universe was bleeding and reaching out for him, bringing him down . . .

# 28

Fascinated and cheery, Szell wandered among the Jews.

He had never conceived that such a place as the diamond market existed, yet here it was in all its ethnic glory, stretching from Fifth Avenue to Sixth along 47th Street. Szell held his suitcase lightly as he stood on the sidewalk and turned around in a circle.

Even the bank on the corner of 47th and Fifth was the Bank of Israel. Perfectly logical, Szell thought; undoubtedly it was set down there so that the Chosen People would not have far to travel after they spent their days in exhaustive haggling.

The names, my God, the names: There was the Diamond Exchange and the Jewelry Exchange and the Jewelers' Exchange and the Diamond Center and the Jewelry Center and the Diamond Tower and the Diamond Gallery and the Diamond Horseshoe—each of them nothing but barnlike areas teeming with tiny stalls, each stall teeming with Jews, hustling and hawking and clutching for shoppers. And in between these larger jewelers were smaller jewelers—smaller but better, private places. Szell was looking for a few of them to talk to later; he had things to learn, and as he passed these private jewelers he saw they were all locked so that you had to ring to gain entrance and their answering *buzz-buzz-buzz* was a constant part of the underscoring of 47th Street, part of the color, along with the delicatessens with their salamis and the young men with their round caps and the old men with their beards.

Knowing he would return shortly, Szell sauntered to Sixth Avenue and took a cab uptown to the bank. He knew it would be open, though he had no intention of going in yet. For two reasons chiefly. First, his plane back to South America did not leave till seven, and the longer he was on the streets with his diamonds, the greater the risk.

Because of Scylla.

That was the second reason. Had Scylla planned to rob him, and was that plan still in effect? If their situations had been reversed, he would have certainly robbed Scylla—who wouldn't make the attempt for one of the larger illicit fortunes in the world, especially since the victim couldn't very well complain to the police?

Was it safe?

The taxi trip took him through Central Park, then out at 90th, by the reservoir, and Szell told the driver to turn up Madison, where the bank was, on the corner of 91st Street, red bricked and lovely.

Now, Szell began to concentrate.

He had a phenomenal memory—chess games, incisor configurations, noses, hands, colors—and he told the driver to continue touring the bank area, noting all the details of upper East Side street life as he went past. He had made a similar trip shortly after eight, slightly more than two hours before, and now he was checking and cross-checking in his mind. Was that the same old woman with the same nurse sitting by the canopied building taking the sun? Were the work clothes on the men digging in the street at 92nd Street of sufficient age to be legitimate? Were any of the people strolling on the avenues the same as two hours ago, and were there doormen who appeared ill at ease, postmen who seemed nervous? Szell missed nothing; he never had, why start now?

Szell finished his tour of the bank area as satisfied as possible, considering the stakes. Everything seemed perfectly normal, though he never trusted "seems." He paid the cab at 93rd and Lexington, got out, and waited till the taxi was gone from sight before hailing another, beginning the journey back to the diamond center.

Because referring to the contents of his deposit box as one of the largest illicit fortunes in the world could either be truth or wishful thinking, he had no way of knowing.

He hadn't the least idea of what a diamond was worth.

Oh, once he had. Once he knew exactly, but that was in a different life, another land. It was crucial that he know at least approximately what he was worth when he finally saw his fortune. The remainder of his life and how well he could afford to live it depended on his knowing. Which was why he was returning to 47th Street. He had questions that needed answering, which was why, when he got to the diamond market again, he paid this driver with a good deal more excitement than he had the one before.

He carried his luggage easily as he walked away from Fifth, reached the first of the two stores he had selected, Katz's. He decided to start small, first finding out the value of a one-carat stone, because if he began asking after giants, it might make them look at him closer than he wanted. He tried Katz's door. It was locked. A buzzer had a "push" sign over it. Szell pushed. The buzzer buzzed. The door unlocked.

And these people thought Germany was a terrible country.

"I'd like to see a one-carat diamond, please," Szell said to the tiny man who all but bounded around the counter.

The man surprised him with "Why?"

"Because . . ." Szell began, but it came out German, "Beecuss," and that was a mistake on this street, and he wondered if the little man had caught it.

" 'Cause if you're just a *see-er*, go window-shop, but if you're genuinely *interested*, if you want the best gem quality rock on the block, I'm your man."

"How much would it be?" Szell asked, nodding, because all his stones were gem quality, the highest.

"Before I tell you, we gotta go to this *independent* appraiser I know, and if he doesn't tell you I'm practically giving the stone away free, I'll get a new brother-in-law." He laughed.

"Please," Szell said, "cannot you tell me just the value of a one-carat stone?"

"Wait—wait—first you come traipsing in asking to see, now you wanna know how much? Money's garbage, it's *value* I sell, and when we've seen the appraiser—he's just upstairs—you'll know I'm your man and no high-pressure artist. Well?"

Szell worked to control himself; he had had his orders followed for thirty years and more, and the insolence of the kike was simply not to be tolerated. You asked a question, *he would not give the answer*.

He turned, wheeled, left, headed more toward Sixth.

Push.

*Buzz.*

Open.

The place was painted mostly blue. There were just two men, one with his back to Szell, a sweating fat one, but the one who came over to him was clearly a gentleman, pencil moustache, dressed to match the walls. "Yes sir."

Szell went British. "I'm interested in the value of a one-carat diamond."

The pencil moustache smiled. "That's like asking me the price of a painting. It all depends."

"My wife and I have been married twenty-five years, and I know that's silver, but, you see, she adores diamonds and I've yet to purchase her one and I'd wait, but that's not till our sixtieth and I don't think the chances of being around for it are all that strong. So I thought, perhaps, a surprise, if you gather my gist."

"I'll tell you the range, sir. You can probably find a one-carat on this street for as low as three hundred fifty. I've got one that goes for four thousand. Now, where in between did you see yourself?"

"Four thousand," Szell replied, thrilled, because he had never bothered with anything remotely that small.

The salesman leaned across the counter. "You're being very smart, sir—always buy top. It's the best investment you can make—diamonds always go up, the top ones, there's never enough of them and the demand won't stop growing. Just for example, a top three-carat would go today for eighteen thousand easy, and by next year it'll be closer to twenty-five thou."

Szell nodded, doing his best to get the numbers straight,

but it wasn't easy, because the fat man on the phone was getting loud. "Arnie, I understand," the fat man was saying. "Arnie, my God, we know each other twenty years, Arnie, for Chrissakes I know she's Jewish, of course she wants a big stone, just give me some idea what you'll spring for. Twelve? Will you go twelve? Because I can get you something she'll cream over if you'll say twelve. Lemme know today, Arnie," and as the fat man hung up and turned, Szell thought, "My God, my God, *I know that Jew, I worked on him!*"

The fat man stood, stretched, glanced at Szell.

He wasn't so fat then, and he must have been strong or he would not have lived, he must have worked at Krupp's or Farben's because of his strength—Christ, how many are there on this street I have worked on?

The fat man was staring at Szell now.

Szell knew he should flee, but he could not, he simply could not. He had dreaded more than anything ever this moment—of someday in daylight meeting a victim.

"I think I know you," the fat man said. "You look familiar."

"I do hope so, I quite love surprises," Szell said, going as British as he dared. He held out his right hand. "Hesse, how do you do." He and the fat one shook. He extended his hand to the pencil moustache. "Hesse, how do you do. Christopher Hesse, perhaps you've been to our shop in London, the missus and mine."

"It wasn't London," the fat one said.

"Well, we've been there since the middle thirties, Hitler, you see, we're Jewish, you see, and we left when we could, our friends thought us genuine hysterics but we went nonetheless, and we've run kind of an odds-and-ends place, out near

Islington, it's quite trendy now, but not when we settled, it was all we could afford, let me tell you. I don't want to seem the braggart but we've done quite well actually." He pronounced it "ectually"—overdoing it, true, but he had earned the right, he was that proud of himself: The fat man was won over, the strange look of remembrance gone.

"I always wanted to visit London," the pencil moustache said.

"Oh, do," Szell said. "And please look us up. 'Hesse of Islington.' Remember now, promise."

"Sure," the pencil moustache said. "You interested in seeing anything?"

"I might be. Let me just sound out the missus, surreptitiously, of course, and gauge her reaction. Four thousand is a goodly amount."

"Shall I hold it?"

"Oh, why not," Szell said, and he smiled, picked up his packages, left the store. He moved by hatted men, aged scholars, hawkers; the street was jammed. And getting hot now. Szell looked at the time and found it well after eleven. Since he planned on returning to the bank as late as possible, that meant he had several hours left to wander, take in the sights, fix Manhattan as firmly as possible in his mind, because you had to give it to the Americans, it was an extraordinary place, everywhere height, the little narrow streets, the spired buildings, and at first, as he sauntered close to Sixth Avenue, he wasn't sure where the word "Engel" was coming from, his mind or some record shop, but then as it repeated, he realized it wasn't just "Engel," it was *"der Engel,"* and Szell felt a slight pulse quickening, which he didn't altogether relish, because now the voice—it was female, and building into a scream—was going *"Der weisser Engel, der weisser Engel!"* and Szell had not heard himself referred to as that, the White Angel, since his Auschwitz time, and then he saw her, directly across 47th Street from him, an ancient bent witch, and she was pointing one hand at him and clutching her heart with the other as she screamed, "DER WEISSER ENGEL—*SZELL—SZELL,*" and she couldn't hold her witch fingers steady but still they were pointed at his heart, and Szell froze for just a moment, because the street was starting to react, and the Spanish walking along kept on walking, and the blacks too, because what did it matter, a crazy old woman shouting something, "sell" maybe, and the young Jews, they didn't stop what they were doing either—

—but then an old man with a beard turned toward her sound and said, *"Szell?—Szell is here?—"*

—and then another old man said, *"Where is Szell?—"*

—and then a giant of a woman with a deep deep voice said, "He is dead—Szell is dead—everyone is dead—"

*"Nein, Nein,"* shouted the witch with the pointing fingers: *"DER WEISSER ENGEL IST HIER!"*

And now 47th Street was starting to explode.

Slowly, as slowly as he could force himself, Szell began walking again toward Sixth Avenue. If he ran it was over, if he ran they would know there was a reason for it and that reason was that he was who he was, the great Christian Szell, and there was no reason for panic, he had only Jews to outsmart, and they didn't know what he looked like. Some of them did—the fat man in the second shop, he remembered, and the witch across the street, who was still screaming, she did too—but not enough of the others. The name, naturally, they knew. The face perhaps a number of them knew. But only a few would see beyond his baldness.

Unless he ran.

Calm, calm, Szell commanded.

Sixth Avenue was up ahead now. Just up ahead. Behind him, though, the noises were getting frightening, his name being shouted along the length of the diamond center, all the Jews suddenly cold with fear but warmed by their numbers, all of them wondering could it be true, could Szell be alive, be *here*, in *America*, and what if they could be the one to catch him?

Slower, Szell ordered his body. You are a sightseer, you are safe, there is no reason for speed.

"He is getting away," the old witch screamed, *"See? See?"*

All the store windows and doors were opening now; he could see them as he moved along, everyone wondering what the hollering was about.

Szell made a pleasant smile at a large lady who was standing in the doorway of her jewelry shop. "The day, it is *très belle*, yes?" Szell said, doing his best with the French accent, forcing himself to behave as if there were nothing going on behind.

"What's all the fuss?" the large lady asked.

Szell made a very French shoulder shrug. "Crazy peoples," he answered.

She smiled at him.

Good, Szell thought. As long as you don't panic, you cannot lose. So slowly. Slowly.

*"I'll stop him!"* the old witch screamed, and without wanting to, Szell turned his bald head, because if they were going to chase him, well, that changed things, and now the witch had plunged across the street, shouting to the traffic, "Room, give me room," and she was slow and very old so the cars should have been able to stop in time, and most of them did but one didn't and one was enough, it braked, the screech was close to painful, but not before it skidded into the crone, and she held her footing for a moment, then fell, unhurt but down, because her voice was louder than ever as she shrieked, "FOOL—FOOL—WHO WILL STOP HIM NOW?" to the driver as he got out of his car and ran around to the front, starting to try to help the old woman to her feet, and Szell continued his stroll, finally making the safety of Sixth Avenue, turning pleasantly uptown, strolling along, the hysteria and shouting of 47th Street behind him now, hopefully a thing of the past, but perhaps not, perhaps the police would come, and if they did, they would hear the old crone's story, and then perhaps they would or would not believe her, that was not for him to control.

All I can control is one thing: myself. And all I can do is one thing: the unexpected.

They would expect him to have guns, which was not now and never had been true. In the first place, he never wanted to train to become adept—he was to be a dentist, what use were guns? And when he did try to learn, he turned out to be a terrible shot. He hated the noise. The gun always bucked. He hit nothing. Not having a gun, of course, was not the same as saying he was unarmed.

He did, after all, have the Cutter.

His Cutter, really; not that he had invented anything—there had likely been knives in existence since we stopped being amphibians—no, his contribution was really just one of refinement. His Cutter was always strapped around his forearm, where, with a simple unobtrusive flick, it would slide, ready for use, into his right hand. The handle was thick, the blade buried deep in hardwood. The blade was pointed, sharp as a hypodermic needle, but only one edge was dangerous, the opposite one being unusually thick, so that all you had to do was swipe with your arm, or slash if you preferred, and the enemy's stomach was wide open, or his throat, wherever you found it convenient to strike. He loved the silence of his Cutter when placed against the horrid sound of guns.

They would expect guns. And they would also expect him to flee.

And so, with a startling degree of calm taking over his body and mind, he decided to stay where he was, since they would *know* that he would, at the first possible opportunity, vacate the area, take a cab, the subway, a bus, anything to get as far from the sighting as possible, but Sixth Avenue wasn't very pretty, the buildings all but blocked the sun, so he turned in after a little and crossed back toward Fifth, got halfway there when he saw a little plaza bathed in sunshine, and made his way toward it, and genuinely gasped in stunned surprise as he stared down on this warm day at the lovely ice skaters whirling around and around just below. Szell moved to a railing and watched.

Incredible.

The best thing yet about America. Here, in the middle of

this jungle city, in the middle of an unnaturally hot day, people were actually behaving like winter. Children were smiling and falling down and old women were skating with old men, hand holding hand, and in the very center were the trick people, professionals perhaps, in any case very good, leaping and turning for themselves, the crowds, whatever, and Szell noticed that most of the really good ones had the same bodies, thick legs, ballet dancers' legs, really, only thicker, and thin upper torsos, thin from the effort of beating their frames into something resembling obedience, not at all fat, like the fat man from the second jewelry shop, who suddenly put his hands on Szell's shoulders, spinning him around, panting, "I knew you weren't English, you murdering son of a bitch," and Szell, as he felt his body turning, flicked his Cutter down, and by the time he faced the fat man, it was already moving, one quick, almost imperceptible gesture with his right hand and the fat man's throat was suddenly and totally laid open, and as the fat man started to fall forward, grabbing for his jugular, Szell began shouting, "*There's a sick man here, there's a man here needs help, a doctor, please a doctor,*" and as the fat man fell over the railing, almost already dead, a crowd gathered, and by the time the fat man could no longer hold his hands around his throat and dropped them, by the time the blood began to faucet, he was surrounded by many people, most of them screaming and none of them Szell, who was half running toward an empty cab, because to hell with the unexpected, storm clouds were gathering over him, bad things came in threes, and the crone remembering him was one and the fat man catching him was two and Szell had no intention of waiting for three to tap him on the shoulder, it was the bank now, the bank and the diamonds, so he told the driver where to take him, and on the trip up he opened his suitcase, and behind the cover of the lid he handkerchiefed his Cutter clean, quickly strapped it back in place, put the handkerchief in the case, closed it, and at shortly before half-past eleven he approached the corner of 91st and Madison.

Well now.

The bank was on the right-hand uptown corner. There appeared to be nothing unusual, but that meant nothing, Szell put even less faith in "appeared" than he did in "seems."

If they were waiting for his exit, if there was a plot, what were his alternatives? The money could stay here, true, but that would make him by Christmas an impoverished fugitive, not the best of positions.

Szell paid, got out, entered the bank.

He had the safe deposit key in his suit-coat pocket and the box number emblazoned in his heart. He moved quickly toward the sign that said "Safe Deposits" together with an arrow. He followed the arrow. Down some steps he went, and there, beyond, was the large locked gate. He could see the guard parading inside. Szell walked up to the woman at the desk on the near side of the gate. Middle-aged, fat, but pleasant-faced for a blackie.

"My box," Szell said, and he brought out the key.

She looked up at him strangely. "I thought I knew 'em all," she said, "but I guess there's new folks every day. Name, please?"

Szell went German—if she was experienced, she must have known his father, who had no ear for languages, so his

German accent must have lingered until death. "Christopher Hesse. I am deputy only. My father—" he said it "fasser"—"suh box iss inn hiss name." He smiled at the black face.

"Old Mister Hessuh," she said, pronouncing it that way. "So you're his boy. Don't think I've ever seen you. Not usual, sending a deputy after so many years." She was still looking at him strangely.

Why was his heart beating? What could she know? "He died," Szell explained.

"Oh my lordie, I'm sorry to hear that," and she sat back in her chair.

"Yess, it iss a sad business."

"That's not what I meant," she said. " 'Course, I'm sorry about him too, but see, we got a law, when there's a death, the box gets sealed till after the lawyers is done examining."

Szell just stood there, blinking.

"I can't let you in's what I'm trying to say."

Bad things *did* come in threes; it was true.

"Maybe you better sit down, Mister Hessuh."

"Pleess," Szell managed, and then he started to cry, tears streaming down his face.

"I can't *do* nothin', Mister Hessuh—ask me, it's a stupid law, but there it is, on the books, I got to obey it."

"Pleess, you go too fast." Szell sank wearily into a chair, buried his head in his hands. "Three weeks more only," he began.

"I didn't quite make you out, Mister Hessuh."

Szell looked at her with his moist blue eyes. "My fasser is dead in three weeks more only. The doctors say this. Cancer, zey say. I beg. Pleess. Pleess. He iss all I haff left for family, make him liff longer, pleess, more zan chust three weeks." He shook his head, turned away.

"Oh, that's a whole different thing," she said. "If he's only sick, 'course you can go in," and they quickly went through the rest of the admission procedure. "George," the blackie said to the guard. "George, you take *young* Mister Hessuh to his box, please." To Szell she said, "Give George your key, why don't you, Mr. Hessuh."

Szell stammered, "Sank you," handed the key through the bars, waited through the clicks and turns until the gate swung open and he was into the box area, following the guard.

"Would you like a private room?" the guard asked.

"Pleess."

The guard took the key, placed it in one lock, took another key, placed it in a second, turned them both, pulled out a very large box. Szell followed the guard to a room. The guard put the box down. Szell thanked him. The guard nodded, left.

Like a child at Christmas, Szell shook the box gently, expecting weight.

It was like a feather.

He threw it open.

It was empty except for a coffee can. One large-sized Melittá coffee can, that was all. In fury, Szell ripped the lid from the goddamn thing.

And the diamonds tumbled out.

Szell decided he'd better sit down. The can had been full to the top. How much was that? He spread the contents of the can all across the bottom of the box.

The sound was louder than he'd intended, so he closed the box fast, in case the guard came running in. When he was secure again, he opened the box and began separating the diamonds. The smallest were the size of pencil erasers, and he wondered what those were in carats. Three? More than three, probably. There were literally dozens of them, and dozens more the size of a thumbnail.

Then there were the big ones.

Many bigger than pecans, and some the size of walnuts. Look at that one—Szell could not keep his hands off the stone—it was as big as a baby's fist—and he suddenly saw a long-dead face, a pretty woman, frail and young and a cousin, she said, of the Rothschilds, and was this enough, it was all she had, would it suffice?

Yes, my dear, of course. More than enough.

Szell's heart was pounding again, because he realized that what he was looking at was more than he had ever dreamed of. I can *buy* Paraguay if I choose. I won't but I could, and—and—

Szell began gathering up the diamonds, banishing thoughts of country-purchasing. He was the possessor of one of the great fortunes, but what good was that if you had to hide in some tropical swamp. There were supposedly, in Turkey, doctors, great surgeons who did things to you, changed your face, could even, if you could stand the pain, shorten you, and perhaps that was the thing—give yourself to these men and let them rape you for their services—if they gave you a different exterior, you could sip champagne on the Continent until gout claimed you at the age of seventy-five. His hands were actually trembling as he managed to sweep the diamonds back into the can, put the can in his case. Then he called for the guard and had the empty box locked up again.

Szell waited through the locking procedure, then followed the guard to the main gate and beyond it to safety, where the blackie said, "My regards to your father—be sure and tell Mister Hessuh that Miz Barstow sends regards," and Szell smiled and nodded and up the stairs he went, out of the building into the sunlight, where he realized that bad things came in fours, threes were nothing, because moving across the sidewalk now was a certifiable madman, a lunatic in running shoes and raincoat.

"It isn't safe," Babe said.

# 29

Szell waited. No sudden moves. Because if this one was alive, that meant that, more than likely, his people were no longer, and that meant that the crazy was armed, probably a gun. Szell noted the bulge in the right raincoat pocket.

Of course, he was armed too. He had his Cutter, so losing was not something he intended. Winning was but a matter of getting close, of being right beside the enemy. Once you were right beside them, it was checkmate. Szell glanced around, looking for a suitable place to get close.

"So what happens?" Szell asked.

"Just tell me where you want to die," Babe said.

"Oh come now," Szell began, but then he saw the pistol butt coming out of the raincoat pocket and he realized this skinny creature, this one he had weeping in the chair no more than a few hours before, had to be taken seriously. All madmen had to be taken seriously. "Put it back—I wasn't mocking you, but there are things you don't know, I have items in my possession, terms can be made."

"Where do you want to die?" Babe repeated. Very soft. His voice was from some other world, human no more.

Szell couldn't believe it. He *wants* to kill me; I hold the wealth of the Indies in my suitcase and suddenly I am confronted with an idiot child who would glory in my death.

"The park," Szell managed, pointing to the entrance a block away. "The park is quiet, we can talk to each other," get close to each other, he did not add; right beside each other.

Babe nodded toward the green.

Szell began to walk. "You must hear me, you must let me tell you," he said. "You are very young, but let me assure you of something: Life can take a very long time, and better live it through with comfort than without."

Babe said nothing.

"You're very young," Szell said again. There was a pleading tone in his voice now. "You are very smart but not yet wise."

"You killed my brother," Babe said.

"No, that is a lie, I was not present, I swear."

"Janeway told me. Elsa did too."

"It had to be done," Szell said. "I didn't want to, I swear."

"Janeway didn't tell me anything," Babe said. "Elsa didn't either. So don't worry about me. I'm fucking wise."

They were getting close to the park now.

"Killing me accomplishes nothing," Szell said.

"Not for you."

"*Nothing.*"

Babe walked behind him. "Faster," he said.

They crossed Fifth Avenue, entered the park.

"Head for the reservoir," Babe said, and they walked up the steps and started around it. It was quiet, and too hot for many joggers. The entire right-hand part of the running path was lined with thick bushes.

"Here," Babe said.

"I must show you! You must see!"

"Get into the bushes," Babe said.

Szell backed down into the underbrush. *"The coffee can, look at it, I beg you, just look at it, that's all."*

Babe took out H.V.'s gun.

"Christ," Szell cried, "one request, everyone grants that."

"Did you?"

"Auschwitz was an extermination camp, not a concentration camp, they were not meant to regain strength."

Babe cocked the pistol.

Szell fell to his knees, flinging his case open, grabbing the coffee can, all the time begging, "—Look—you must look—I ask no more—*please*—"

"I don't want your diamonds," Babe said softly. "I don't even want you crawling, I just want you dead," and then he said "Jesus," because by that time Szell had the lid off the coffee can.

"You see? Millions—so many millions for us both—deals can be made—"

Babe hesitated, shook his head.

*"At least look at what I'm offering you!*—come down and look, consider it, *I beg you,* come down here next to me, *come right beside me and decide,* that is my last request, you must grant that!"

Babe hesitated one more time, then moved down into the dark covering of the bushes beside Szell, who waited, waited, and then when Babe was right beside him, the Cutter began to move.

Szell was candy.

Babe squeezed the shot off, and it exploded at close range

into Szell's chest. Szell spun backward as if yanked, then lay on his face in the dirt, trying to gather strength to move.

Babe sat comfortably on the ground, holding the gun, talking quietly. "I don't know that you'll understand this, but once upon a time, long ago, I was a scholar and a marathon man, but that fella's gone now, dead I suppose, but I remember something he thought, which was that if you don't learn the mistakes of the past, you'll be doomed to repeat them. Well, we've been making a mistake with people like you, because public trials are bullshit and executions are games for winners—all this time we should have been giving back pain. That's the real lesson. That's the loser's share, just pain, pure and simple, pain and torture, no hotshot lawyers running around trying to see that justice is done. I think we'd have a nice peaceful place here if all you warmakers knew you better not start something because if you lost, agony was just around the bend. That's what I'd like to give you. Agony. Not what you're suffering now. I mean a lifetime of it, 'cause that's the only degree of justice I think we're ready for down here yet, and I know any humanist might disagree with me too, but I don't think you will, because you had a lot to do with educating me, I'm like you now, except I'm better at it, because you're going to die and I've still got a long way to go."

Szell charged. He pushed himself forward like a tackle when the ball is snapped, trying to reach Babe, who didn't bother moving, just fired again, and Szell's stomach split and he spun back down.

"You know it gets easier? You're the fifth I've killed today, and Karl went first, *whap* through the eye, and if I'd had time, I would probably have tossed my cookies over what I'd done, but each death it gets easier. I'm kind of enjoying this. Does it keep on getting better? Tell me, I'd really like to know."

Szell was a bull of a man, and like a bull he made his final charge.

Babe waited until he was very close this time, then fired three or four times.

Szell screamed and collapsed, and there was blood coming from all over now.

" 'Groin' is a funny word," Babe said quietly. "I don't know the German for it, but I'm sure you do." He began to talk more quickly then, because he could tell Szell was starting to die. "Oh, maybe you didn't see it in the papers, but they've made this fabulous theological discovery, do you know what they've found? People don't go to heaven or hell, they all go to one spot first, sort of a way station, and that's where things happen, because, you probably won't believe this, but some people on this earth have been known to do bad things to other people, innocent people, and at this way station, the innocent people wait, and then when their savager comes, they get to exact a little portion of revenge. God says revenge is good for the soul. Do you know who's waiting for you, Mr. Szell? All the Jews. They're all there, and you know what else? They've all got drills, like you used on me—remember how you said how wonderful it was, anyone could learn that, how to use them? Well, they have and they're waiting, and I don't know about you, but I think it's gonna be terrific."

Szell was almost dead now, but Babe just had time to get it in.

"Have a swell eternity," Babe said . . .

# AFTER THE END

# 30

The cop came tearing along the reservoir, and he was big, and he had his gun out, and he looked efficient as hell.

Inside he was panicked.

He was not yet twenty-four, had been on the force less than a year, and he'd just been minding his own business on the corner of 90th and Fifth when the backfires started—that's what he'd hoped the explosions were, anyway. Just backfires. Nothing to cause you trouble when it was this hot and you were stuck wearing the heavy uniform. The second explosion more or less convinced him that he wasn't going to get his wish, and when the third shot came, he knew that's what he'd been listening to: gunfire.

So he took off into the park, and it sounded like it had been a hassle near the reservoir, so he started there. "Hey," he called to a kid. "You hear any shooting?"

The kid nodded, pointed to some bushes. "From there."

The young cop took a peek. "Hey," he said to the kid. "There's a guy lying in these bushes. He don't look so hot."

"He's dead I think is why."

"Oh, right," the young cop said, and suddenly he realized a number of things: a) the kid wasn't any kid, he was older, in his twenties maybe, wearing sneakers and a raincoat; b) there was a pistol on the ground beside him; c) he was on the wrong side of the reservoir fence, the inside, so he must have climbed it, and that was illegal, there were signs posted all over. "Hey, you shouldn't be in there."

"I won't be much longer."

The young cop approached the fence warily now. "Nice gun," he said, keeping his voice as casual as he could. "Yours?"

"It was my father's," Babe said.

The young cop was starting to get excited now—he'd never been involved with a murder before; hookers and junkies, sure, but he'd never been able to really crack the big time. "You didn't, by any chance, just use it?"

"You mean, did I kill him?"

"Kind of like that, yeah."

Babe nodded.

The cop quick cocked his pistol. "No funny moves," he said.

"Can't I just finish what I'm doing?"

"What *are* you doing?" He was just standing there, holding what looked like a coffee can, and was skimming marbles or pebbles across the reservoir.

"I've only got a few more to go," Babe said. "Once I got four bounces." He whipped another couple out across the water, wondering if the cop would let him sprint around the reservoir before they went in, it might be just the thing to clear his head. Babe glanced at the cop. Probably he'd say no, and anyway, it wouldn't make you think straight, you're tired, sleep's the only thing that'll do that, but no one's gonna let you sleep for a while, not once this explodes. God alone knew which way the blast would hurl him, but there was about to be one hell of a detonation, that much was sure; he was either going to end up serving five hundred years in prison or as the biggest thing since Sonny Tufts. Babe skimmed a few more, watching the circles widen.

"Hey, it's hot, let's go," the cop said.

Babe nodded, tossed away the empty can, got rid of a final handful.

. . . skip . . . skip . . .

. . . skip . . . skip . . .

. . . skip . . .

## About the Author

William Goldman has been writing books and movies for more than forty years. He has won two Academy Awards (for *Butch Cassidy and the Sundance Kid* and *All the President's Men*), and three Lifetime Achievement awards in screen-writing. His novels include *The Temple of Gold* and *The Princess Bride.*